FIGHTING THE GOOD FIGHT—

As long as there are people there will be clashes, and as long as there is more than one side to any issue, there will be warriors to champion one cause or another. Some will fight with swords, spears, guns, or other tools of destruction, some with magic, some with logic, some with words. But however the battles are fought, won, or lost, there will be those ready to cheer their chosen warriors on. And in WARRIOR FANTASTIC, the fighters and the challenges they face occur in such fascinating territories as:

"As Good As a Rest"—Being an archetype had been fine in olden times, but what was a warrior maiden to do when all she knew was hacking and slashing and she really wanted to make a career change?

"Spirit Warrior"—From ancient Egypt to modern-day America the power of healing will always fight the darkness that seeks to claim mortal souls. . . .

"Conscript"—He'd been commandeered as a foot soldier in a wizards' war, and though all he really wanted to do was go back to being a wood-carver, he'd made the mistake of becoming the object of a wizard's attention, and now there was no turning back. . . .

More Imagination-Expanding Anthologies Brought to You by DAW:

BATTLE MAGIC *Edited by Martin H. Greenberg and Larry Segriff.* The spells of war are conjured up for you in this all-original volume of tales by some of today's finest fantasy strategists from John DeChancie, Josepha Sherman, and Rosemary Edghill, to Jane Lindskold, Mickey Zucker Reichert, Julie Czerneda, and Charles de Lint. From classic settings to contemporary locales, from battles waged between demon and mortal to those between the mightiest of sorcerers to wars that entangle innocent and evil alike, here are stories certain to hold your imagination captive.

CIVIL WAR FANTASTIC *Edited by Martin H. Greenberg.* The War Between the States is synonymous with romance, tragedy, bravery, and lost causes. The only war fought by Americans against Americans, it nearly tore the nation apart. Yet America did survive, though at a terrible cost. Even today, more than 130 years after the end of the Civil War, people are still fascinated by this pivotal point in American history. Writers, too, find this a fruitful period to investigate. And in *Civil War Fantastic,* some of science fiction's finest—from Nancy Springer, Robert Sheckley, Mike Resnick, and Josepha Sherman to William H. Keith, Jr., Gary A. Braunbeck, David Bischoff, and Kristine Kathryn Rusch—take us back to this turbulent time with their own special visions of what might have been.

SPELL FANTASTIC *Edited by Martin H. Greenberg and Larry Segriff.* Fantasy is fueled by spells, from those cast by simple love potions to the great workings of magic which can alter the very nature of reality, destroy seemingly all-powerful foes, offer power or punishment, immortality or death. In *Spell Fantastic* thirteen of today's finest word wizards—including Kristine Kathryn Rusch, Nina Kiriki Hoffman, Robin Wayne Bailey, Jane Lindskold, Dennis McKiernan, and Charles de Lint— have crafted unforgettable tales with which to enchant your imagination.

WARRIOR FANTASTIC

Edited by
Martin H. Greenberg
and John Helfers

DAW BOOKS, INC.
DONALD A. WOLLHEIM, FOUNDER
375 Hudson Street, New York, NY 10014

ELIZABETH R. WOLLHEIM
SHEILA E. GILBERT
PUBLISHERS

First Printing, December 2000

1 2 3 4 5 6 7 8 9

DAW TRADEMARK REGISTERED
U.S. PAT OFF AND FOREIGN COUNTRIES
—MARCA REGISTRADA.
HECHO EN USA

PRINTED IN THE U.S.A.

ACKNOWLEDGMENTS

Introduction © 2000 by John Helfers.

At Sea © 2000 by Thranx, Inc.

The Walnut-Hued Man of Sutton Passeys © 2000 by Jean Rabe.

A Two-Edged Blade © 2000 by Diana L. Paxson.

Heritage © 2000 by Fiona Patton.

As Good As a Rest © 2000 by Tim Waggoner.

A Game of Swords © 2000 by David Bischoff.

Airs Above the Ground © 2000 by Janet Pack.

Demon Hunter © 2000 by Pauline E. Dungate.

Suspended Animation © 2000 by Nina Kiriki Hoffman.

Spirit Warrior © 2000 by Kristin Schwengel.

Conscript © 2000 by Jody Lynn Nye.

Final Score © 2000 by Bradley H. Sinor.

Barbarian © 2000 by Bill Fawcett Associates.

Bright Be the Face © 2000 by Gary A. Braunbeck.

Making a Noise in This World © 2000 by Charles de Lint.

CONTENTS

INTRODUCTION
by John Helfers

THE warrior has enjoyed an exalted place in fiction since the beginning of time. In every culture around the world, there have been plenty of men and women willing to fight anyone, anything, any time, anywhere. In ancient civilizations as well as today, a warrior stands apart from everyone else around him. A person who has dedicated his life to the art of combat, of going out and defeating a foe by whatever means necessary, a warrior has a philosophy of life and death different from anyone else in the world.

For there can be no doubt that when a warrior takes up his sword, bow, or rifle, that he is picking up whatever weapon he uses with one goal in mind—to kill. Once battle is entered, he does what he's been trained to do. The samurai of feudal Japan understood this better than any civilization before them, and were therefore able to train their warriors to go into battle expecting to die, fighting each battle as though it was their last, thereby conquering their fear of death. When a warrior no longer fears his own demise, he is beyond worrying about keeping himself alive, and is free to concentrate solely upon combat. It is this single-minded dedication, the willingness to go forth into battle knowing that he might not come back, that sets the warrior apart.

But combat is just one aspect of the warrior's art. A

true warrior is also a master of strategy and tactics, choosing not only which battles to fight, but where, when, and how to fight them. Eventually, assuming he survives the battles he participates in, a warrior can also become a leader of men, and accomplish more in that role than he could with an entire lifetime of simply fighting.

History has been full of warriors. Whether fighting for their country, their religion, or simply their families, men and women have answered the call to arms throughout the centuries. Alexander the Great, Boudicca, Sun Tzu, Julius Caesar, El Cid, William Wallace, Genghis Khan, Joan of Arc, Napoleon Bonaparte, Miyamoto Musashi, Oda Nobunaga, Frances Marion, Robert E. Lee, Wyatt Earp, Geronimo, Audie Murphy, and Douglas MacArthur are just some of the many men and women whose exploits have passed beyond history into legend.

Of course, no discussion of warriors would be complete without mentioning the warriors of myth and legend, those whose daring and exploits on and off the battlefield formed the basis of many cultures' mythologies. The stories of such warriors as Odysseus, Hercules, Achilles, Cuchulain, Finn mac Cumhaill, Beowulf, King Arthur, Don Quixote, and many others form a body of stories where the warrior is often triumphant not by force of arms, but by his intelligence and cunning. To be sure, physical prowess does play a large part in any warrior story, but it is how that prowess is used that often leads to the most interesting tales.

That is what we asked of the stellar collection of authors assembled in this book—new stories about warriors both past and present. From Alan Dean Foster's tale of a ship captain whose prayer for help is answered in an unusually divine way to a poignant tale by Charles de Lint that explores what being a warrior means in this modern age, here are fifteen stories of warriors wise and wondrous, men and women who live and die as much by their wits as by the sword. So turn the page, grab your weapon, and prepare to march into the world of the warrior fantastic.

AT SEA
by *Alan Dean Foster*

Alan Dean Foster was born in New York City and raised in Los Angeles. He has a bachelor's degree in Political Science and a Master of Fine Arts in Cinema from UCLA. He has traveled extensively around the world, from Australia to Papua New Guinea. He has also written fiction in just about every genre, and is known for his excellent movie novelizations. Currently, he lives in Prescott, Arizona, with his wife, assorted dogs, cats, fish, javelina, and other animals, where he is working on several new novels and media projects. His recent books include the third volume in the Journeys of the Catechist series, *A Triumph of Souls*, and *Dirge*.

"HOY, CRUZ—there are five horses on the stern!"

Sandino was a big man with a squinched puss and huge arms the color of old bratwurst. Right now, his expression was slowly subsiding into his face like a back street into a Florida sinkhole, swallowing his features whole. It was left to his voice, which had the consistency of toxic cheese-whip, to convey his confusion.

Although he was on board a modern longline fishing

boat, Cruz didn't know much about fishing. That did not matter, because he didn't care much about fishing. Boats, however, were something else again. Boats could go where planes and cars could not. As far as fishing boats were concerned, the best thing about them was that they stank. The big swordfish boat reeked of blood, guts, fish oil, and sea bottom. This made it perfect for Cruz's purpose. This was his ninth run on the *Mary Anne*, and there was no reason to believe it would be any less successful than the previous eight. No one suspected it carried any cargo beyond the limp mass of dead swordfish in its hold. No one suspected that one particular dead swordfish contained twenty million dollars worth of top grade pure cocaine that did not normally form part of a billfish's diet. Compressed into dozens of waterproof, odor-proof, break-proof packages, this highly inhalable product of the Peruvian hinterland fit neatly into the chosen fish's hollowed-out body cavity.

Cruz did know enough to realize that the presence of five horses on the stern of the *Mary Anne*, one hundred and twenty miles out from Providence, was not in accord with normal fishing procedure. Even if the horses had been dumped at sea, they could not have climbed aboard. Since he had not heard the metallic bang-and-rattle of the big winch that hauled in the long-lines, they could not somehow have been lifted aboard.

It occurred to Cruz that Sandino might be enjoying a joke at his expense. A single hard stare was enough to put that possibility to rest. There was a lot of meat on Sandino, but not much of it was gray matter. Nor was it the sort of gag that Truque or Weatherford would concoct. Lowenstein, now, that was different. The computer and communications expert was clever. Cruz's brows furrowed. Too clever to come up with a dumb line about horses on the stern.

"I don't have time for stupid shit now, Sandino. We'll be having to look out for Coast Guard soon."

Cruz turned back to the thick port glass that looked out over the foredeck of the *Mary Anne*. Sullen and silent as they always were in the presence of the unusual passengers, the crew of the fishing boat went about the business of securing their ship for the night. They didn't like Cruz and his unpleasant companions; didn't like the way they comported themselves while on board. Didn't like the way they hectored and taunted Captain Red and his son David. Didn't like the way they acted as if they owned the *Mary Anne*. Why the Captain tolerated their presence on so many trips even his closest friends did not know. But when queried, Red just stared off into the distance and mumbled something about old obligations, and told the questioners to carry on. Because they loved Red, and because he always found swordfish and made them money, they ground their teeth and held their peace.

"Nice cloud cover," Cruz declared conversationally to Gunnar "Red" Larson as he peered up at the night sky. "Fog would be better."

"For you. Not for me." Larson kept his gnarled fisherman's hands on the ship's wheel and his eyes straight ahead. He strove to focus only on his instruments; on the radar, the GPS, and the weather scan. Others spread across the broad glowing console he could ignore, knowing as he did the way back to the *Mary Anne*'s home berth the way a puffin knows its flight path back to the North Sea cliffs of its birth. He hated the wiry, soft-talking son-of-a-bitch standing next to him. Hated the man's face, his manner, his clothing, the smelly Indonesian clove cigarettes he chain-smoked, and his friends. Most of all, he hated Cruz's business.

No, he told himself as the ulcer-sparked pain that would not go away spasmed through his gut and made him wince imperceptibly. Most of all, he hated the old gambling debt that had put him in bondage to Cruz more than six years ago. The debt he could not seem to satisfy. The debt from which he had begun to fear he would never emerge.

Three years back he had stumbled drunkenly out of Portuga's Bar and Grill on Sixth Street, his arm around David's shoulder, and on a quiet night in the middle of the river park had broken down and confessed all to his only son. David, fine young college-educated boy that he was, had listened in stony but sympathetic silence while he waited for his tough-as-hooks father to stop sobbing. Then he had proposed that Red immediately unburden himself to the police. The old man had violently demurred. He knew people like Cruz, he explained. Had known them most of his life. Lock up Cruz and his minions, and others of his filthy kind would take vengeance. Not out of any love for Cruz— who, after all, was a sly and successful competitor—but as a warning to others. To keep their mouths shut. To pay their debts.

Besides, old man Larson had mumbled, it was only one or two trips a year. Just one or two trips. Meet the courier boat in the open Atlantic, transfer the noisome illegal cargo, stuff it in a conscript sacrificial swordfish, and it was done. No violence, no confrontations. At the wharf, that one fish would be purchased by a certain buyer from New York, and that was the end of it. Year after year. Soon the debt would be paid, he had assured a dubious David. Soon they would be free of Cruz and his grinning, scornful face. Soon, soon. . . .

Was "soon," Red Larson reflected as he stared resolutely out the port at his sulking crew and the gathering night, ever to come?

"Fog is better for you," he repeated. "Not for me. I am responsible for the boat."

Puffing on one of his sweet, execrable cigarettes, Cruz looked away and chuckled. " 'Horses on the stern.' You'd think Lowenstein, that squeaky little nerd asshole, could come up with something better."

Unconsciously, Larson looked away from the black water athwart the bow and over at his noxious passenger. "What the devil are you talking about?"

"I know what he is talking about. The brigand is insulting our mounts."

Uttered in a most distinctively steely feminine voice, the observation was bizarre enough. Turning simultaneously there on the bridge of the *Mary Anne*, the sight that Cruz and his sulky captive captain beheld was stranger still. But not, a captivated Cruz reflected, in any wise unpleasant. So taken was he by the unexpected vision that he barely gave a thought to connecting it to the putative presence of multiple horses on the stern.

Crowding into the bridge were five of the most stunning, gorgeous women Cruz, or Larson, or Nick Panopolous, who was standing with his mouth open at the far side of the chart table, had ever seen. All of them were blonde. Startlingly blonde, except for one scintillating redhead, and all had eyes of electric blue save for two who flashed green, including the redhead. Variously attired, none were dressed for open-ocean deep-sea fishing. Common to all of them, though visible on some more than others, was scarlet underwear. One wore a severe off-the-shoulder black dress suitable for performance with a symphony orchestra, and carried a violin case. Despite this, her appearance was no more incongruous than that of her four companions. Lost in the rear of the crowd, though not unhappily so, was a visibly dazzled David Larson.

"Hi, Dad," the young fisherman called out. "I'd like you to make the acquaintance of some new friends of mine."

Before a flabbergasted Red Larson could reply, the suddenly animated Cruz stepped forward. "It is lovely to meet you all, señoritas. Though I have no idea how you come to be here, in the middle of the ocean, I openly welcome you aboard." He leered at the nearest woman. She wore a comfortable brown business suit, practical flats, and stood five-nine, maybe fine-ten. She was also the shortest member of the group. "I was not insulting your mounts. Though I am always available to such charming company to discuss matters of mounting."

Pushing past him without a word, the blonde confronted the bewildered captain. Hands on hips, she looked him slowly up and down, leaned forward to peer deep into his eyes, reached out to take several of the thinning hairs atop his head and rub them between thumb and forefinger, all the while sniffing at him with a nose that was as pert and perfect as the rest of her. She smelled, old man Larson decided, of wild honey and expensive leather, of crisp fresh air and slow-warmed cognac. Married for thirty-six years to the same woman, he nonetheless felt dizzy in the presence of this professionally clad golden goddess.

"Do not be alarmed," she told him forthrightly. "My name is Herfjötur."

"Say what, girl?" Even though she was facing away from him, Cruz continued to stare at her, and not at the back of her head.

She spun around to confront the smirking Colombian. "War-Fetter, to you, blackguard." Raising a hand, she gestured at her watchful companions. "These are my sisters. That's Sigrdrifa. Next to her are Hrist and Róta. The tall one behind them in the evening gown is Skeggjöld." The "tall one," Red Larson noted, towered over his son, who stood six foot one in his stocking feet. "When in his misery and desperation a true scion of the Old Believers called out to us," she indicated David Larson, "we came as soon as we could. The others would have come as well, but they are presently occupied." She glanced enigmatically back at the confounded captain. "We are wiring Asgard, you know. Being on another temporal plane creates problems that most installers cannot imagine."

"War-Sister is too modest," declared Róta. "In this plane she works for Nokia, you know."

The one called Sigrdrifa nodded. "Having companies like hers and Ericcson right in our ancestral backyard has helped immensely."

Hrist was shaking her head slowly. "Between battles, Odinn insists on being online. And Freyja is simply impossible."

It was a tentative Gunnar Larson who stuck his head around Herfjötur to inquire cautiously, "You're not . . . ?" Beneath bushy brows his eyes grew a little wider. "By my Grandfather's soul, you are, aren't you?"

The spectacular blonde who was resting an elbow on David Larson's shoulder essayed a divine smile. "Don't you recognize us? Of course, we have to adopt our dress

to the present time, or we would draw the stares of the
meddlesome curious while living and working among
them."

As if you don't draw stares as you are now, the old captain mused.

With a polished fingernail painted fire-engine red, Skeggjöld flicked one of the long earrings that dangled alongside her neck. It took the form of a pendulant hatchet
fashioned from rubies and diamonds. "These sign my name,
fisherman. Can you know it?"

Larson struggled to remember the old tales his grandmother had told him, over hot cocoa beside crackling fires
on midwinter New England nights. He nodded. "Yes, I
know you. 'Wearing-a-War-Ax.'"

Skeggjöld shrugged exquisitely. "I do what contemporary fashion allows."

Cruz, who had been watching and listening to the mean-
ingless byplay, was interested in only one thing. Well, two
things. But matters of importance must perforce come first.

"How did you get on this ship?" He glanced out a port.
Outside, it was now black as the inside of a deserted Bronx
tenement. "I didn't hear or see another boat pull up alongside."

"We did not come by boat," Róta informed him coolly.
"We flew."

"Low," Hrist added. "You have to, these days, to stay
under the coastal radar."

Cruz frowned. A glance at the stupefied Sandino showed
that no plane or copter had been observed approaching.
The smuggler was not entirely displeased with the attempted
subterfuge. It would be a pleasure to get the truth out of
liars as attractive as these.

"I don't know why you're telling me these loco stories. You've been on the *Mary Anne* all along, haven't you? That's it!" His gaze narrowed and the false veneer of good humor vanished. "I could almost think you were agents, planted here for purposes of entrapment. But why only women? And in such clothing?"

" 'Maybe," Sandino rumbled from beside the starboard doorway, "they're hiding something."

"*Seguro* . . . sure." Cruz's smile returned. Sandino was a good man. Dedicated, loyal. It was time to reward him. "Why don't you have a look and see? But pick on one your own size."

A wide, wicked grin of realization slowly oozed across the face of the muscle. Advancing, he reached unhesitatingly for the bodice of Skeggjöld's elegant evening gown. As he did so, she reached down and lifted the hem of the exquisite dress, in the process exposing more leg than Cruz or both Larsons or Nick Panopolous had ever seen in their lives.

She also revealed, running from hip to knee, a custom-fitted leather scabbard on which was embossed the cognomen "Gucci." From this she pulled a mirror-bright short sword with bejeweled pommel. Swinging it around and down in a single incredibly swift, smooth arc, she hacked off the impertinent approaching forearm of the shocked Sandino. Screaming like a baby, he staggered backward, clutching at the stump of his arm as blood fountained across the bridge. Some of it spattered Róta, who brushed at it in obvious displeasure.

"For damn! This has to be dry-cleaned."

All thoughts of mastery of the situation and any ancillary activities fled from Cruz's mind as quickly as his balls shriveled inside his scrotum. Fumbling for the pistol he always kept holstered beneath his weather jacket, he shouted for help. In moments, the interior of the bridge had become bedlam.

Clutching his AK-47, Truque came hurtling through the rear door. As he tried to bring the weapon to bear on Skeggjöld, Róta ("She who Causes Turmoil") removed from the violin case she had been holding a double-bladed ax that could have done duty in a television commercial for men's razors. Her howl of battle reverberated through the enclosed space as she leaped into the air, kicked with both feet off the chart table as a stunned Panopolous fell backward out of his chair, and brought the ax down blade first.

"Skull-splitter eats!" she screamed, in a piercing but not unattractive soprano.

Dropping from Turque's suddenly limp fingers, the automatic rifle fell to the floor. It was followed by a substantial portion of his brains. Behind him, Weatherford came barreling in, a pistol clutched in each hand. One blew a hole through the center foreport just as Red Larson dove for the deck. The other dropped from the big man's fingers as he felt himself lifted off the floor in Hrist's astonishing grasp. Long ago, Weatherford had played a couple of seasons of semipro football, before finding that he could make a lot more money in a game with far fewer rules. He weighed well over three hundred pounds.

Hrist banged him headfirst into the ceiling, then rammed his flailing form into the nearest porthole. The thick, storm-resistant glass did not give. Not right away. When it finally did, Weatherford was already unconscious, his skull crushed by "The Shaker."

Of Cruz's people, only Lowenstein had enough sense

to avoid the furious cataclysm that filled the bridge. It did him no good. Perceiving the advent of most welcome sea change aboard the *Mary Anne*, members of the long quiescent crew chased the terrified computer specialist twice around the ship, finally cornering him on the bow. There was no need to weight the screaming, kicking passenger when they threw him overboard. It was over a hundred miles to the nearest land, and even in the tepid Gulf Stream, the open Atlantic at night is not a kind place to weak swimmers.

Though he held his pistol tightly, Cruz had yet to fire a shot. The fight had ended so quickly, and so spectacularly, that he had been stunned into immobility. Shocking enough it was to see his hand-picked, street-hardened professionals disposed of by a bunch of tall blondes, but the manner of their dispatch had been so brutal as to scarcely be believed. He felt as if he was partaking of a bad dream from which he would soon awaken.

Something hit him in the middle of his back and pushed him forward. Behind him, teeth clenched, Red Larson had taken out six years' worth of frustration in that single shove.

"Paid off," the captain growled. "My debt is paid, Cruz. Go back to New York. Tell your people to leave me and my family alone." His eyes glistened as he regarded the five women; all beautiful, all breathing hard, and all drenched in the blood of his enemies. Behind them he could see concerned members of his crew, good friends all, bunching up in the ship's corridor as they tried to steal a glimpse into the bridge.

Cornered in the center, Cruz had nowhere to turn. That these women were rather more than what they appeared to be was brutishly self-evident. That he could not fight them, where experienced killers like Truque and Sandino had failed, was equally apparent. But he had not survived in his chosen profession for as long as he had by turning pussy in the face of adversity. Whirling, he stepped behind the old captain and put the pistol in his right hand to the other man's temple.

"All right now! I don't know who you are or what you are, but I have a cargo to deliver." His voice was threatening, steady. "Don't think you can frighten me, because there are people I work for who are more terrible than you can imagine. If I fail, they will kill me slowly. So—put down your weapons and back out of this bridge, now. Stay below, out of my way." He pressed the muzzle of the pistol harder into Larson's neck, so that it forcefully dimpled the flesh. "Otherwise this man dies before you can do anything to me."

Exchanging glances, the women did as they were told. Ax followed sword in clattering to the floor. Cruz started to relax a little. Whatever these bitches were, they were not omnipotent. He only had to stay awake until they made port. Another day and night. He could do that. He had done similar things before, on other desperate occasions, and had always survived. Did they have any idea who they were dealing with?

One by one, the women started to file off the bridge. David Larson would not go with them, would not leave his father. That was fine with Cruz. Two hostages were better than one.

A sudden coldness brushed past the smuggler's face, chilling his skin. It was unusual to feel such on the bridge, which was always kept warm in defiance of the sometimes brutal cold outside. Taking his eyes off the doorway for just an instant, he glanced upward in the direction of the breeze.

The needle-pointed icicle falling from the ceiling that had been flash-frozen by Sigrdrifa, alias Victory Blizzard, went right through his left eye.

Staggering and screaming, he stumbled away from old man Larson, who perceptively fell to the deck as several wild shots from the agonized smuggler's pistol rang out. They hit nothing but a framed antique chart on the wall and a surprisingly sturdy metal purse that Hrist thrust forward to shield the younger Larson. Striding over to the wildly sobbing figure that was now rolling about uncontrollably on the deck, Sigrdrifa dispatched the half-blinded Cruz with a single swift, quick slice of the sharply curved blade she took from her slim attaché case. The body kicked violently several times before quivering to a stop.

"So perish all enemies of good fisherfolk." Turning, she ululated a victory cry that was taken up and amplified by her sisters. The *Mary Anne* shuddered with the power of it, and members of the crew who were used to hauling in longlines in howling Atlantic gales were compelled to cover their ears.

Reassembling on the bridge, with the wide-eyed crew once more crowding as close as they could to the gore-soaked scene of battle, the quintet of bloodied blondes (and one redhead) confronted Red Larson and his son.

"We go now," the blood-soaked Róta informed them.

"Yes." Hrist checked her Phillipe Patek chronometer. "I have a meeting in Zurich tomorrow at nine, and with the time difference I will get little enough sleep as it is."

Sigrdrifa nudged Cruz's body with a high-heeled shoe. "Sorry about the mess. It was not exactly Ragnarok, but it is good to still be able to do battle on behalf of a noble cause now and then." Raising her stained short sword, she licked blood from the flat of the blade. "Keeps a girl in shape."

Red Larson swallowed hard. "I hardly know what to say, how to thank you. . . ."

Herfjötur smiled. Stepping over Truque's body, she put a reassuring hand on the captain's shoulder. "Thank your son, who in a moment of desperate need had the foresight to call upon those of us who have watched over your kind for millennia." Leaning forward, she gave him an encouraging peck on the cheek. The old man did not blush, but he was glad his wife was not present.

As for David Larson, he was the dazed recipient of kisses from every one of the women. It was enough to make a weaker man succumb, but David had been toughened by years of hard work on the *Mary Anne*. Still, when she bent him back to buss him most soundly, Skeggjöld nearly sprained his back. Her ax earrings fell forward, tickling his cheeks as he felt the salt of her tongue slide into his mouth. The salt, he knew, came from the blood she had licked off her sword. This realization somewhat mitigated his otherwise complete enjoyment of the moment.

Too awestruck to talk among themselves, the crew gathered on the stern deck to watch as, one by one, the women mounted their snow-white steeds. With a kick and a leap, they soared away from the *Mary Anne*, calling out boldly to one another as they rose into the night sky. Most prominent among them was the beauteous Herfjötur, who was still upset that in the heat of battle she had broken the heel of one of her handmade Spanish pumps.

"We'll have to get the bridge cleaned up before we make

port," a soft-voiced Panopolous whispered to his captain. "The stains don't look like fish blood."

"At least we have the supplies to do that." Red Larson looked and felt better than he had in a decade. The curse that was Cruz and his business had been lifted. The mysterious disappearance at sea of the smuggler and his henchmen should be enough to keep any curious fellow businessfolk away from the *Mary Anne*. And if it was not, Larson mused, why, his son could always put in a call for help to an escort service the likes of which was not to be found in the Providence *Yellow Pages*.

Above them, the Aurora Borealis suddenly flashed to life, filling the night sky above the smoothly chugging fishing boat with shimmering luminescence.

"You know what they say causes the light of the aurora, David?" Larson put an arm around his son's tired shoulders. "It's light flickering off the shields of the Valkyries."

The younger Larson nodded. "I wouldn't expect anything less from designer-name armor."

THE WALNUT-HUED MAN
OF SUTTON PASSEYS
by Jean Rabe

When she's not typing away on her out-of-date computer, Jean Rabe watches the goldfish swimming happily in her backyard pond, tugs fiercely on old socks with her two dogs, listens to classical music and noisy cows, and thinks up things to write about. She is the author of ten fantasy novels, including her first hardcover: *Downfall, the Dhamon Saga Volume 1,* and more than a dozen fantasy and science fiction short stories. She lives in rural Wisconsin across from a dairy farm.

HIS dreams rode on the exquisite blade that shimmered in the light of the full moon. He put all of his strength and skill behind the weapon, his years of careful study. He imagined the point crying out for blood, aimed straight at the heart of his most-hated enemy. The keen edge sparkled, like his eyes sparkled in morbid anticipation. He lunged so fast that he was certain he heard the weapon whistling as it drove faultlessly through the air, forward and true and . . .

. . . missed.

"Not this night, my Lord Sheriff!" his enemy taunted,

grinning mischievously and springing back a heartbeat before the blade would have connected.

Another leap and the outlaw was beyond his second swing, and his third—which, in his desperation, was clearly awkward. The fourth was worse, so clumsy now that he caught his own cloak, slicing through a voluminous fold and drawing the hissing snickers of the townsfolk who'd come out of their cozy homes to watch.

"Damn you, Robin of Locksley!" the sheriff hollered, rushing forward and slashing furiously again and again, each time missing his agile foe by inches. "To the pit with you, I say!" The sheriff knew he needed to compose himself, needed to drown the ire that made him woefully inept in the presence of Sherwood's famous outlaw. He silently shouted at himself to relax and focus—but the doing of it was not within his capabilities. At least not this night.

Despite the ungainly way he was wielding the weapon, the sheriff was an accomplished swordsman, riding with the king a few years past on one of his all-important crusades. In his reasonably short life he'd cut down dozens of skilled warriors, perhaps hundreds. But he could not put more than a scratch on this one despicable foe—no matter the weapon he chose to use. This night, it was a heavy Mascaron sword, embossed with gold on the crosspiece, an expensive gift from a visiting Spanish noble.

His collection of bladed weapons included the finest Damascene steel, one with a basket hilt layered with silver and bronze; folded blades from unpronounceable far-eastern villages; an elegant Italian malchus; a singular French rapier said to have belonged to a prince; a silver-edged Moorish three-point; an ancient parazonium—that he flaunted on his hip, but never used for fear it would break; a broadsword taken from a Saracen chief; and more. He practiced daily, save during tax weeks, and no man in the castle could last more than a few minutes with him in a sparring session.

But this man . . . this one very arrogant and insolent man. This man was truly beyond him.

Why had Robin Hood come to Nottinghamshire this evening? Supplies for his Merry Men most likely, as the sheriff's guards spotted him skirting a wall in the merchants' quarter. The guards were assembling a force to take him, but the sheriff bid them to keep their place, intending to take Robin Hood alone and claim all the glory and notoriety for himself. It was not the first time the sheriff had tried this stunt, and the way the duel was going now he was certain it would not be the last. Clearly, if he had gathered enough guards and soldiers, Robin would be captured and on his way to the dungeon at this very moment. But the victory that he so profoundly craved . . . no, the victory he so desperately needed . . . would not be his. He must take the man alone.

Robin said something, but the sheriff didn't catch it, too deeply lost in his musings. The daring outlaw was several feet away, clearly illuminated in the moonlight, dressed in greens the color of wet fern leaves. His long brown hair fluttered about his shoulders in the slight breeze, and his mustache curled up on the edges as his smile grew wider. Robin was a handsome man, only a year or two younger than the sheriff, and the sheriff yearned intensely to deeply scar that pretty, unblemished face.

The sheriff spat—this, too, missing the outlaw. Through clenched teeth he cursed his foe again. "Damn you, Robin Hood!"

"It is not your place to damn me, my good sheriff. Only

God can do that." Robin feinted to his left, the sheriff following him, sword leading and jabbing and missing wide when the outlaw unexpectedly pivoted to the right. "And I'd like to think God is on my side, Philip Mark. The good friar prays for me every night—right after dinner, you know."

The sheriff tried a feint, too, a move that did not catch the outlaw off guard. It only made Robin laugh louder. The outlaw was quick, spinning to the left again, darting right, his own blade flicking out like a striking serpent. It caught the sheriff's tunic, slicing through the laces and causing the growing crowd to cheer. Another deft flick and he'd cut through the cord that held the sheriff's cloak. For a moment the black velvet hung suspended like a giant bat, then it fluttered to rest around his ankles.

"In need of a new tailor, my Lord Sheriff?" Robin's mocking voice was musical and light. "I could recommend one." The outlaw danced forward then, suddenly slashing with a speed that made his inferior blade sing.

Startled, the sheriff stepped back, his feet becoming tangled in his cloak. His sword flew from his fingers as he fell to his rump, and Robin thrust forward, skewering the sheriff's hat. Then the outlaw continued on his way, flicking the hat to one of the onlookers and grabbing up the sheriff's lost sword. He bowed and twirled in front of a comely young woman as if he were at a dance, then he effortlessly hurdled a horse trough.

By the time the sheriff had picked himself up, Robin had melted into the shadows and was no doubt out the gate or over the wall. Heading back to the refuge of his blessed Sherwood Forest.

The townsfolk were murmuring, casting amused glances at the sheriff as they returned to their homes.

"Aye, not this night," the sheriff whispered, recalling the outlaw's words. "But soon, Robin Hood. I shall have you very soon."

He grabbed up his cloak, tossing it over his shoulder, not wanting to leave it on the street as physical evidence of tonight's debacle. The sheriff drew his tunic together, lamented the loss of an expensive, unique blade, and strode purposefully toward the castle.

"Eustace!" the sheriff stormed into the great hall, brushing by a pair of guards and dismissing them with an angry wave. He slammed the door shut behind him and glanced up the staircase. "Eustace!"

It was late, only a few candles flickered in the room and caused ghostly shadows to cavort along the walls. Did even the specters of Nottinghamshire mock him? he wondered.

"Eustace!" he bellowed once more. "Come down here at once!"

Heart hammering wildly in wrathful indignation, the sheriff dropped his ruined cloak on the table and tugged free the tunic. He turned to stare up into the mirror that hung above the mantel. "Why can't I beat him?" he moaned. The image that looked back had no answers. The sheriff's ropy muscles gleamed with sweat, his chest rose and fell rapidly. He ran his fingers over his taut stomach and up to his face, which was angular and darkened by a hint of stubble. There was a thick scar leading from his jaw to just above his ear, the end disappearing in his jet-black hair—Robin Hood had given him that memento early last year.

"Eustace!"

There were hurried footfalls in the stairwell beyond, accompanied by the soft swish of fabric.

"Yes, my Lord Sheriff."

"Eustace of Lowdham, if you manage to get any slower, I will . . ."

"I was sound asleep, Philip. One of your guards just roused me . . ."

Philip Mark glared at his deputy.

". . . and told me what happened near the merchant district. Robin Hood again. Pity."

Philip's eyes narrowed.

"You can't beat him, Philip. Not alone. You should have called the guards. They would have caught his sorry carcass." Eustace glided farther into the room, the hem of his robe dragging on the floor behind him. He was quite a bit smaller than the sheriff, and the overlarge garment made him look frail. "All you need is the element of surprise and enough men," he continued. "In fact, Philip, if you had . . ."

The sheriff moved quickly, reaching Eustace in two steps and bringing his hand up to the man's throat, pushing him back until he hit the wall. The smaller man's skin blanched and his eyes grew wide like a frightened doe's.

"You will not talk to me that way!" The sheriff spat each word for emphasis. "You are my deputy, Eustace of Lowdham, serving at my behest, and I'll warrant that if your tongue wags with such insolence again, you'll be on the first ship headed toward—"

"I'm sorry, Philip," Eustace gasped. "Truly sorry." The smaller man's eyes successfully pleaded with the sheriff to relax his grip. Eustace sagged against the wall and rubbed at his throat. "Forgive me. I wasn't thinking."

Philip Mark paced in front of him. "A favor to your family. That's why I selected you. That and your knowledge of all the villages that litter this land. You're an expert in intrigue, my good little Eustace. And you've a remarkable memory. People don't consider you a threat, and so they aren't very careful with their secrets when you move about them."

Some of the color was returning to Eustace's face. "Secrets? What secrets do you concern yourself with so late this evening?"

The sheriff seemed not to have heard him. "A favor to your family. And now you'll do a favor for me." He stopped in front of his deputy, noting that the smaller man seemed more than a bit nervous at the closeness. It brought a faint smile to Philip's lips that he could so intimidate Eustace of Lowdham.

"You have a Yorkshire connection."

Eustace nodded.

"And you're well known in the Barnsdale area. And throughout Derbyshire for that matter."

Another nod.

"You know of the swordsmen there."

"You are an excellent swordsman, my Lord Sheriff. Certainly one of the best in . . ."

"*The swordsmen there*," Philip repeated through clenched teeth.

"There are several my Lord. . . ."

"The *very best* swordsmen. Someone better than me, far better than the men in my service. Someone even better than that damnable Robin Hood."

Eustace studied the sheriff, trying to figure out precisely what he was up to. The shadows continued to dance around the room for several silent moments, occasionally teasing the sheriff's sweat-slick face. Finally, Eustace took a deep breath and spoke. "There are a few legendary swordsmen in Nottinghamshire, men who rode with the king a long time ago, and some of whom you know. Local heroes, I suppose you could call them."

"I don't want a local hero! I want someone relatively obscure. A very private man. Not one of the wizened old fools who can't even lift a weapon anymore. And not one of those braggarts who wraps his hands around a tankard of mead every night instead of the pommel of a sword. I want the very best, Eustace. Do you understand?"

Eustace cleared his throat and gestured to the table. Philip nodded, and the two of them selected seats opposite each other. They lowered their voices, talking in hushed whispers more because whispers were the stuff of conspiracies rather than because they did not want any passing guards to overhear them.

Eustace suggested swordsman after swordsman, Philip rejecting them all as either too celebrated or not good enough. "Someone who is not known to any of the nobility of Nottinghamshire. Someone whom I have not heard of. Someone who keeps to his little village and keeps to himself. Surely there must be such a swordsman. Someone who has fallen out of memory," Philip hissed. "This is a very private thing."

The deputy sheriff sat back in the chair, running his fingers through his hair as if he were trying to stir up some recondite recollection. The sheriff drummed his fingers on the table and waited.

"There is a man in Sutton Passeys," Eustace began. "I believe he is still alive." He leaned forward until he was practically forehead to forehead with the sheriff. "He is an old man, but not so ancient as to be infirm. Keeps to himself—now. But two decades or so past he was with the king on one of those years-long crusades. I believe his name is Aruze."

"An unusual name. What one might call a cat or a dog."

Eustace steepled his fingers. "It is what the villagers call him, in any event. But those outside the village refer to him as the Walnut-Hued Man. And those in Nottingham proper know nothing of him."

Philip cocked his head. "This Walnut-Hued Man. Is he a Moor? In Sutton Passeys?"

Eustace shrugged. "I've never met him, only seen him once or twice as I passed through collecting taxes. He looked a little exotic. Definitely a foreigner."

The sheriff crooked his finger, indicating he wanted more information.

"I've heard tales about the man, from the more talkative folks in Sutton Passeys. Seems they all welcomed this stranger into their midst several years ago, even though he lives in a shack alone. And if half the tales are true, he was indeed a formidable swordsman years back. Tends livestock now with the rest of them, sheep and—"

"Take me to him in the morning."

Eustace let out a deep breath, the sound of leaves rustling across the ground. "My Lord Sheriff, tomorrow the Court-neys . . ."

". . . will be coming to Nottinghamshire," Philip finished. "Yes, I know." His voice was so soft now that Eustace had to strain to hear him. "There are plenty of people in this castle to entertain the old man and his sons and that hawk-nosed daughter of his. Enough people to keep up appearances. And we should be back well before nightfall, in plenty of time for the feast. Besides, we will be made more important to the Courtneys by our tardiness."

Eustace yawned and pushed himself away from the table, stood and brushed at a wrinkle in his robe. "At first light, then, my Lord Sheriff." He waited for Philip to wave his hand, officially dismissing him. But the sheriff's gaze was locked on a whorl in the tabletop, concentrating on something far from this room. "My Lord Sheriff?" Louder: "Philip?"

The sheriff waggled his fingers. "All right, go. But be ready at first light."

Eustace glided toward the stairs and caught up the hem of his robe. "Philip?"

The sheriff almost reluctantly raised his head.

"This trip will be for folly, you must realize. The Walnut-Hued Man will not fight Robin Hood for you. No matter that he rode with the king. Or that he might have been noble in whatever country he's originally from. He's one of the common people now, whom we tax to death. His sympathies most assuredly will be on the side of the outlaw. If you want a swordsman who will face Robin alone, I can . . ."

Philip Mark smiled. It was a wicked-looking expression that held all manner of maliciousness within it and sent shivers down Eustace's back. "I don't want him to *fight* Robin Hood, my dear Eustace of Lowdham. I want him to teach me. And I don't care what side his sympathies are on. *He will teach me.* Of that you can be confident. I can buy his sympathies. Every man has a price."

*   *   *

"Teach you? The likes o' you? Teach the Sheriff of Nottinghamshire how to use a sword?"

"I know how to use a sword," Philip Mark returned tersely. From the back of his horse, he looked down at the old man and thumped his fingers on the basket hilt of a long sword that had been specially made for him. "I can use any blade quite well. I merely wish to improve on the skills I already possess."

"Me. Teach the Lord Sheriff?"

The man was dark-skinned, though not near so dark as to be considered a Moor. His skin was more the shade of walnut shells, free of wrinkles despite his years. Perhaps he was from Italy or lands to the east of it, Philip mused. His head was shaved, like a man from the Orient or from a reclusive order of monks. The sheriff looked closer and shuddered, discovering no hair on the back of the man's hands or forearms or on his face, as if a horrible disease rather than a religious sect had robbed him of it. Age had certainly robbed the man of his posture. He walked stooped over, one shoulder slightly below the other, and one foot turned in. His clothes were in tatters, though reasonably clean, and a shade or two darker than his skin. He looked up at the sheriff, squinting into the sun.

"Me? Teach you?" He let out a clipped laugh. "I haven't heard somethin' so silly in all o' my days." His voice sounded like gravel bumping around in a bucket. He looked over his shoulder. A few villagers milled about, kept far enough back by Eustace and the guards that they couldn't hear all of what was being said, but desperate to at least see what was transpiring. Whispers of "more taxes" passed from one man to the next. The old man nodded to them, offering them some measure of reassurance that he wasn't going to be carted off to the dungeon for some silly offense.

"I guess I was mistaken that you could teach me anything," Philip Mark stated evenly, turning his horse so his back was to the rabble, yet so that he could still watch the old man. "I had heard that at one time you were an expert swordsman."

But the shriveled wreck before him was far from a swordsman, the sheriff could see that. The dark-skinned old man would be hard-pressed to even make a worthy peasant. And Eustace would find himself entertaining the Courtney woman this evening for mentioning this walnut-hued lout and dragging him out here so early in the day.

"It would seem that I am looking for someone else. Someone named Aruze. Someone who once rode with the king."

The dark-skinned man returned his attention to the sheriff, his eyes needlelike slits.

"I am Aruze," he said after a while, opening his eyes wider. "But I'm a shepherd, not a warrior."

The sheriff would have left then, thankfully abandoned this quaint village that smelled strongly of sheep dung and poverty. Indeed, he was looking forward to watching Eustace squirm before that ghastly Courtney woman. But there was something about the old man's eyes that held him like a vise. A cunning intelligence flickered in them, something that the years and the harsh conditions of this life couldn't chase away and that the sheriff found fascinating and hypnotizing. Philip's hands tightened on the reins. He should leave now, but . . .

"I used to be a swordsman," the man finally acknowledged. "It was a long time ago. And many miles from here."

"And so you've forgotten those skills," the sheriff baited, his eyes still captured by the old man's. A small part of Philip's mind again told him to leave, screamed that he should not waste another minute of his precious time chatting with a dirty commoner who did not even address him as "sir" or "my Lord Sheriff." Why, if Philip were home in the castle right now, he would have servants trimming his hair and measuring him for new clothes. And the hawk-nosed Courtney daughter would be fawning over Eustace, throwing herself at the smaller man and making everyone quite nauseous. Did she still marinate herself in sickeningly sweet perfume? "What was I possibly thinking . . . Aruze . . . that one such as you might . . ."

"I've forgotten nothin'." The man made an effort of straightening himself.

Philip Mark slid from his horse's back, his eyes still not leaving the peasant's. Closer to the old man, he could *smell* him. There was a sharp, musky fragrance to him, no doubt from spending his days and nights with sheep. "Forgotten nothing? Then teach me what you know."

"Why?"

"Does it matter?"

Aruze dug the ball of his good foot into the ground and slowly shook his head. "I've schooled many a man in the blade. Here, and in my homeland. But I'll not teach the likes o' you." Then the old man dropped his gaze to the toes of his worn boots, releasing Philip's gaze.

The sheriff blinked to clear his head. He should have the man whipped for refusing. No. Not enough. He should have him hung or drawn and quartered. Then he should find a swordsman not as old or as crippled, but every bit as obscure. He should get back on his horse right now and . . .

"Teach me," Philip found himself saying. "I will make it worth your while, old man."

Aruze spat at the sheriff's feet. "I don't like you. I don't like your kind. Nothin' you could do would make it worth my while to help you. Nothin'.."

The sheriff spun, looking across the rundown village to the men and women kept back by the guards. They were a pitiful lot, all poor and broken and dirty.

"I'll not tax Sutton Passeys for two months."

Aruze raised his head, again meeting the sheriff's gaze. He drew his lips into a thin line, as if considering the offer. "No."

"Three."

"Five months."

"Done."

"Not quite." The old man smiled thinly, and his dark eyes sparkled. "Five months worth o' tax money you will return to this village before we begin."

Philip clenched his fists. It was his turn to refuse.

"And you'll not tell a single soul that it's for swordplay lessons. You'll say all o' that taxin' was a mistake. You simply took too much. The people here were overburdened. And you'll say you're sorry for it."

Philip vehemently shook his head.

"I don't like you, Sheriff o' Nottinghamshire. And I don't trust you. If I teach you for a month, you might well turn around and start taxin' us again."

The sheriff forced himself to relax and offered the man

a slight nod in appreciation. Taxing them again was indeed what he would have done.

"So you'll return five months worth o' tax money. If you want me to teach you."

Words flitted through the sheriff's mind. He should call this man an impudent cur, should throw him in the dungeon, increase Sutton Passeys' taxes for spite—though he was certain from the looks of these indigent folks he wasn't likely to get more than another coin or two.

"Very well," Philip said softly. "We shall start tomorrow. I shall bring the tax money with me."

"And . . ."

The sheriff cocked his head, anger glimmering in his eyes.

"You'll bring me a sword. A fine one, as good as what you're totin' on your hip."

"That I won't agree to."

"Then we don't have a deal."

Philip balled his fists and set them on his waist. "I am being more than generous as it is, old man."

"Swordplay lessons are expensive. And the time of even someone like me has value." Aruze smiled, showing a row of yellow-brown teeth. "Besides, I don't have a sword, my Lord Sheriff. And I'll need one to teach you . . . sir." The words showed contempt, not respect. "I was forced to sell my favorite sword last year to pay your taxes."

"A sword, then."

"As fine o' one as that." He pointed to the sheriff's long sword.

"Tomorrow morning."

Aruze shook his head and dropped his voice to a harsh whisper. "Tomorrow night. There is an old stable a few miles south, down this road. It has no roof and is barely standin'. But it will do. Come there. Bad enough that I will teach you my craft. I cannot let my fellows here know what I am doin'. It wouldn't do at all to let them know I've sold my soul for tax money and a fine blade."

The sheriff clenched his jaw tight to keep from smiling. No tales of this endeavor would be spread! The foreigner was ashamed at this bargain. "Tomorrow night, Mister Aruze." Then he was on his horse and riding hard from Sutton Passeys. Eustace and the guards hurried to catch up.

Philip was tired. The ordeal with the Courtney nobles lasted well into the early morning hours, and a noon meeting with the Merchants' Guild prevented him from sleeping late. He had considered sending Eustace to find the barn and tell the old man he would meet him in a few days. He should have, he told himself.

But here he was, alone and yawning and traveling south from Sutton Passeys. The horse's saddlebags chinked with coins, and he halfway worried that Robin Hood and his men might rob him. They might have, had he been dressed properly. But he was wearing commoner's clothes that Eustace had fetched for him, drab garb that kept the people of Nottinghamshire from recognizing him as he rode out the gates on a sway-backed, aging mare.

The barn loomed ahead, and he pulled on the reins, stopping well short of it. "What am I doing?" he whispered. "All of this skullduggery because I wish to best one man."

Perhaps Eustace of Lowdham was right, this was folly and he should simply summon plenty of guards and soldiers when he caught sight of the outlaw. "But for pride and my obsession," he said, as he slid from the horse's back and led the animal to the barn.

He had expected it to be dark inside, but with no roof the moon shone in. There were gaps in the walls, and Philip wondered if a strong breeze would topple the thing. The old man was there, standing crookedly in the center, carefully regarding him. "I didn't expect you'd show," he said, the gravelly voice still sounding unpleasant to the sheriff's ears.

"Neither did I." Philip dropped the reins and fumbled about on the saddle, tugging free the tax money and tossing it to the ground. "Your fee."

"And . . ."

He retrieved a rolled blanket, and from it he pulled a sword. It was an unusually thick-bladed rapier with a steel hilt, one embossed with brass designs. Near the half-basket the sword was scalloped, and the indentations were edged in silver and bronze. The moon caught the sword and made it gleam, as the old man's eyes were gleaming.

"A very fine blade," Aruze said, a hint of awe in his rough voice. "A most superb weapon."

"Worth more than the five months of taxes collected from your village," the sheriff added, as he tossed it to him. Worth far more than your sorry hide, he added to himself. The old man caught the sack of coins and continued to admire the sword, which was one of the lesser pieces in the sheriff's collection. "I trust, Mister Aruze, that this sword will . . ."

"More than suffice, my Lord Sheriff." Respect in the voice this time. "My thanks to you. And I trust you will not be disappointed with my tutelage."

"Let us hope not," the sheriff swore under his breath.

As the night wore on, the sheriff discovered that the bent and crippled man still possessed a considerable measure of grace, and that he moved with a speed belying his years. There was an awkwardness about him because of his crooked foot and dropped shoulder, but it was evident that the man had adapted to his deteriorating condition and had compensated with other moves. Philip suspected that Aruze had been a masterful warrior in his youth, one the king was proud to have with him—no matter what foreign land he came from.

The sheriff found himself struggling to keep pace with Aruze, finding that it took all of his effort just to parry the old man's blows. There was little strength behind Aruze's swings, but they were accurate, aimed at vital organs and stopping short just in time. The sheriff inwardly beamed when, as the evening grew older, the peasant praised his techniques. And he surprised himself when he did not get angry when the old man in turn said he had a long way to go to match him.

Eventually the old man tired, announcing an end to the first lesson. He carefully placed the rapier on the ground, then he sat next to it, this move taking a bit of work because of his misshapen foot. He let out a great sigh and looked up at Philip, who'd led his horse to the door. Then he dropped his gaze to the sword and reached a finger out to caress the crosspiece.

"My Lord Sheriff, you are a passable swordsman."

Philip nodded.

"So I am curious why you have a need to be better. And why you came to me."

No answer.

"I am no one, my Lord Sheriff. No songs are sung of my deeds. Few know of my talent with a sword."

"There are a few tales," Philip said.

"So I am still curious. Why do you need to be better? Do you fear someone from within the castle? The king did and so became more skilled."

"You taught him, Aruze?"

No answer. Instead, another question. "Is it your deputy? The young fancy man from Lowdham. Does he want your position? Some lesser noble scrabblin' up the Notting-hamshire ladder? There is always intrigue among your kind. Plottin' and schemin' and . . ."

"I want Robin Hood."

Aruze wiped at something on his tattered pants. "The outlaw?"

A nod.

"He's good. Very good with a sword and very good for the common folk."

Philip instantly cursed himself for telling the old peasant the truth. He could have easily fabricated something, gone along with the notion that Eustace of Lowdham was out to get his title.

"But I don't like him," the old man continued. "Good that I know who you plan to face, my Lord Sheriff."

Philip cocked his head in a question.

"Makes the lessons different." There was still a question on the sheriff's face, and so the old man went on. "Saw Robin Hood once, fightin' some o' your soldiers on the road near Sutton Passeys. He fights from his heart, doesn't use any techniques taught by any masters. Taught anywhere for that matter. He's unpredictable. And he taunts those he fights, his words workin' as a second sword that pricks at their hearts."

Philip found himself agreeing.

"So we will have to make you unpredictable, too. And, o' course, we will teach you to close your ears to his babble."

The sheriff gave the old man a genuine smile. "You say Robin Hood is good for the commoners, yet you'll help me best him. Why?"

Aruze looked at his beautiful sword. "It is wrong, all this stealin' he does. I'll make you better than him."

"How long shall that take?"

The old man shrugged, the motion exaggerated because of his bent body. "Depends on you, my Lord Sheriff. How quick o' a learner are you?"

"Tomorrow night, then?"

Aruze nodded. "And can you bring some wine?"

The nights blurred, and in them Philip learned to improvise and to anticipate the unexpected. He discovered that by studying an opponent's eyes he could judge where the man's sword would lead. He forced himself to shut out his opponent's words, be they hurtful or filled with pleas for mercy. And all those steps and thrusts he'd studied in his youth, he hid away in the back of his mind and instead relied on what the Walnut-Hued Man taught him.

When nearly three months had passed, the old man announced there was no more he could pass on to Philip Mark—though he could always learn more by finding an even better instructor. There existed a hint of friendship between the student and teacher, one that was guarded by the difference in their stations. Still, they had closed each session with fellowship by drinking wine and feasting on whatever the sheriff brought; this last night he offered up the very finest from his cellar. Aruze would recount a battle or two from the crusades or from a duel he fought in his faraway home, and Philip would tell of some of the goings-on in Nottingham Castle, though he never spoke of the more nefarious activities. This last night the sheriff even told Aruze of his many losses to Robin Hood.

"I don't like the man," Aruze admitted again. "But I like life. A part o' me regrets givin' you the skills to kill him."

"Everyone dies," Philip said evenly, his tongue thick from the alcohol they'd been sharing. "I only intend to hurry his death along." He noticed a sadness in the old man's eyes, and he cursed himself for feeling compassion for a mere peasant. "But I will make it quick," he added for consolation.

Aruze offered his hand.

And the sheriff almost took it.

Four nights later, Philip Mark found his green-clad foe at the edge of the merchants' quarter. Robin had been skulking, hood pulled tight over his head and keeping close to the shadows. His bags were filled with goods he'd either stolen or purchased with ill-gotten gold, and he barely had time to drop them and pull his sword before the sheriff was on him.

Philip was using the Saracen chief's blade this night, finding the balance perfect now that he had more strength in his arm. This night when he lunged, Robin wasn't able to so easily dance away. Indeed, the outlaw struggled to keep pace with the sheriff, and the merchants who climbed out of their cozy beds and opened the shutters were quiet as the men traded blows.

The sheriff tried a feint, one the old man taught him early in their sessions. It caught Robin off guard, and Philip spun to his right, slashing and cutting Robin's cloak. He could have run him through, but he needed to prolong this fight, he needed to relish his victory, and he needed more witnesses.

"It is you, perhaps, who are in need of the tailor now, Robin Hood!" The sheriff swung again, and a thin line of red appeared across Robin's arm.

Robin didn't offer a reply, putting his effort instead into parrying the sheriff's expert swings. The duel took them past the merchants' businesses and into a courtyard near the front gates, where the moon shone down unobstructed. The guards turned from their posts to watch the display. People were coming out onto the street, some wrapped in blankets, others struggling into cloaks. There were no giggles this time, and no words against the sheriff, only wide-eyed stares of disbelief and gasps of surprise as he forced the outlaw to defend himself.

As the fight continued, there were murmured speculations that the sheriff for once in his life would indeed defeat Sherwood's favorite son. Robin's leggings were slashed, the moon showing that the sheriff had drawn more blood.

"No," the sheriff told him. "On second thought, you won't be needing a tailor this night. You'll be needing a priest. To pray over your grave."

Philip's swings grew bolder and wilder, the moonlight flashing along the edge of the blade as it clashed against Robin Hood's sword. Then the moonlight caught the outlaw's weapon, just as Robin began to vary his thrusts.

It was a fine and unusually thick-bladed rapier the out-

law was wielding, one with a steel hilt embossed with
bronze. There were scallops near the half-basket, edged in
silver and brass that sparkled like the stars.

"It can't be!" Philip hollered, as with that realization he
now found himself working to parry Robin Hood's blows.
"It is not possible!"

The moonlight showed no hair on the back of Robin's
hand, and when the outlaw lunged, his hood flew back,
showing a shaved head.

"By all that's holy, no!"

"By all that's holy, yes," Robin returned.

There was no stoop in the posture, no dropped shoulder or crooked foot. But the eyes were the same, glimmering with a cunning intelligence. Robin rained a series
of blows against the sheriff's heavier weapon. Then he
darted in and jabbed at his thigh.

"Why?" Philip gasped. "Why the game? Why teach me?"

"I needed a better sparring partner," the outlaw continued. "One worthy of my efforts. And I thank you for providing me with one."

"How?" But in the back of Philip's mind, he began to
answer that question. Robin had stooped his posture and
turned in his foot, shaved himself. But darkening the skin?

Philip's musings stopped when Robin further increased
the tempo of his swings, the tip of his rapier catching the
basket of the sheriff's sword and sending it flying from his
grasp. Robin darted forward again, slashing at the laces on
the sheriff's tunic, again cutting the cord that held his cape.
The garment fluttered to the ground. "We must do this
again sometime, eh, my Lord Sheriff?"

Then the outlaw was scampering toward the gate, catching the pulley rope and hauling himself up it. Before the

sheriff and the guards could react, he was over the wall and on his way to Sherwood.

Philip turned and retrieved his cloak. Then he headed toward the castle.

"Eustace!"

The sheriff slammed the door shut behind him, dismissed the guards with a wave and tromped into the great hall.

"Eustace of Lowdham, if you . . ."

The deputy sheriff was scrambling down the stairs, the hem of his robe gathered in trembling fingers.

"My Lord Sheriff?"

Philip glared, clenching and unclenching his fists, taking a step toward Eustace, then stopping himself.

"Robin Hood?" Eustace risked.

The sheriff nodded. "Indeed. Robin Hood."

Several moments of silence passed between the two, the flickering candles sending shadows dancing across the walls, specters to mock the Sheriff of Nottinghamshire.

"I will have him, Eustace. I will have him twitching on the end of my sword. There will be no force of guards to take him. I won't use soldiers. I will take him. Alone!"

"Philip, I . . ."

"To my last breath, I will work. Do you understand? He can't kill me, Eustace. He wouldn't dare kill the Sheriff of Nottinghamshire. And so I am safe. But not him. I will have him!"

"Philip, perhaps I . . ."

"Swordsmen, Eustace, you will find me the very best. I don't care if they're known. I don't care where you get them. Tomorrow at first light, you will . . ."

"Philip, I . . ."

"But this time you will make sure that they are indeed who they claim to be. No imposters, or I will find myself a new deputy sheriff and I will send you on the first ship to . . ." The sheriff glanced up into the mirror that hung over the mantle. His face was red from ire and exertion, his chest rose and fell rapidly, and he could feel his heart hammering in his chest. Through the gap in his tunic, his broad chest gleamed, and the outline of the muscles in his sword arm rippled. He had to admit he was better and stronger. But he was not yet good enough.

"The Walnut-Hued Man, Philip . . ."

"Was Robin Hood," the sheriff spat, returning his attention to his deputy. "In disguise. Aruze, Eustace. Aruze! He was, indeed, a ruse. And I—with your eager help—played right into his hands. But I will have him. You will find me a better teacher. And I will have him very soon."

The sheriff strode from the great hall, brushing by Eustace and nearly knocking the slighter man over.

"My Lord Sheriff . . ." Eustace began. "The Walnut-Hued Man is real. I saw him in Sutton Passeys. He can't have been Robin Hood. The tales . . ." But the deputy sheriff's words were lost in the shadows. Philip Mark was on his way to his armory to practice with his swords.

An old man walked south on the road past Sutton Passeys. His skin was dark, branding him a Moor, not painted on from the juice of crushed walnuts—as Robin Hood's complexion had been. His gait was slow, his foot being turned in and his shoulder dropped from age and injury. Still, it was a determined pace he kept up. The old man knew not to stay in these parts, as the sheriff would be angry at the ruse he and his student Robin Hood had concocted. It had been his idea, in truth, wanting to give the outlaw a more formidable opponent. And when Robin embraced the idea, the old man had volunteered to do the teaching. But Robin wouldn't have it, not wanting to risk the old man's life—and not wanting to risk the possibility that the sheriff might become too skilled. And might possibly defeat him.

And so the old man was headed . . . somewhere. His purse was heavy with gold coins, payment from Sherwood's beloved outlaw. And on his hip hung a fine Mascaron sword, a singular weapon that a Spanish noble had once gifted to Philip Mark. And a blade that the old man knew how to use very well.

Author's note: Historians differ on who they believe was the "Sheriff of Nottingham" of Robin Hood fame. One candidate is Philip Mark, who acted as the sheriff of Nottinghamshire and Derbyshire from 1209 to 1224. Another possible candidate is Eustace of Lowdham, who served as Philip's deputy from 1217 to 1224. Eustace himself served as the sheriff from 1232 to 1233.

A TWO-EDGED BLADE
by *Diana L. Paxson*

Diana L. Paxson is a writer of fantasy living in the literary household called Greyhaven in Berkeley, California. She has sold over seventy short stories and twenty novels, most recently an Arthurian novel, *The Hallowed Isle*, which is now appearing in two paperback volumes. The entire novel was published in a single hardcover as a Science Fiction Book Club alternate. She has just finished *Priestess of Avalon*, a collaboration with Marion Zimmer Bradley.

"A Two-Edged Blade" tells the story of an early episode in the career of Hengest, better known as the leader of the Saxon invasion of Britannia. His later exploits are recounted in *The Hallowed Isle*.

> "Then Hunlaf's son laid on his lap,
> 'Battle-bright,' best of blades,
> whose edges well by Jutes were known."
> (*Beowulf* 1143–45)

RAVENS swirled like flakes of ash in the wind that was driving the ship toward the gray shore.

"That way!" cried Frithuwulf, leaning out along the

carved figurehead to point. "The channel is just beyond those pines!"

"Winter hunts hard upon our heels. Just as well we've come to our journey's end," muttered Hengest, reaching out to grab the boy's belt as the helmsman leaned on the tiller and the ship heeled over.

For a moment Frithuwulf's weight strained his arm, then the deck heaved back and he had to scramble for balance as the boy was flung against him. In another moment King Hnaef had grabbed him, laughter stamping the faces of uncle and nephew with a momentary identity.

"There it is! Finn's burg!" Frithuwulf cried as they rounded the headland, pointing across the waste of dune and marsh through which the channel wound inward from the sea.

Frithuwulf was the son of the Frisian king, but in face he was his mother's child, and five years as Hnaef's fosterling had only strengthened the bond with his Danish kin. Would he return to his father's hall as a stranger?

At least Frithuwulf had a home to return to. For a moment Hengest's lips twisted with a bitterness he had thought forgotten. He came of the line of Wihtlaeg, the Anglian prince who killed Amlodhi, the last Jutish king, but his own father had been a second son who died young, and Hengest's only inheritance from his royal relatives was a strong right arm and his pride.

And so the descendant of Wihtlaeg led a mix of Danes and sons of the Jutish chieftains who had sided with his great grandfather, guarding the Dane-king who ruled Jutland now. And Hnaef was a good lord. With only a few years more under his belt than Hengest's twenty-three, he

treated his Anglian thane more like a brother than a fol-
lower.

And it is to Hnaef that my oath is given, thought Hengest.
Where he is, I have a home.

They were moving into the channel now, sail furled and
oars lifting and dipping in unison. Behind them the second
boat was turning, its wake doubling their own as they passed
into the brackish water of the marsh. Frithuwulf danced
with excitement as he picked out landmarks. Fifteen, and
newly granted the arms of a warrior, in that moment his
face was still that of a boy. They were still some distance
from the burg, but the mound on which Finn's settlement
stood, the carven timbers of the king's meadhall lifting
above the palisade, was clearly visible—the only place in
that coastal plain that was significantly higher than the sea.

"They've sighted us—" said Sigeferth, the oldest of the
Jutes in Hnaef's houseguard, as gesturing figures appeared
at the gate. Behind him, two dozen warriors cast an in-
stinctive glance toward their weapons, even though they
had come by invitation to keep the feast of Yule with the
Frisian king.

"I see a woman whose headdress is woven with gold,"
said Hengest. "Is that your sister?"

"You have good eyes," answered Hnaef. "I suppose it
must be, but I was younger than Frithuwulf when Hildeburh was sent away to marry Finn. Still," he added, grinning as he picked up his sword belt and buckled it over
his mail, "I daresay I'll have changed more than she has
in the last fifteen years!"

Hengest's gaze followed the movement of the sword. It
was called Battle-bright, the blade that Wihtlaeg had carried when he killed the Jute-king and later given to Hnaef's

grandfather when he made alliance with the Danes. Finn's queen would be hard to please if she was not proud of her brother and her son, he thought then, considering them. They were both long-boned, ruddy men with a smile that was like the break of day. He himself was ash-fair, the moon to Hnaef's sun, though there was strength enough in his big frame.

The two ships eased around another turn in the channel, where little black cattle grazed on the frost-bleached grass. The burg lay directly before them now. Through the open gate Hengest glimpsed a series of longhouses clustered around the royal hall. More dwellings lay outside the walls where years of occupation had extended the mound. Women were waving; from somewhere beyond them came the rich scent of cooking food. Hengest found his own lips curving in a smile. Yule was a time when men hung up their swords and drank deep before a blazing fire to drive the demons of the winter dark away. It would be good to spend this hallowed season in Finn's high hall.

The keel slid up the muddy bank as a last thrust with the oars grounded the ship. A golden torque glinted from the neck of a man, wiry in frame and a little stooped now, whose red hair was fading to gray. That must be the king. Hildeburh was beside him, a great silver-mounted drinking horn in her hands. Her younger son Frealaf clung to her skirts, staring wide-eyed at the brother he scarcely knew.

Hengest clambered over the side, jabbing the butt of his spear into the mud for balance, Sigeferth at his shoulder. Others were splashing shoreward, spreading out to flank Hnaef and Frithuwulf, who could not keep from grinning, though he had taken a correct position a step behind the Dane-king and a little to one side.

Hnaef thumped his chest with one fist in salute. "Finn Folcwalda, Frisia's King, Wassail!"

"Finn of the Frisians welcomes Hnaef Hocing in frith to his hall!" answered the king. Hildeburh started forward with the horn.

Sigeferth hissed suddenly and Hengest turned, stiffening as he met the furious gaze of a man who stood just behind the Frisian king. He noted grizzled hair and rich clothing, and a youth with the same stamp of feature at his side.

"Guthulf, here!" muttered Sigeferth. At Hengest's lifted eyebrow the old warrior's smile grew grim. "Here's one who will give neither you nor me any good welcome. He counts himself as Amlodhi's heir. . . ."

Now Hengest could see other faces darkening as the murmur passed among Finn's men. He had known, of course, that the defeated adherents of the last Jutish king had taken refuge in the surrounding kingdoms, but he had never expected to find a royal Jute in the houseguard of the Frisian king.

But Hnaef had already raised the horn to pledge frith between his house and all at Finn's burg. They had no choice now but to follow him into the hall.

"My king, let us enjoy Finn's hospitality tonight, but it would be better if we took our leave tomorrow," said Hengest softly. "The storms may hold off long enough for us to come safe to Jutland once more."

The benches of Finn's mead hall were crowded with men. The glow from the long fire pit down the center and the torches fixed to pillars on either side showed faces flushed with food and drink. But the laughter was muted. Even the native Frisians and Hnaef's Danes could sense the tension between the two groups of Jutes sitting there.

"Do you think these Jutes more dangerous than the seas?" Hnaef shook his head in disbelief. "They are Finn's sworn men. He will not allow them to break his peace in his hall!"

Both men glanced toward the high seat where Frithuwulf sat between his father and the queen. The boy was laughing, telling his mother about some exploit among the Danes. But Finn's brow was furrowed beneath the ginger-gray hair.

He is a peace-king, thought Hengest. *He has never had to deal with the madness that seizes men who see an enemy sitting with them in hall.*

"He may try.... Your folk came to the land after Amlodhi's wars," he said aloud. "You do not understand how deep the old hatreds run. Even I find it hard to comprehend— but I am a generation farther from the conflict. Men like Sigeferth and Guthlaf drank in the poison with their mother's milk. And though Finn may be a good king, he is no warrior. If tempers grow hot, will he be able to hold his men?"

"Maybe not," growled Hnaef, "but I will hold mine. I came in peace to this hall."

Hengest sighed and held out his horn for a passing maidservant to fill. But he did no more than taste the mead. Finn had signaled for his scop to come forth and sing. The murmurs quieted as the bard finished tuning the strings stretched across the narrow soundbox, painted with an interlace of birds.

The first chord silenced conversation.

> "Ho! Hear now, ye highborn heroes,
> Boasting on mead-bench, bold deeds many,
> How Aurvendill was avenged by Amlodhi,
> Crafty-mad, he killed Haethcyn ..."

The scop drew breath to begin his story, but before he could speak a bench crashed backward. Gethwulf was on his feet, face reddening with rage.

"Silence! You shall not speak of Amlodhi when his slayers' kin sit unpunished in this hall!"

The scop took a step backward, looking to his lord in alarm.

"Perhaps a different song—" Finn started, clearly not yet understanding just how great a mistake that choice had been, but Gethwulf was already whirling, snatching the sword that hung behind him on the wall. Steel scraped as he drew. His son Garulf grabbed his own blade and leaped up to guard his back, halting the warriors who had surged forward to intervene.

"Dane-king, stand away!" Gethwulf roared, "You have traitors in your train—spawn of kin-slayers, king-slayers, following Wihtlaeg's heir. Their presence pollutes this hall!"

"Put down that blade!" cried Finn, starting from his seat, but Gethwulf was beyond hearing. He leaped onto the table, sword swinging, and young Hastred, who had the misfortune to be sitting across from him, fell back, blood spurting from a great wound in his breast. Sigeferth snatched up the dagger with which he had been cutting his meat and threw it, and Gethwulf fell back into Garulf's arms with the blade embedded in the muscle of his upper arm, sword slipping from his hand.

Suddenly everyone was shouting, but Hnaef's great cry of "Hold!" overbore the rest. In the silence, all could hear the harsh gurgle as Hastred breathed his last.

"I will pay you his weregild—we will bury him with honor—" babbled Finn, but Garulf snatched up his father's fallen sword.

"That was a first payment on the weregild owed *us!*" Red drops spattered as he shook the blade, "This blade will not sleep until they all lie where that dog is now!"

"You will kill no more of my men!" grated Hnaef, reaching for his own weapon. Hengest stepped in front of him.

"This is a Jutish quarrel," he said desperately, "and no business of Frisian or Dane. If blood must be shed to settle the matter, do you stand aside, my lord—you and the Frisian king. Let *us* fight it out and have an end!"

"You are no Jute, Hengest—" Hnaef said gently.

"I am the great grandson of Wihtlaeg, and these are my men—"

"And you are *my* man," the Dane-king replied in the same soft tone. "Do you think my oath of less value than your own? I will stay with you in the hall."

Hengest shook his head despairingly as Frithuwulf came down from the high seat to stand at his uncle's side. "And I will stand with the man who fostered me, lest I be dishonored by allowing my father's men to attack a guest in his hall!"

Hildeburh's face had gone dead white, but by this time Finn had recovered his wits enough to set a line of Frisian warriors between Gethwulf and Garulf and their foes.

"This fire blazes too high for the matter to be decided now." His voice was tight with strain. "King Hnaef, I and my men will leave the hall. Tonight you may sleep here securely. Perhaps in the morning, when tempers have cooled, we may reach some accommodation." He made a sharp gesture, and Gethwulf and his followers, still glowering, allowed the Frisians to escort them out of the hall.

* * *

"Wake up!" Guthlaf turned from the door he had been guarding. "The gables are blazing!"

Hengest rubbed his eyes, surprised to find he had been dozing. Despite the cold, they had left the doors at either end of the hall ajar and set men to guard them. There was no smell of smoke, but a pale glitter of light flickered beyond the opening. His mail jingling softly, for he and Hengest had armed themselves as soon as the Frisians and their allies departed. Hnaef moved to look over Guthlaf's shoulder.

"Nay, lad," Hnaef said grimly, "this is neither a dragon nor the dawn, nor does Finn mean to burn down his own hall. That is the gleam of moonlight on armor that you are seeing as Mani slips in and out behind the clouds."

Eaha peered out the door he was guarding and stepped back with a short laugh. "You were right, Hengest—Finn couldn't hold them. Gethwulf and his rabble are out there, sure enough, shivering in the snow!"

"Arise now, my warriors!" the king's voice rang suddenly, "Bring this old feud to an end! You there—" he turned to the sleepers, "get your mail on! It's time for deeds, not dreams! Come on Dunwalh!" He dropped the boy's helmet into his lap. "Brace up, man, and stand proud. We'll need all our resolution now!"

Cursing as pounding heads protested, the men got into their armor and picked up their shields. Sigeferth joined Eaha by the main doorway and Hengest followed Ordlaf to back up his brother Guthlaf at the other end of the hall. From the side Eaha was watching came the sound of argument.

"But it is my right!" came a young voice. "You are already wounded, and I am the heir. The honor of the first attack belongs to me!"

"That sounds like Garulf," whispered Ordlaf. "I marked him for a hothead before."

A glory-mad child, thought Hengest bitterly, the same age as Frithuwulf, who stood at his uncle's elbow, eyes wide, as if he had not believed until this moment that things could really come to such a pass.

"You *are* the heir, the last child of my blood, and your life is too precious to risk against desperate men," came the answer. It must be old Gethwulf out there, despite his wound.

"Would you have me dishonor the blood we share?" exclaimed the boy. "Oath breakers, I challenge you! Which of you poor *wrecces* thinks he can keep me from coming through that door?"

Hengest stiffened, for that was a term that could be applied to him as well.

But the Jutish warrior answered with a burst of laughter. "Sigeferth is my name, chieftain of the Secgan clan, a *wrecce* whose mighty deeds are widely known!" he answered, giving the other meaning to the word. The *wrecce* was a two-edged sword—he could be the most wretched of men, landless and lonely, or a hero without a master, free to seek fame on the roads of the world. "I have known many woes and bitter battles—" Sigeferth went on. "Whatever you seek, you'll find it here!"

The scorn in his voice would have stung a more seasoned warrior. Suddenly swords rang at the doorway; light from glancing blades flickered through the hall. Watching from the other end, Hengest could not quite see what happened, but the cry of despair that rose when the swordplay ceased told its own tale. Young Garulf had paid the price for his boldness, and if there had been any hope of reconciliation, it was now gone.

In the next moment a spear thudded into Ordlaf's shield. Guthlaf locked his own shield into place beside his brother's, effectively blocking the door, while his own point darted out like a striking serpent, seeking the life of his foe. The man fell back, yelling, and Hengest laughed, set free to fight at last. He remembered then that it was always so when the die was cast and the only choice was whether to defend himself or be slain.

He and Hnaef had already settled what they must do if it came to battle. He moved now among the half of the men assigned to hold his end of the hall, choosing some to rest and some to stand ready. The usual strategy would have been to force the defenders out by setting the place on fire. So long as Finn refused to let them do so, the sixty Jutes and Danes in the hall should be able to hold the hall.

"Stand steady, men," he murmured, "and let them come. Their fathers fled before yours—it's time to see if the blood runs true!"

In the next few days, they proved it. There were wounds, especially once the shields had been splintered, but none of Hnaef's men fell. It was the attackers who were dying, each day reducing their advantage in numbers as they dashed themselves against the Danish defenses. Nor could they starve out their foe. Every morning the queen and her women would bring water and food and firewood to replenish their supplies. No one dared forbid her—her son was in that hall.

Sometimes the Danes could hear Gethwulf cursing the wound that had kept him out of the fighting, and Sigeferth

would grin in his beard. Sometimes also, they heard the
Frisian king, asking some warrior who had retreated, mail
pierced and shield in fragments, if the two young men, his
son and his brother-in-law, still stood unscathed.

We will get through this, Hengest told himself as the
days went on. *We have only to hold on until they realize
that they cannot win.*

And so it went on until the sixth night, in the darkest
hour of the out-tide when the limbs grow cold and men
lie locked in the coils of sleep. Even the men guarding the
doors must have worn out their vigilance, for with each
day the vigor of the attackers had lessened. Old Hunlaf, at
the western entrance, started upright with a shout as Dunwalh, who stood beside him, went down with a spear
through his gut. Arms stiffened by inaction could do no
more than raise his shield before a rush of attackers sent
him sprawling.

In the next moment the rest of Hnaef's men were rousing, reaching for the weapons they slept with, but the attackers were already inside, striking and slashing like
wolves in a sheepfold. The bloody darkness rang with the
screams of dying men.

An overturned bench rolled into the fire pit, and in the
sudden swirl of sparks Hengest glimpsed Gethwulf laying
about him like a berserker.

"Guess his arm is better," gasped Hnaef. He staggered,
and Hengest reached out to steady him, his gut tensing as
he saw the widening stain of red on the Dane-king's breast.

"My lord, you're hurt!" He got an arm around the other
man's waist and dragged him toward the high seat.

Hnaef nodded. "Through the armhole, under my mail."

He sank heavily on to the cushion and sagged back against the carven slats of the back.

A shape loomed up and Hengest whirled, stabbing, wrenching his blade free as the dead weight of his enemy bore it down. He turned back to the king. Hnaef's eyes were closed. "No . . ." he whispered, and saw Hnaef's lips twitch in the ghost of a smile.

"Scyld's ship is coming . . ." whispered the Dane-king, "to take me to Woden's hall. . . ."

"Hnaef, you must live! We need you!"

"Take care of my men. . . ." came the answer, and then his breath departed in a bubbling sigh and he was still.

For a long moment Hengest simply stared. Then reason was overwhelmed by a red tide of rage and sorrow. Sword wheeling in great arcs, he plunged back into the fray.

When next he came to himself, he was staring around the charnel house that had once been the proud mead hall of the Frisian king. In the cold light of dawn the bodies of Danes and his own Jutes, nearly half the sixty men who had come with them, lay mingled with those of their enemies. Hnaef slumped in the high seat, the sword Battle-bright still gripped in his cold hand. Hengest had taken a step toward him when he heard a gasp of surprise.

"Woden! This was an evil night indeed!" Hunlaf was staring down at Frithuwulf, who lay with a spear in his side, eyes fixed in surprise.

The women, finally, had ceased their wailing. After the first great cry Hildeburh herself had maintained a frozen composure, but since the terrible moment when Finn had emerged from the hall, staggering with his dead son in his arms, the other women had mourned him. Now, the only sound was the crackling of the flames, and the hiss and pop of the flesh burning on the funeral pyres.

The fire is the only victor here, thought Hengest, wincing as a shift in the flames brought a momentary glimpse of wounds that the heat had caused to bleed anew. *Greediest of spirits, it devours friend and foe. . . .*

It was the queen who had taken charge on that gray morning, while Finn sat weeping, Hildeburh who had ordered the Frisians to take in charge those few Jutes of Finn's houseguard who had survived, to prepare the bodies of the dead, and to build a great funeral pyre before the royal burial mound. Gold glistened from the bodies with a brighter flame, cups and platters brought from Finn's treasury to honor the fallen, torques and arm-rings and the gilded boar-crests on royal helms.

Hnaef lay there, and the queen had commanded them to set Frithuwulf beside him, uncle and sister-son burning in one fire. Sigeferth was with them, and nearly thirty of the men they had brought with them, both Jute and Dane. But Gethwulf and Garulf burned with twice that number on the second pyre,

My lord has a fine escort to Waelhal, Hengest thought numbly. *I should be among them.*

The shame of his own survival had haunted him since he saw the life leave Hnaef's eyes. In the last moments of the battle he had tried hard enough to spend his life in vengeance, but no blade, it seemed, would bite him, and when it was over, standing in the midst of the carnage he had looked around at the groaning survivors and remembered his promise to watch over Hnaef's men. But a thane should die with his lord or else avenge him—every tale ever told by scop before the fire made that duty clear.

Hengest's gut knotted with tension, his own flesh fighting itself, as the kindred lutes had warred not so long ago.

Wind gusted in from the sea, sending black smoke swirling to clouds nearly as black. Wet snowflakes touched his cheek, bitter as the kisses of the waelcyriges who bore away the spirits of the slain, but they could not damp the fury of the fires. Beyond the marshes the sea frothed. His first thought had been to take his little band home to Jutland as soon as the funerals were done, but winter had come, and no ship would sail these waters until it was over. They were trapped among their enemies.

By the day's ending, when the fires had burned down to coals, the sun appeared for a brief moment beneath clouds that glowed as if she had lighted her own funeral pyre upon the waves. Someone murmured in surprise, and rousing, Hengest saw that Finn was making his way toward him, leaning on the arm of the queen.

"Your king feasts now in Woden's hall, but you and your men still hold mine," said Finn.

Hengest frowned, wondering what the old man was getting at. "That is true," he said evenly. "And there we will stay until we are able to take ship for home. Whether we do so in peace or hostility depends on you."

"Yes, yes," the king answered with a nervous glance around him. The Frisians in his guard numbered scarcely a dozen. It would take him time to gather together a new *comitatus*, Hengest thought grimly, and until then, the Danes held the upper hand. "It is a firm pact of peace that I offer you, as my wise old men have counseled me. Spend this winter here as my houseguard, sharing equally in the golden gifts with which I reward my Frisian thanes."

"Serve the king whose men slew our own dear lord?" exclaimed old Hunlaf. "We would be shamed!"

"No man of mine shall break the pact," Finn said earnestly, "nor mock the Danes for doing what necessity has laid upon you. And if any Frisian should speak amiss to one of your Jutes and bring the feud to mind again, the sword's edge shall guarantee it, in the name of Tir, I swear!"

He needs us, thought Hengest grimly. Honest folk kept close to home through the winter, but there were masterless men, wretches indeed, who would fall on Finn and his treasures like ravening wolves if it were known he was unprotected here. *And we need him . . .* he told himself then. His gaze searched the faces of the survivors—the Jutes whose ancient allegiance to his house had caused the feud, and the Danes, over whom he had only what authority they chose to grant him. After a moment old Hunlaf nodded.

"Very well, we will stay and defend your burgh," Hengest told the Frisian king, thrusting his rage back to gnaw like a serpent in his gut, "until spring opens the sea lanes once more."

The feast of Yule, that should have been passed so mirthfully, was no more than an occasion for men to drown their sorrows. In the days that came after, a storm howled in from the North Sea, lashing the land. Hunlaf, who at times had the troll-sight, swore that he had seen the Wild Hunt thundering through those roiling clouds, Hnaef riding with them with Frithuwulf at his side. Gethwulf and Garulf were there also and many another, for friend and foe alike must ride together, all enmity forgotten, when Woden hunts the winter skies.

In Middle Earth it was otherwise. Finn had been as good

as his word, and expanded and fitted out one of the other halls to be a fit home for Hengest and his men. But some contact was unavoidable. In the long dark of the first month of the new year tempers shortened. A Frisian insult led to blows, and a holmgang in the snow. Finn's man died, but in the thaw that began the month of Hretha, the first small band of warriors who had heard of the Frisian losses arrived, and though the seas were still uncertain, a small but steady trickle of reinforcements, seeking a place in Finn's service, made their way across the marshes. Nothing was said, but Hengest could see his superiority in numbers decreasing daily, and the serpent in his belly began to twist once more.

Just after the equinox, Ordlaf and Guthlaf set out one morning, intending, as they said, to go hunting, and did not return. Hengest, noting that their father did not seem particularly worried, and remembering that they had gone well-provisioned and somewhat overly burdened with gear, forbore to send out searchers. Had duty not constrained him, he would have been off to Jutland himself.

The days lengthened and spring, most glorious of seasons, laid a mantle of fragile green across the marshes. The air grew clamorous with the cries of migrating waterfowl. Hengest longed to wing northward with them, but though some of the men grew restless, he did nothing, though he was himself uncertain what held him there.

And then, on a day when a warm breeze from the south set the blood to singing in the veins, the sons of Hunlaf returned. Hengest wondered if Finn believed their tale of having lost their way and spent the rest of the winter with a farmer whose daughters had persuaded them to stay. Ordlaf and Guthlaf had not come slinking back like dogs from a bitch, but tense and watchful as wolves.

That night, when the Danes had left the meadhall to return to their own lair, the Hunlafings came to Hengest where he sat gazing into the fire. He roused only when they knelt before him, the short hairs rising on his neck as he recognized the unsheathed blade that Ordlaf was holding out to him,

"Battle-bright!" he named the sword. "I thought it had burned on Hnaef's pyre!"

"Our father, as eldest among the Danes, took it into his keeping," Guthlaf answered softly. "Now we offer it to you. . . ." Light glanced from the gold in the hilt and flickered along the serpentine ripples in the steel of the blade, bright as the flames of Hnaef's pyre.

"My forefather Wihtlaeg once bore this blade," Hengest's voice cracked. "He carried it when he carved out his kingdom. Its edges are famous among the Jutes—"

"Even more famous now," Ordlaf agreed grimly, "but Hnaef is unavenged—" He lowered the sword until the hilt lay in Hengest's lap. "We have brought a shipload of warriors from the Dane-mark. They lie now in the Boar Wood, awaiting my signal. Will you take up this blade and lead us against the Frisian men?"

The hall was silent, every eye fixed upon Hengest as Dane and Jute alike waited to see what he would do. Hengest understood then that he was not the only one to have harbored a serpent of rage in his belly through the dark winter days. Grief and guilt had gnawed all those who survived that night when the Jutes killed their king. He understood now the anguish that had eaten at Gethwulf all those years. There came a time when only more blood would ease the pain. Moved by some force deeper than will, Hengest's fingers closed upon the cold hilt of the sword.

Afterward, it seemed to Hengest that this single movement had been like the spark that falling into waiting tinder, ignites a holocaust. Events unfolded with a dreadful inevitability, as if they had spent the whole winter planning. Perhaps they had done it in their dreams. But the dreams of the Danes were Finn's nightmare.

Guthlaf had gone off first, to guide the hidden warriors to Finnesburgh. When they came, they bore bundles of brushwood on their backs to add to the kindling Hengest and his lutes brought from their own hall. By now it was the out-tide, but the cold no longer chilled Hengest's bones. His heart was burning like the torch with which they set the wood they had stacked around Finn's mead hall ablaze.

When the smoke awakened the sleepers inside, they allowed the women, the children and the thralls to escape through the one entrance they had left unbarred. The warriors charged out through the door with swinging swords, to be cut down in a brief and bloody battle by the waiting Danes. And after a time there came no more men, only the hot breath of the flames as the timbers burned through and the roof of that ill-fated hall where Hnaef had died fell in.

Then the Danes and the lutes of Hengest's band raged through the burgh. The goods and treasure they could carry were gathered up, and the rest put to the torch. The smoke of burning buildings made a red haze of the dawn.

"Was Finn killed in the fighting?" asked Hengest, gazing at the charred timbers of the hall.

Eaha shrugged. "He never came through the door. I think it likely that the meadhall was his pyre. The younger son, Frealaf, was brought out by a nursemaid and is nowhere to be found. No doubt they have spirited him away into the countryside. We could search. . . ."

Hengest shook his head. "Let him go. We have done enough ill to the Frisians. I will not kill a child." Suddenly he felt very tired.

"Let us be going, then," answered Eaha. "The wind is fair."

Hengest lifted his head, scenting, as the smoke shifted, the bracing, bitter breath of the sea.

"Yes . . . in Woden's name let us be gone from here!" He turned, and limping a little from a sword slash he had not noticed until now, made his way to the storeshed, very nearly the only building left unburned, where they had put the queen.

"My lady—" He bent to go through the door. "It is over. We will take you home now."

Hildeburh looked up, and the desolation in her gaze chilled his soul.

"I have no home," she said in a still voice. "My home was not a place, but people, and you have slain them all. My heart died with them. With my body you may do what you please. . . ."

Hengest could find no words to answer her. He backed out of the shed and gave a terse order to Guthlaf to escort the lady to the landing while the rest of them loaded up the spoils of Finnesburgh.

"The Danes will call you a hero, when the scops tell tales of this day," said Hunlaf. He swayed as the ship rounded the headland and leaped suddenly before the wind. Only one of the two craft in which Hnaef's people had come to Frisia was still seaworthy, but the survivors were scarcely enough in number to man it. The other ship, that Hunlaf's sons had brought back from the Dane-mark, danced over the waves ahead of them, seeking the sea.

Hengest looked at the still, set, face of the queen who sat beneath a canvas awning by the mast, and shook his head. Hildeburh had been right. The Dane-mark was not his home. With Hnaef he had lost land as well as lord, and there was now no hearth where he could claim a welcome.

I am a wretch, not a hero, he thought then, *and where now shall I wander to find a home?* Perhaps he could leave the north coasts entirely and seek his fortune in Britannia, where he had heard that the Romans were hiring men.

Behind him, ravens circled, and the smoke of Finnesburgh stained the morning sky.

Note: My interpretation of the Finnesburgh story is based on J.R.R. Tolkien's "Jutes on both sides" theory, as expanded by Alan Bliss in Finn and Hengest *(Houghton-Mifflin Co., 1983)*

HERITAGE
by Fiona Patton

Fiona Patton was born in Calgary, Alberta in 1962 and grew up in the United States, returning to Canada in 1976. After a series of schools and a series of jobs including carnival ride operator, electrician, and group home counselor, she sold her first book, *The Stone Prince*, to DAW in 1997. Two other books in the *Branion* series followed with *The Painter Knight* and *The Granite Shield*. *The Golden Sword* is due out in 2001. She now lives in rural Ontario with her partner, four huge cats, and a tiny Chihuahua who thinks he's a fierce farm dog.

"ALEXANDRA TATIANA!"

Pravitni Sasha Nikorov jerked her gaze from the horizon as the harshly spat sound of her formal names snapped her from her reverie.

Mentally cursing herself, she came to attention, the ax held like a musket at her side. This was only her second day at the garrison of Petrokolymsk and already she'd broken her father's first piece of advice. *Don't get noticed.*

The Gvardia Starski who'd shouted her name stalked forward and shoved his face to within inches of hers. In a tone of sarcastic politeness, he repeated the question she'd not heard. "Do we see something of interest on the steppe, Pravitni Nikorov?"

There was only one answer to make. "I thought I saw a wolf, sir!"

He gave a yellow-toothed snarl in response. "No doubt. The gray wolves of Skovetskoe are as big as a full-grown man, and can bring down a buck elk each one alone, and they travel in packs of fifty or more. You wouldn't last one night out there alone with them, would you, Alexandra Tatiana?"

"No, Gvardia Starski."

"Then pay attention, or you'll find yourself guarding a frozen river at midnight this winter!"

"Sir!"

He looked her up and down, his sharp face twisted in disdain. "You're from Kyvansk."

Her father's second piece of advice, *Don't argue with superiors,* looked to be broken as fast as his first, but the Kyvanski lived on the border of hostile Iliatsi, and were rumored to be closer to their southern neighbors than to their fellow Velinkans. Better to be thought a troublemaker than a traitor. That her grandmother, whom she strongly resembled had been Kyvanski, come north to find work, was better left unsaid.

"No, sir, Takolov Province."

"Then you've seen plenty of wolves," he grated.

"Yes, sir."

He made to dismiss her, then stopped, his eyes narrowed.

"Takolov Province, eh? You'd be kin to Pieter Nikorov, then."

It was not a question and Sasha could see some of the

older soldiers turn to glance in her direction. There was nothing for it but to answer.

"My father, sir."

The Gvardia Starski's heavily seamed face paled slightly. He looked about to say something, then abruptly gestured her back to work and stumped away.

Trying to ignore the stares of the others, Sasha swung her ax, biting deep into a young birch tree.

"Looks like *you've* made a friend. Must be your sparkling personality."

She spun about, an involuntary snarl on her face, but bit back the retort when she saw who'd spoken.

Yuri Pavel Sazonov was a small, irrepressibly good-humored young man who'd spent most of the month-long march to Petrokolymsk trying to convince Sasha to sleep with him. Finally, tired of his humorous advances, she'd had a serious talk with him, then pushed him toward a local whore with instructions to stay there until he wore it out. They'd been friends ever since despite his sense of humor and her lack of one. It was impossible to stay angry with him, so she contented herself with a warning frown in his general direction before returning her attention to the tree.

Yuri took an armload of green logs to the wagon, but as soon as the Gvardia Starski was well out of earshot, he sidled up to her again. "So who's Pieter Nikorov?" he asked curiously.

"My father, fool, like I said." The ax bit deep, sending a triangular-shaped piece of wood flying out at him. Yuri merely stepped to one side, then returned to his original position.

"Sure, but why did old stone-trousers react like that? What'd your father do?"

"It was before your time," Sasha answered evasively, and one of the older veterans snorted.

"It was before you were born." Hauling a tied bundle of limbs onto his back, he glared at the two recruits. "And it's a tale better left untold."

Sasha watched him trudge toward the wood wagon, and then, under the sudden baleful glare of the Gvardia Starski, swung her ax at the tree again. "He served against the Il-iatsi in the garrison of Tagansk, okay?"

"But weren't they all. . . ?"

"Yes." Her father's third piece of advice had been un-spoken but understood by them both. And as equally fu-tile as his first two, she thought with a grimace. They'd been foolish to think they could have hidden the truth. Sol-diers have long memories. Better to get it all out in the open so it could be forgotten about. She turned to face Yuri.

"They were all wiped out in the winter campaign eigh-teen years ago. All of them, except my father."

"Wiped out?"

"Killed. By wolves."

Turning her back on his questioning look, her eyes found the horizon and the vague, flitting shape she'd thought she'd seen out of the corner of her eye.

Beside her, Yuri followed her gaze, saying nothing.

"You've been stationed where?"

Her mother had laid the plate down on the table and turned, the tone in her husband's voice making her frown. Sasha, the feel of her new uniform coat an unfamiliar weight on her shoulders, had simply handed over her orders. Her father had held the paper as if it were unclean.

"*Petrokolymsk.*"

The war was over, had been over for five years, but the Velinkan Empire still maintained a ring of forts across its eastern borders, and Petrokolymsk was the easternmost garrison, now that Tagansk lay in eighteen-year-old ruins.

Her parents had traded one apprehensive glance and then her father had simply handed the paper back with a grunt.

"*When do you leave?*"

The family never spoke of that year, that winter, when the Iliatsi, guided some said, by the Kyvanski, had stormed her father's garrison one dark night. The survivors had been driven out into a driving blizzard to freeze. The wolves had found them before the storm could.

Her father had been the only one to come home.

"Sasha!"

"What!"

Pulled from her thoughts yet again, she stared unseeing at the bit of sausage Yuri held out to her, then accepted it with a rueful smile. Around them, the rest of the wood-cutting detail were pulling out canteens and packages of food.

Biting into the spicy meat, she allowed Yuri to fish her canteen from its place beside her powder horn and take a long swallow before she snatched it away. Life was good, she counseled herself. She had friends, she had work. If she distinguished herself, she might even be promoted. There was no reason she should fear the past or the future.

She finished the last of her canteen, muttering, "Serves you right for finishing yours," in response to Yuri's plaintive expression, and purposely turned her back on the steppes. She had no reason to fear them either.

In the distance she thought she heard a wolf call.

Some hours later, as the late autumn sun cast orange bands across the horizon, the wood-cutting detail exchanged axes for muskets and made their way back to Petrokolymsk. For now they marched easily, their weapons hung loosely over their shoulders with their powder horns and ammunition pouches. When winter came, she knew, they would be more vigilant.

"Take him, Sasha."

Yuri, whispered the words urgently in her ear and she jerked her head at him to be quiet. Two hundred yards away a hare nibbled at a piece of foliage poking up from the snow, unaware of the hunting party crouched in the nearby stand of pines. Pushing up the brim of her kiver, Sasha squinted down her musket barrel and pulled the trigger. One shot, and the force of it kicked the animal into the air.

"Meat tonight," Yuri hooted, bounding from his place beside her as the others grinned.

The hunting party was on its way back from a three-day sojourn, two elk strapped to poles carried between the four of them. The elk was for the garrison, the hare would be for them.

Holding it up by the ears, Yuri allowed its blood to drip onto the snow as the others came forward. Sasha paused to load her musket again, carefully shielding the flint from the wind, before joining them. Winter had come early to Skovetskoe, and hunting parties went out armed and ready to defend themselves and their catch from the barely tamed Kyvanski and from the wolves.

In the distance they could hear the now familiar cry of a pack out hunting its own game on the frozen steppe. The hair on the back of Sasha's neck rose. Turning, she scanned the horizon, but the pack was too far away to be seen. Reluctantly, she lowered her weapon and joined the others.

A natural tracker and seemingly unafraid of the danger beyond the garrison walls, Sasha had often been sent out that autumn to chase the moving herds of elk. At first, she'd gone as a junior hunter, but as the weeks passed, and her prowess had become clear, she'd found the veterans relying on her skills more and more often. Soon she accompanied every hunting party, rarely spending more than one or two nights at a time in the fort.

Although relieved to be free of the stifling atmosphere of winter garrison life, and pleased that her skills had been noticed, Sasha often suspected there was more to it than that. In the four months she'd been at Petrokolymsk very few of her fellow soldiers had been able to look her in the eye. Too many remembered Tagansk. After that first day, the Gvardia Starski had ignored her, but Yuri had told her he'd said that she represented bad luck for the garrison. The howling of the Skovetskoe wolf packs, growing more frequent as the winter took hold of the countryside, seemed to agree.

The stares and the questions no one dared ask were oppressive, so she was always relieved when the Kapitan called for a hunting party. Finally, he'd simply put her in charge of three others and sent them out with instructions to find food.

Now, in the company of Yuri, Nadya, and Jacek, she felt

free. Yuri kept up a steady stream of jokes and nonsense, and the others, plains hunters from northern Uzakh Province, were a solid and sensible pair, used to the cold and uninterested in the past.

All four of them now wore the long Kyvanski tunics of heavy pelts over their greatcoats and fur kubankas on their heads. Sometimes it seemed they had more in common with the hide-clad Kyvanski than with their own comrades. As the winter set in with a vengeance and only Sasha and her party dared the frozen steppe and the wolf packs to find meat, the few Kyvanski hunting parties they met were the only other humans to be found.

Walking a little away from the others, Sasha scanned the horizon. Nothing moved. The wolf pack, farther away than they sounded, would be closer tonight. Sasha ordered the others to make camp. They would wait.

That night, wrapped in a thick blanket by the fire, she cradled her hands around her musket and squinted into the darkness beyond the fire's light. They had a good defensive position tonight and the moon was full. It would be a good night for killing.

In her shirt pocket, a letter from her mother crinkled against her skin. She was worried about Sasha's father. Since winter had set in, Pieter had become withdrawn and silent, worrying, her mother wrote, about Sasha. Couldn't she write more often? Surely the garrison duties let up enough to allow one letter to her parents now and then.

Sasha had read the note impatiently. She *had* written, although only once since autumn, she had to admit, but garrison life was dull, and her thoughts would not have comforted her parents, thoughts about the hunt, and the kill, thoughts of her rivals, the howling wolf packs, and the pelts that warmed her party on the long nights. And once out on the open steppe she had no thoughts for anything but the hunt.

In the distance something moved.

Squinting in the darkness, Sasha eased the musket up. It was early yet. The whole pack had yet to gather, but she had patience. The pack leader would show itself soon enough and that was the one Sasha wanted.

Moments passed and she continued to stare into the darkness. The sparks and smoke from the fire obscured her vision, then a shape that might have been a figure, swirled into her line of sight and out again. She thought she saw a face, a length of smoky-gray hair flowing in the icy wind, a mocking smile, one hand beckoning, and then she saw a muzzle in the firelight and knew it was time.

Easing the hammer back, she took aim as she worked her foot from the blanket and kicked Yuri. He woke quickly and silently, one hand moving to the musket at his side, the other touching Nadya on the shoulder. She was slower to react, but roused Jacek, and soon all of them were ready. It was an old game. One they had played with increasing success all winter.

The wolf leaped and Sasha fired. Throwing off their blankets, the others brought their own weapons up as the pack came into view.

Some distance away, a pair of glittering eyes watched the fight, assessing the strengths and weaknesses of the new pack in her territory and of the new leader making her challenge.

*　　*　　*

A week later Sasha and her squad were back in Petrokolymsk for refitting. It had been three weeks since their departure and the garrison was buzzing with news. Word was that since peace had held for over five years the more distant forts were being decommissioned. The new Emperor wanted money for new pleasures and soldiers to guard his new palaces. Come spring they were all being transferred to other duties, and Petrokolymsk was to be destroyed, consigned to the same fate as abandoned Tagansk. In the barracks there were murmurs of unrest. The soldiers hadn't been paid since autumn and none had been granted leave. Morale was low. The kapitan had taken to drink, and he neither knew nor cared how long Sasha's party had been away. They stayed one night and were back out on the frozen steppe before dawn.

"Do you see her?"

Sasha had whispered the words to Yuri that night weeks ago as she'd stared into the darkness, and then, as now, Yuri had shaken his head. He never saw the gray-haired woman with the glittering eyes who stood just outside the circle of firelight. The woman who watched and waited and sent her wolves in to test the accuracy of their aim and the limit of their weapons. The woman whom Sasha had fired upon each night, and who returned each night to be fired upon again. Whether she was an apparition or a mortal being Sasha could never tell, but each night as she raised her musket, she began to believe that the woman was her own personal vision.

The team now hunted for themselves, holding up when Sasha said it would storm, moving when she said it was safe. They walked with the pelts, both elk and wolf, strapped to their backs, and traded them with the silent Kyvanski for gunpowder, shot and foods other than meat. The Kyvanski seemed neither hostile, nor friendly, merely watchful and Sasha had Nadya do the trading when they came to their camp so that she could maintain a watchful position of her own.

They hadn't been to Petrokolymsk in over a month. None of them seemed to miss it.

Then one day, they came upon the ruins of a stone-and-wood palisade.

Sasha stood upon a broken rampart, watching as the others explored the site. Finally Yuri climbed up beside her.

"The buildings are all in disrepair. Holes in the roof, doors broken in. It looks like fire went through it. Actually it looks like an army went through it."

"One did."

Her voice was distant and Yuri shuddered, his usual humor dampened. "Tagansk."

She nodded.

"The Kyvanski say it's haunted."

"It is."

"Are we staying?"

"We're staying."

That night the wolves circled the outside of the fort. Nadya and Jacek were stationed just inside the gates, but none of the animals ventured inside. Yuri stood beside Sasha on the top of the ramparts, waiting.

On a small rise to the east of the fort, an old woman with long, flowing gray hair also stood waiting. After a moment a shot rang out and one of her wolves fell. She was not concerned. There were plenty to replace it. She had called, and the packs had responded by the dozens; more coming in every day. There was another shot, followed by a muffled curse. The young one had missed. She was impatient. The old woman smiled, her silvery teeth glinting in the faint moonlight. She had time. The young one would not travel any further this winter. She had come to this place of her father's to take her stand. She would defend her territory to the last bullet, as he had, and then the true test would begin.

As the moon rose in the night sky, the old woman raised her head, and sniffed the breeze. Spring was still a long way off. Satisfied, she dropped to all fours and padded down toward the fort, the moon turning her pelt a silvery gray. Time to awaken the young one's blood again.

Days had passed. Sasha was no longer sure how many. Nadya and Jacek now went out alone to hunt in the morning and returned with their catch well before dark. Sasha and Yuri tracked the wolf packs, trying to find their lair and their leader. The nights were spent on the walls.

They'd repaired some of the outer defenses, dug a few traps, but mostly they waited, each with their own position, each taking their turns at sleep and watchfulness. Waiting, for the pack leader to show herself.

But the pack leader was also waiting; waiting for the young one's ancestry to rise to the fore, for the night she would no longer be content to crouch behind the human defenses of wood and stone, but would come down to fight for dominance on the steppe. It would be soon, the pack leader knew. She could smell the change on the night's breeze.

The next day Nadya and Jacek returned with only a single hare to show for their day's sojourn. The herds had moved too far away, fleeing the growing number of predators in the area. They would have to leave the fort if they wanted to find food.

Sasha heard the news silently. They had enough meat and wood stored for two weeks, and powder and shot for a week beyond that. They would wait.

The others accepted her decision without comment, only Yuri glancing at her with a worried frown.

In the distant hills, the pack leader slept in the midst of her wolves, and smiled in her dreaming. It was time.

That night it began to snow. Soon a blizzard drove the others to the relative safety of the ruined barracks and Sasha alone stood on the walls. Wrapped in heavy furs, she ignored the wind and snow, staring down into the night. A long, undulating cry sounded in the distance, a cry of challenge and battle. The hair on the back of her neck rose, and her throat strained with the effort not to howl her denial in reply. Instead, she lifted her musket and shot blindly into the storm.

On the rise, with her wolves crouched about her, the pack leader laughed at the sound. She stood, and with a rippled motion dropped to all fours. Touching noses with one of the great, gray wolves she turned and together they flowed down the hill toward the fort.

Sasha saw them coming and jerked her weapon toward them, but at that moment she heard a shot. Spinning around, she squinted into the fort's courtyard. Gray shapes appeared through breaks in the storm and, with sudden clarity, she knew the wolves were somehow inside the fort.

Leaping down, she ran toward the barracks. There was another shot, a bullet whizzed past her and she threw herself to the ground. In her muffling pelts, she must look exactly like one of the attackers. The best she could do was find a defensive position and add her firepower to that of her people. She began to crawl toward a pile of rubble, but before she reached it, she heard a scream. The barracks door was open, gray shapes pouring into the breach. She had one sight of Jacek on his back, two wolves at his throat, before she leaped in, swinging the butt of her musket like a club.

It connected with a solid thunk, and one of Jacek's attackers was flung aside by the impact. The other turned, standing over Jacek's prone body, growling its challenge.

Sasha screamed in reply, her lips drawn back over her own teeth, her face twisted in a furious grimace. She swung the musket again. The wolf dodged aside. They circled each other warily, each staring into the other's eyes, each waiting for the other to make a mistake. Sasha felt rather than saw another form appear beside her, knew it to be Yuri. She heard his shot, saw the wolf kicked out and fall.

They had just a moment to catch their breath. Yuri, his eyes wide and shocky, blood dripping from a wound in his arm, nonetheless calmly reloaded his weapon and looked to his leader. She nodded her reply and they turned, back to back, waiting for the next attack, but the wolf pack had vanished.

* * *

Morning saw the end of the storm and the end of Tagansk. The wind had pulled most of the palisade down, the wolves had done the rest. Jacek was dying, raving in pain by the fire, and Nadya had disappeared. Heavy drag marks and blood on the snow, almost obliterated by the storm, betrayed her fate.

Crouched by the fire, Yuri held his arm up for Sasha's inspection.

"Will it have to be cauterized?" he asked, attempting a light tone of voice, but the pale flesh about his eyes and mouth betraying his fear.

Sasha shook her head. "Sewn."

"Oh, only that. Well, you'd better get it over with."

He'd only screamed once, a tight little sound that had leaked between his clenched teeth, but after Sasha had bound his arm with strips of shirt, and hide, he'd thrown up.

Jacek died two days later. Unable to dig in the frozen ground, they wrapped him in the fresh pelts of the two attacking wolves and tucked him into an old bread oven, jamming bits of wood into the hinges to secure the door. It was as good a vault as they could find for him. There was little to say in eulogy and the two of them merely stood in silence a while before turning away.

That night they stood on the top of the palisade looking down at the steppe. The wolves had not returned since the attack, but something in the air told Sasha they would be back soon.

The full moon illuminated the snow, casting a series of gray shadows across the hills.

Yuri stirred beside her.

"We're just about out of ammunition."

Sasha nodded.

"And powder."

"I know."

"It's a long time until spring, Sasha, and I don't want to die here."

"You won't."

They said nothing for a long time, and then Yuri stirred to her again.

"Sasha, why did we come here?"

She shrugged. "We just stumbled on it, Yuri," she answered. "I wasn't aiming for it."

"But was she?" He gestured toward the hills, and Sasha frowned.

"I don't know. Maybe."

"So why did we stay?" he asked, watching her expression, grown so feral in the last few weeks.

She shook her head. "I stayed because I had to . . . I still have to. There's something I have to do . . . something I have to face. I can feel it. The others stayed because, well, they stayed because I was their leader."

"So why did I stay?" Yuri asked quietly, almost to himself.

"Because you're mine."

"Yes, but your what?" The old, teasing sound was back in his voice, though a little strained.

Sasha didn't bother to turn her gaze from the steppe. "Just mine."

Giving up the attempt at levity, he followed her gaze. "So what do we do now?" he asked after a time.

"We wait."

"We can't wait too long."

"We won't have to."

"We don't have much of a defense."

"It doesn't matter."

The wolves came that night, over a hundred of them flowing over the broken palisade like gray water in the spring. Sasha and Yuri shot until they ran out of bullets, then swung with their muskets until they were overrun. As the pack rushed in, snapping and snarling, a new cry was heard over the steppe.

Moments later, the pack leader entered Tagansk for the second time.

Spring came late that year. When the rivers finally thawed, sending great chunks of ice flowing into the sea, and when the grass began to show a faint greenish glow amongst the dead, yellow stalks, the Emperor's messengers came to Petrokolymsk. They brought word of the garrison's disbanding and of strange findings out on the steppes. A dead man had been found to the west, a living man to the south. With the help of the garrison, the living man was identified as Pravitni Yuri Pavel Sazonov of Petrokolymsk. He'd been wandering the steppes, dressed in ragged wolf pelts and living on raw meat. He was half wild from hunger and cold and had run from them at first. He had bites on his body and an old, badly healed wound on his arm, wrapped in dirty linen. He didn't speak, hadn't spoken since they'd found him. They brought him to Petrokolymsk and tried to make him comfortable.

The dead man had been found frozen in the lee of a pine tree where he'd obviously crouched to hide from some winter storm. In his pocket they'd found the scrap of a note addressed to one Sasha Nikorov. Their officer had read it, then burned it, but not before the Pravitni who'd found it had shared its contents with the rest of the troop.

The note had been almost obliterated by ice, but some of the words had been clear,

> . . . *dear Sasha . . . wish . . . told you sooner, but . . . need to know . . . the truth . . . never should . . . let you . . . east. Please do not . . . Petrokolymsk . . . Grandmother . . . not Kyvanski . . . Volkiasti . . . Do not . . . among them . . . they will claim you . . . tried to . . .*

The troop had discussed this nervously, and finally the Starski had raised enough courage to ask their leader the meaning of the strange word. The woman had shuddered.

"It's a Kyvanski word," she'd explained. "It means Wolf-Kind. Set extra guards tonight."

The garrison moved out one week later, Yuri Sazonov carried in a litter. As they passed over the plains they heard the cry of the wolf packs, but none ventured near the large party of armed soldiers. Soon the steppe gave way to the rolling hills of the western provinces.

The Velinkan's final night on the plains, two women crouched on a low rise, looking down on their camp. One had long, flowing gray hair, the other, black and tangled locks just growing out of a military haircut. The young one leaned forward eagerly.

"Are we hunting tonight?" she asked.

The old one shook her head.

"There are too many of them. They have guns."

"We could get guns."

"We don't need guns."

The young one stirred impatiently. "But we could still *get* guns," she muttered.

The older woman quelled her with a glance.

"Your Yuri is down there," she reminded her. "I thought you wanted him saved."

"I do, I guess, but . . ."

"But . . . ?"

"We could kill *most* of the others and take their guns."

The older woman laughed at the young one's newfound ferocity but shook her head again.

The young one glared down at the intruding camp, trying to call up the smiling face of the young man but the memory was already becoming a blur. Yuri. The old one's bargaining piece. Sasha's life for Yuri's. She'd agreed.

The pack had taken him to the edge of a Velinkan settlement, and melted away, Sasha in their midst. Weeks in their hands had addled his mind somewhat, but she believed he would recover. At any rate, he wasn't dead.

Already she was unsure of why she'd wanted him saved.

Rubbing at a new scar on her shoulder, she resisted the urge to turn and chew at it. It had been a hard few weeks. Many had wanted to challenge the new Volkiasti stripling with the strange ideas about weapons and defenses, but the old one had stood by her.

Looking down at the human camp, the young one knew she needed the pack leader for now, but one day there would be a new challenge, and on that day they would get guns and the challenge would go out not just to the Volkiasti, but to the Kyvanski, the Iliatsi, and finally to the Velinkans.

Her eyes glowing a dark amber, she turned at a gesture from the old one and together two gray wolves padded back toward their pack, away from the human camp and the man who would dream of flitting gray shadows for the rest of his life.

AS GOOD AS A REST
by *Tim Waggoner*

Tim Waggoner has published more than fifty stories of fantasy and horror. His most current stories can be found in the anthologies *Civil War Fantastic*, *Single White Vampire Seeks Same*, and *Bruce Coville's UFOs*. His first novel, *The Harmony Society*, will soon be available. He teaches creative writing at Sinclair Community College in Dayton, Ohio.

THE door to the office of Archetype Management burst open, and into the sterile reception area stalked a tall, broad-shouldered, well-muscled woman dressed in skimpy leather-and-bronze armor covered completely in gore.

The receptionist shouted as gobbets of bloody flesh slid off the warrior woman and landed on the plush ginger-colored carpet with meaty-wet plops.

"Look at the mess you're making!" the thin, bird-boned woman said. She stood, eyes blazing over the tops of her granny glasses, hair bun so tight it looked as if her head might explode any moment. She stabbed a slender finger at the door. "Get out of here before you make it any worse!"

The blonde swordswoman—the very picture of a Norse Valkyrie with a touch of Stone-Age savage thrown in for

good measure—dropped a callused hand to the hilt of the
sword hanging at her side. "I would consider it a personal
favor if you wouldn't speak to me in that tone," she said
evenly.

The receptionist's face reddened in anger, and her jaw
muscles tightened. The already severe lines of her suit
seemed to become sharper, sharp enough to draw blood.

"Don't think you can intimidate me, Ms. Tugenda. As
Mr. Abernathy's executive assistant, I deal on a daily basis
with all manner of archetypes, from thunder gods to
demons. I don't threaten easily."

Tugenda didn't usually encounter this sort of resistance
and wasn't quite sure what to do next. She decided to try
to bull her way through. "I've come to ask for a reassign-
ment. Is Mr. Abernathy in?"

The receptionist glanced toward a closed door behind
her immaculately ordered desk. "Yesssss . . . but he's
booked solid. Perhaps you could return tomorrow? After
you've bathed a dozen times or so," she finished cattily.

Tugenda gritted her teeth but otherwise ignored the taunt.
"I can't stand another day of mindlessly hacking my way
through barbarian hordes. I must insist on speaking with
Mr. Abernathy." She scowled darkly. "Now."

The receptionist's expression hardened. "That's not possible, Ms. Tugenda. You'll have to make an appointment."
She took a seat at her desk once more and flipped open
her appointment book. "How about next Thursday at
11:15?"

In answer, Tugenda drew her sword in a single swift
motion, raised it above her head, and brought it down on
the appointment book. Pages scattered into the air as the
book, as well as the desk beneath it, split in two.

The receptionist didn't so much as blink. "I take it Thursday isn't good for you. How about Friday?"

Tugenda didn't bother to reply. She sheathed her sword and stomped toward Mr. Abernathy's door, leaving bloody bootprints on the carpet behind her.

The receptionist dashed forward to block her way. "I simply cannot allow you to see Mr. Abernathy without an appointment! It isn't—"

"That's quite all right, Clarisse," came a pleasant voice from within the now open doorway. "I always have time for a client as important as Ms. Tugenda."

The receptionist frowned, clearly not approving, but she stepped aside and Tugenda walked into the office. Mr. Abernathy, a small, rather rotund man in a charcoal gray business suit, gave Tugenda an overly practiced smile and stuck out his hand.

"Good to see you."

Tugenda displayed her gore-slicked fingers. "I think you'd prefer that I didn't shake just now."

Mr. Abernathy's smile faltered. "I see what you mean."

Tugenda realized then that Abernathy wasn't alone in his office. Before his desk sat a massive man in an ill-fitting but expensive navy blue suit. His long dark hair was pulled back and bound in a ponytail, and a leather briefcase sat on the floor next to his chair.

Tugenda was about to ask who he was, when she recognized him. She was shocked. The Cimmerian looked quite a bit different than the last time she'd seen him.

"I'm sorry," she said. "I didn't realize you were here. If I'd known—"

He held up a huge, powerful hand to forestall Tugenda's apology. "That's all right. I was just about to leave anyway." He stood, bent to pick up his briefcase and stuck it awkwardly beneath one arm. "I have to get going to my new assignment." He sounded like a beaten man, with none of the fire and passion she was familiar with.

He turned to Mr. Abernathy. "One last thing: can you tell me exactly what in Crom's name a *tort* is?"

Mr. Abernathy chuckled and patted his client on one of his log-sized arms. "You'll figure it all out, don't worry. After battling monsters and wizards for so long, I think you'll find your new assignment with Hyperborean Law to be a breeze."

The man snorted doubtfully, turned to Tugenda, nodded once, and then left the office. Mr. Abernathy followed and closed the door on the sound of Clarisse spraying a can of industrial-strength air freshener into the reception area and muttering to herself about how in the Omniverse she was ever going to get these bloody footprints out of the carpet.

Mr. Abernathy smiled at Tugenda once more and gestured to the now empty chair. "Please, sit down."

Tugenda did so, ignoring the wet smack of her blood-smeared body as it came in contact with naugahyde.

Mr. Abernathy looked as if he suddenly regretted inviting her to sit, but he said nothing. He sat behind his desk and clasped his hands together before him. "So, what can I do for you today?"

Tugenda got straight to the point. "You can reassign me. I'm sick to death of slicing and dicing hordes of enemies. And I've really had it with this outfit." She wriggled uncomfortably. "Not only doesn't it provide much protection during battle—not to mention against breezes!—but it chafes like a bear!"

Abernathy shrugged. "I always thought that what it lacked in practicality it made up for in style."

"I doubt you'd give much of a damn for style after you've picked as much troll flesh out of your cleavage as I have. But it's more than my outfit. It's the saddle sores from riding all day on a flatulent excuse for a horse. It's not being able to get a decent date because I'm too busy toppling an evil monarch or questing after some fabulous magical artifact. And when I finally do meet a man, he's either afraid of me or, if he's a warrior, he's only interested in the sort of empty-headed submissive females that evil priests are always serving up as sacrifices to their gods.

"And just try to have a decent conversation! All sorcerers ever want to talk about is how they're going to conquer the world and how much better everything will be once they're running the show. And all male fighters want to discuss are fighting techniques and sexual positions—and not in that order." She brushed a clumpy, matted lock from her forehead. "And do you have any idea what blood does to a girl's hair and skin?"

"I can see why you're so unhappy with your current assignment," Abernathy said with just the right amount of understanding. "Actually, it's rather fortuitous that you came to see me today. I was just about to send for you."

Tugenda was surprised—and more than a little suspicious. "Oh?"

"Recently we've been updating some of our assignments, trying to bring them more into line with today's needs."

She jerked her head toward the door. "Is that what you did with him? Bring him 'into line'?"

"Sometimes an archetype needs a bit of modernizing in

order to stay relevant." Abernathy smiled. "He'll still be a warrior, just a different sort."

Tugenda thought of the way the barbarian fighter had almost slunk out of the office. He hadn't looked much like a warrior to her. "And you intend to do the same with me?"

"Yes, we do. It's true that your particular archetype—that of the battle maiden—has grown in popularity over the last few decades, but we feel it's time to move on, to explore new and more exciting possibilities. After all, that's why you came to see me today, isn't it?"

True, but Tugenda didn't relish the prospect of ending up like her male counterpart. She'd do her best to make sure that didn't happen.

"Very well. But there's one thing, Abernathy."

"Yes?"

"If you ever refer to me as a 'maiden' again, I'll have your balls for earrings."

Abernathy's ever-present smile faltered. "I'll, uh, try to keep that in mind. Now let's see what we've got for you." He turned to the computer on his desk and worked the mouse for a few moments. "Ah!" He turned back to face Tugenda, smile once more in place. "Tell me, have you ever heard of something called a sitcom?"

*   *   *

INTERIOR, EVENING—THE IVERSON HOUSEHOLD.

TUGENDA IVERSON, home from a busy day at the office, rushes into the kitchen, carrying an armload of groceries that are about to spill. Running in behind her are the three adorable but smart-aleck Iverson children, five-year-old BILLIE, eight-year-old JOEY, and sixteen-year-old DIANE.

HOLD FOR AUDIENCE APPLAUSE.

TUGENDA lays the groceries on the counter just as the bags rip, spilling boxes and cans everywhere.

LAUGHTER.

TUGENDA

By Caolan's cast-iron girdle! (TUGENDA looks up at the audience. In a demanding voice.) What's so damn funny?

MORE LAUGHTER.

TUGENDA's hand reaches toward her side, as if for something that should be there, but isn't. She scowls.

DIANE

Mu-therr! I swear, you are such a klutz sometimes!

BILLIE

I think she's getting old.

JOEY

Maybe we should start looking at nursing home brochures.

LAUGHTER.

TUGENDA

Why you little mud-sucking plague worms! (She grabs for her terrified children as the audience roars with laughter.)

Enter FRANK IVERSON.

FRANK

(Pausing for applause.) Hey, everybody, I'm home!
(Noticing that his wife has all three of his children in head-
locks.) Ah, there's nothing like family togetherness!

LAUGHTER.

TUGENDA

(Looking out at the audience and bellowing.) SHUT UP!

FRANK

Honey, I hate to spring this on you at the last moment,
but my boss and his wife are going to be coming over to
dinner tonight. (Checks watch.) In about forty-five minutes, to be precise. Do you think you can whip up one of
your famous gourmet meals by then?

TUGENDA roars her fury, grabs a knife from the butcher
block and slaughters her entire family.

RIOTOUS LAUGHTER.

TUGENDA

(Looking out at the audience and grinning maniacally.)
Now it's your turn! (Brandishing her blade, she leaps into
the crowd.)

ASSORTED SCREAMING.

*   *   *

Tugenda sat before Mr. Abernathy's desk again, this time
wearing a business suit and skirt, but still covered in blood.
Abernathy sighed. "That assignment wasn't to your lik-
ing, I take it."

"I fail to see how it related to my archetype," she said stiffly.

"The strong modern woman trying to have it all, juggling husband, kids, career, all the while maintaining her sense of humor . . . Don't you see how it applies to the role of a warrior maid—er, I mean, a warrior? I admit, it's a bit on the abstract side—"

"I'm a swordswoman," Tugenda said. "I kill things. I don't do abstract."

Abernathy furrowed his brow in thought. "You know, you might consider going the route of your male counterpart who was in here the other day. Despite his initial hesitancy, he's thrown himself into his new role with gusto. He's already won a class action suit against Eldritch Pharmaceuticals, and he plans to take on Stygian Tobacco next."

Tugenda wasn't sure. Still, it if was good enough for *him* . . .

* * *

"So you unequivocally deny that you killed your wife for the insurance money, Mr. Carcosa?"

The defendant—a wormy little man with pale, pockmarked skin—answered calmly. "Yes, I do. I couldn't have. I . . . just don't have the heart to murder anyone, let alone my own wife." A slight quiver of his bottom lip, a hint of tears welling in the corners of his eyes.

The defense attorney, a wolfishly handsome thirty-something male, flashed Tugenda a quick, self-satisfied grin as if to say, *Some performance, huh? We've got the jury right where we want them*, before turning to the judge. "No further questions, your honor." He strode back to the de-

fense table, strutting like a particularly vain peacock dressed
in a four hundred dollar suit.

The judge, a white-bearded man with stern hawkeyes,
looked at Tugenda. "Do you wish to cross-examine, Prosecutor?"

"Uh . . ." The former warrior rifled through the papers
scattered on the table before her, unable to make heads or
tails out of the chicken-scratchings which covered them.
Reading wasn't exactly a prime job requirement for a barbarian.

"Prosecutor?" The judge was beginning to sound an-
noyed.

Tugenda looked up from the bewildering papers and
took a deep breath. "Yes, your honor, I would." She stood
and approached the witness stand, her high-heel shoes
clack-clack-clacking as she crossed the highly polished
wooden floor.

She could feel the jury leaning forward in anticipation
as she carefully framed the first question in her mind. "You
claim to be innocent?"

A small smile, as if he were thinking, *That's the best
you've got?* "I don't claim. I *am* innocent."

Tugenda nodded. "Very well, then you will have no
qualms about facing me in ritual combat."

The defendant blinked. "Excuse me?"

"If you are truly innocent, then the gods shall lend
strength to your swordarm and you will defeat me. If not,
then I shall defeat you."

The man turned to the judge. "Your honor?"

The judge scowled. "Ms. Tugenda, if this is your idea
of a joke—"

Tugenda ignored the old man. "Defend yourself, Carcosa!" She lunged for the defendant.

* * *

"The man was dead before he hit the floor," Abernathy said, a trifle queasily.

Tugenda grinned. "At least I learned one thing: he *did* have the heart of a murderer." She reached into a blood-soaked suit jacket pocket. "I have it right here if you'd like to take a look . . ."

"NO! I mean, thank you, that won't be necessary." Abernathy fell silent as he thought for a moment. "It's clear that you need a career that will allow you to be more . . . physical. Something with opportunity for a bit of adventure." Abernathy consulted his computer. "It appears we have an opening in romance novels."

Tugenda had to admit that the law did have its rewards—she patted her wet pocket—but overall it was a little too mundane for her tastes. She wasn't sure exactly what a romance novel was, but the adventure part sounded appealing.

"I'll take it."

* * *

Tugenda stood on the swaying deck of a sailing vessel, the strong breeze carrying the scent of saltwater, gulls crying above her, the sound almost lost in the creak of the ship's rigging and the singing and shouting of sailors at work. The summer sun blazed down upon her, its heat at once unbearable and somehow stimulating.

She wore a blue-and-white dress which had been beautiful at one time, but was now little more than tattered rags barely covering her lush and ample form.

Standing before her was the captain of the vessel, shirtless, with long, flowing blond hair. He was well-built, his chest hairless and coated with a sheen of sweat. His black pants hugged his legs and trunk, leaving nothing to the imagination. A thin rapier (nearly useless as a weapon, Tugenda thought) hung at his side.

Not bad. Nothing to compare with a certain barbarian turned lawyer, but she wouldn't kick him out of bed. Not until she was finished with him, anyway.

"My love," said Captain Ignazio as he struck a pose and flexed his pecs, "these last few days have been a gift from God, a blessed respite in the wearying struggle that is a pirate's life."

Tugenda had trouble understanding him, the man's accent was so thick.

"Uh, yes, for me, too. I guess."

He gestured dramatically toward the port side of the vessel. "Even now my twin brother's ship, *The Revenge*, draws alongside, and we shall finally settle our long-standing feud once and for all!"

Tugenda glanced at the oncoming ship. "Twins, huh?" This assignment was looking better all the time! She began contemplating the geometric possibilities when another thought intruded.

She turned back to Ignazio. "What are you doing going around in this sun without a shirt? You'll burn like crazy! And your hair looks awfully bouncy and full-bodied for someone who spends a lot of time in this salty air."

"Never mind that, my treasure." He put his arm around

her waist and drew her manfully to him. "We have only moments before my brother attacks. We must make the most of them."

Tugenda grinned. "Now you're talking!" She undid Ignazio's sword belt, dropped his rapier to the deck, grabbed the waistband of his pants and yanked downward.

The pirate captain pulled back, horrified. "What are you doing?"

"You said we only have moments, so let's get to it, sailorboy!"

Ignazio stumbled backward, feet caught in his pants, and fell onto his posterior. "But you can't do this! Y-you're a lady!"

Tugenda sighed. It was the same old story. Men were all hands and sweet talk—as long as they held the reins. But let a woman show the least bit of aggression in romance, and they acted like confused little boys.

"Never mind, Ignazio. I'm not really in the mood anymore." She reached down and picked up his ridiculous excuse for a sword. It wasn't much, but it would have to serve.

"What do you intend to do with my rapier, my sweet?"

Tugenda faced the oncoming ship. "Find out if your twin is a better man than you are, Ignazio." She swished the blade through the air a couple of times to test it. Then she glanced back at the still prone—and pants-less—captain. "And whether or not his sword's bigger than yours."

* * *

"One hundred and twenty-three dead, including the captains of both ships," Abernathy said.

Tugenda shrugged. "I was bored." She stood in front of Abernathy's desk. She was so covered with blood and other less-identifiable substances that he'd refused to allow her to sit this time. "That was hardly a suitable scenario for my archetype."

"What do you mean? A woman in a rough-and-tumble man's world, trying to survive—and perhaps win a little love—with only her wits and femininity to—" He broke off and sighed. "Yes, I suppose it was something of a stretch." He turned to his computer once more. "I'll check to see what else we have, Tugenda, but I have to be honest with you, the prospects don't look good. I don't know if we have anything that falls within the parameters you've outlined."

"Actually, I've been thinking about that." Tugenda wiped a clotted dark-red mass off her forearm and flicked it onto the floor. "Even though fighting day in, day out gets a little tiring at times, I *am* awfully good at it."

Abernathy eyed her crimson-soaked frame. "I'd say."

"And it does satisfy me in a way nothing else seems to. So maybe I should go back to doing what I do best."

Abernathy hesitated. "There's a slight problem with that."

Tugenda frowned. "Oh?"

"We've reassigned the particular milieu where you used to work. It's being used for computer role-playing games now."

Tugenda stepped forward and put her hands on Abernathy's desk. She leaned toward him until her nose was just touching his. A drop of pirate blood ran onto him and rolled down his cheek.

"Then find me another *milieu*, whatever in Caolan's name that is, and be quick about it!"

Abernathy swallowed and got to work.

*   *   *

Tugenda stood amidst a decayed cityscape, photon sword held high above her head, its hungry thrum announcing its bloodlust to the world. Surrounding her was a horde of misshapen creatures that supposedly had once been men, though there was little sign of humanity in them now. As one, the mutants charged, bellowing as they came.

Tugenda thumbed the switch on her forearm control panel to activate her battlesuit's defenses. The hi-tech armor was still skintight—and its molding quite unnecessarily exaggerated her feminine attributes—but at least she wouldn't have to worry about any nasty bits and pieces of mutant sliding down her front.

She lay about her with the energy weapon to the accompaniment of sizzling flesh and shrieking, dying monsters, quickly falling into a familiar, comfortable rhythm: hack-slice, hack-slice, hack-slice.

What the hell, she thought as she decapitated yet another mutant. *It's a living.*

A GAME OF SWORDS
by David Bischoff

David Bischoff is active in many areas of the science fiction field, whether it be writing his own novels such as *The UFO Conspiracy* trilogy, collaborations with authors such as Harry Harrison, writing three *Bill The Galactic Hero* novels, or writing excellent media tie-in novelizations, such as *Aliens* and *Star Trek* novels. He has previously worked as associate editor of *Amazing* magazine and as a staff member of NBC. He lives in Eugene, Oregon.

THE land trembled with aftershocks of magic. It was as though the Earth were shivering with disbelief that such tragedy could occur on what had been, mere hours before, a grassy field through which a creek zigzagged like some lazy garden snake. Now that waterway ran thick red with blood, and the green fields lay blasted and scorched black. Fires crackled in once magnificent ficklewood trees, splintered now as though by great lightnings. Greasy smoke smelling of singed flesh and dark sorcery wound sinuously to the moody blanket of overcast which moved like an inverted ocean of dread to cast waves upon the distant Myrrhrock Mountains that made this field a valley. But scarred as this once-pleasant field was, its horror and pain were nothing compared to what lay upon its surface, racked upon the trees, or bobbing in the water: Bodies of warriors bristling with arrows. Bodies of tall men and short men, young and old, cloven with ax wounds and cut in twain by ripping shocks of spell-guns. Even now buzzard hawks fluttered down lazing from their cowardly gyres to pluck at strewn entrails, jelly-clouded eyes. The air here was tainted iron with blood and ruin and doom.

From a twisted pile of pikes and slaughtered horses, a survivor pushed up like the sprouting of a seedling from a abattoir yard. Coughing, the armored figure staggered. She tripped, then steadied herself upon a pile of shattered and mangled corpses. A shudder jangled her armor and her spurs, and the dented plate of her breast gleamed and glittered in the sweep of fire from a nearby ravaged gorse-bush. The figure moaned and sighed, and then, slowly, reached out and grabbed a long sword by its knotted hilt. Jamming this into the bloody ground, the animated armor pushed itself back up into an erect position and lodged the long sword top into its armor for support. Then, creaking, arms lifted up the silvery helm. A face streaked with sweat and grime, smoke and blood appeared and sodden blonde hair glistened in the somber firelights. A long braid of yellow hair, bound by a topknot, tumbled down over the armor.

Sofia de Christabel stared out over the sea of the dead for a long moment. Then a sob wrenched up from some deeper dimension, beyond her sturdy but limited body, and broke through her blistered lips. "My faithful. My valiant! Oh, eyes! Oh all senses! Say that you are rank liars. Say that I am amongst my people again and they are amongst the quick!"

No voice answered. No words refuted what her eyes told her. The only sounds that came to her ears were the crackle and sputter of the fitful fires and the flap of vulture wings and the rip of flesh as they fed. Memory dribbled back, carrying horrid visions of ringing steel and gushing blood, frenzied charges and brave stands against hordes of bristly creatures sprouting from leather cuirasses that shone with protective weavespells. As her vision cleared now, she saw the occasional patch of bloody fur and twisted fangs amongst the fallen: dead boxorks. Even in death, they looked larger than life, fearsome and bestial subhumans cooked up in some nullgod-chemist's vat. However, slaughtered men and women, her ravaged, defeated army, outnumbered these creatures by far. Oh, and so many! How she hoped that some of her people had seen defeat imminent, had turned and sprinted for higher ground at the least, and perhaps even bounded away, back to Alexandria to alert those sacred halls to the coming hordes.

And had those dark armies already swept past? What would have stopped them? Certainly not a fallen commander beneath a pile of bodies. Why, oh, why had she not stood back as her armies had desired? Why had she rushed in to do battle? And then she remembered. For such was the nature of her power, her demigod's magic that her sword swinging against the Dark would fill the swords and pikes and daggers and arrows of her armies with that same puissance. A fool's mission, perhaps, and the Wisdom in her needed no Prophecy to have told her that. However, it was her sworn duty to defend her sacred trust, to place her sword and herself between the Night and the Illumination. This is what she had done and now, if she could push back this overwhelming grief that leaped from her heart, threatened to burst through her breastplate, threatened to dissolve her eyes all into tears—that mission was what Sofia de Christabel must set out for again.

She walked, and even as the tasses knocked against her tuille, the plate above her thigh, and her chainmail rattled wearily, she heard—no, *sensed* more than heard—a distant clanking, a rumble, an antediluvian *presence*. Sofia de Christabel looked up and saw, upon the ridge, a line of soot-dark armor and winks of fire in helms. The army of boxorks in line formation stretching fully two leagues across the horizon. Spears and morningstars and maces and broadswords and more dreadful and more alien Between-Star weaponry pushed up above their beavered helmets, like spikes and spines on some dreadful serpent.

Sofia de Christabel took a deep breath. Her first inclination was to turn and to run back through this valley past the Twilight and Dusk Peaks; to run and to take her stand before Alexandria, the city of Knowledge, and thus make a better stand. But run in full armor? Even a demigod could not accomplish so much. There were no living horses about, and whatever spells, whatever magic she could still pull up from her DeepPouch after the day's travail would surely exhaust not only her supply but her ability.

Even as she debated what course she should take—the foolish or the stupid or perhaps the totally hopeless—a rider broke free of the ranks upon the ridge and began to gallop down the slope toward her.

Both rider and mount were dressed all in shades of black, from serge through night, obsidian and stygian. From a lance fluttered a sole streamer: dove white. A truce? But how could this be, she wondered. The victory was surely theirs. The victory and more . . . However, even as her surprise gave way to suspicion, Sofia de Christabel prepared her heart and her soul for what was to come. For she realized that surely, when mere words were weapons, then the battle ahead could be for more than mere life or death.

The horse was huge, a big-chested steed crested with a ceremonial plumage of a Black Dawn Cock that made it seem even larger. Its eyes were fierce agate, and they glittered with the sheer force of the power reflected from the rider, a tall stately figure in rococo armor heavy with curlicues, ridges, and polished gleam. From the aiette draped an elaborate surcoat, stitched in spun gold, silver, and platinum, holding diamonds and sapphires and rubies of astronomical splendor, brought together in patterns denoting a cosmic heraldry. Mount and rider stopped amidst the slaughter, just short of the opposite crimson shore of the creek.

Slowly, a gauntlet lifted and pushed back the visor. The visage revealed was that of a beautiful dark-haired woman, eyes twin coal flashes in a perfect face, cheekbones high and noble, nose a bold but feminine beak above a hard but full and sensuous mouth. As the mouth opened to speak, ivory teeth with just the suggestion of points were revealed, and Sofia was reminded of nothing so much as a summercat regarding a grounded, fluttering bird.

"There you are, Sofia de Christabel," said the mounted Lordette. "I knew that you were not dead, but with so much offal, it was hard to detect your pulse. We had but to wait for you to show yourself, and so you did. I thank you." Her voice was a mellifluous alto with a faint bite of BetweenStar sarcasm. It felt like mountain water running over glacier ice; twinkling and beautiful but cold, cold.

"Do your worst, Archon. I am ready. You will pass

through only over my riven and lifeless corpse." She held up her sword to underscore her determination.

"You will not surrender? No—wait. Do not answer until you have heard me out!" Her words were spoken with the regal cadences of a leader used to obedience. Sofia said nothing. In such confrontations between great powers, time could only aid her cause, if only so that the universe had another few seconds to treasure the Light that was Alexandria; and thus, in some distant nether Age, its healing reflection might be all the brighter.

"Speak. I am going nowhere."

The rider leaned over, regarding Sofia with an unblinking, intense gaze. "No indeed, woman. You are not." With balance and poise, the armored Lordette General lifted herself from the ornately carved leather saddle and stepped onto a bare spot betwixt bodies and a severed head. During the dismount, somehow the Archon kept her eyes upon her prey in a feral, feline fashion. "Sofia de Christabel, I have a message from his Holiness the Demiurge Himself. 'Kyra,' he said to me. 'Kyra, Sofia would be welcome in my Many Mansions if she would but bow down and service me' . . . but wait a moment. Perhaps I am not the proper one to bear the full message." From a belt, the woman drew a rapier and with this rapier she stabbed through the severed head. She hoisted this up and blood dribbled down the blade. It hung for a moment like a memento of an execution stuck upon a pike. A breeze tousled the long, curly hair. A fly buzzed. Then, the eyes opened. A crackle, a soft nimbus grew from around the edges of the head, seeming to separate it from this reality, outlining it in bold relief. A chilly scent, as though from the depths of a black sea or from the reaches of a Netherworld touched the air. The bloody mouth worked, and a voice rang out:

"Sofia! Sofia, my darling! I long for you! Light of my night, you do me wrong by keeping yourself from my chambers." The voice, beautiful as a reed instrument, had a shrill sharpness that cut it through with sarcasm. "Can we but parley a while? Come to the Great Hold of my Palace and join me in wine and feasting, and we will discuss the situation in a more convivial atmosphere than this death-stink." The eyes ogled about and the nose sniffed and the mouth twisted with disdain. "Then, if you decide that you do not care for the heavens and earths, I should like to place at your dainty feet— Well then, you can be returned to this place forthwith and you may have what Fate and my armies can offer."

"Great Creator," said Sofia de Christabel. Her curtsy was not without a mocking quality. "Lord of the Dusk, and King of Yesterday and Tomorrow. That very well may be, and I well know the virtues of your table, your hospitality, oh, Demiurge. And yet, that would remove me from the path between your armies and Alexandria. That I will not, cannot do. The Library and the Wisdom, the Knowledge of the Truth—those are what I defend. Not my own life."

"But you would have my word of honor, Sofia!" said the bloody head. "Come, come! This is no place to parley. My Archon, my armies need rest besides. Come and let us take our leisure."

"You do not think I do not consult the books and the histories of my library," said Sofia. "I am not merely Guardian, Creator. I am Master Librarian of Light!" She drew up her sword, gripping it by the blade so that it formed a cross. "In the name of the Christos whose name I bear, whose light inhabits my heart and animates my mission— I rebuke thee, False, Foul Creator . . . Beast of Illusion, Master of Darkness. Kill me if you like, but I shall remain true to the True, and not harbor beguilement by the fleshly, rotting stuff that is the fabric of your temptations."

The head smiled. "Had I shoulders, I should shrug. Very well. I will proceed in good conscience. You wrong me with your words. You imply that I am evil. There is no evil. There is only reality, and reality is the law by which I live, the science of my methods. Farewell, then, Sofia de Christabel. I would have enjoyed whiling afternoons in debating philosophy. Instead, reality must be rid of you and your ilk."

Then, the head became just a head, and the Archon tossed it aside. It rolled back amongst the corpses. The Archon pointed her rapier at Sofia. "Your execution has thus been ordered. Shall it be mere ceremony, or would you enjoy a playful duel? A game of swords, if you will?"

Fear convulsed through Sofia, a lava flow of terror threatening to erupt through her brain. However, she caught it in her throat, swallowed it back. She fought her instinctual physical urge to turn and run, run with every last bit of strength she had, cut and retreat in total gibbering panic. Her mind, however, knew that this was not merely caused by the impulses that imbued her flesh; there were exterior forces at work. With her will, and the concentration of the Illumination within her, she rallied, and she fought back, and the dark forces pushed in on the scream of her sinews to Survive! Survive at all Costs! Mere survival was never an option. Never. Never! Her flesh was but to serve her Cause, and if there was pain and indignity—so be it. The alternative was shame, which was far, far worse than defeat could ever dream of being.

The great steed splashed across the crimson creek. The silky frocks around the goldworks of its saddle fluttered like lightning and smoke. The Archon Kyra slapped her visor down with a clang, and then raised herself up full in her stirrups. Her knees bit into the creature's flanks, urging it forward faster, and the fluttering neighs of the creature sounded like a dragon's roar. Through the helm of the attacker bloomed a primeval blaze, which spread, sparking, up her right arm as it lifted. The fire shot round the weapon, making the rapier the black spine to a blazing long sword.

Sofia did not even attempt to put her helmet back on. Neither metal nor flesh could withstand this force, she well knew. Nonetheless, she raised her own sword despite the talons of fear and gravity that would keep it down, and she stood, straight and defiant, in the path of her attacker.

Just as the armored Archon was almost upon her, and the air was raging with the bright sweep of her sword, Sofia Christabel's left hand left the sword hilt and dove down to the nearly empty SpellPurse dangling at her side. With a shriek like a million needles across cold marble, the sword of the Archon named Kyra descended upon her. It roared through the air, stinking of immolation. The blade met Sofia's blade, and the explosion of light clashing with black hurled Sofia back—back into Memory.

The Mother sat quietly by the altar, waiting for her as she stepped into the vast, mysterious room. Ropes of incense hung in the air, smelling of camphordaze and frankenmyrh and sandalspring and a delicate mixture of braided sacredness. The duskmonks had just been here, Sofia could see: the drifting fog of censer pots hung in the air, drifting down amongst the racks and rows and shelves of the library to become a groundfog, soon to melt away.

Sofia approached the Mother. She felt apprehensive. The paper message she clutched had been tersely worded with no polite salutations. This usually portended a disciplinary meeting of some sort; and Mother's punishments were strict, to the point and generally unpleasant. Alas, Sofia well knew there was good reason for discipline in her case. There was a Trespass on her soul.

She curtsied politely. When there was no response from the Mother, Sofia coughed. Still no response. Sofia felt a touch of impatience mingling with her unease. She was a spirited youth, and she'd been disciplined before. She just wanted to get it all over with. She had been summoned into the Chamber, away from her usual time of Dueling. She enjoyed swordplay. Competition intrigued her, and it was great fun to see surprise in the eyes of the young men when she would best them with subtle parries and ripostes. She was quick, Sofia was. Quick and Smart, her Swordmaster had said. . . .

Always though, with the satisfying feel of sweat on her brow, and the earthy smell of exertion about her, she was all too happy to give up the slapdash of exercise and return to her studies in the Library. Studies that would continue until evening vespers, when the Staff would close up the musty, musky halls of books and the Community would join together for evening meals, plays, music, board games, and other delights of the mind and intellect. Even the most monkish of the monks, though, who rose in the cold long before the crow of cock, to abase the flesh and be mind-

ful of the Glories of the Light beyond even as they fumbled in the Dark—they, too, saw the benefits of the recre-
ation and celebration that evenings afforded.

After the games, Sofia and others had other little, secret games they played. Those comprised her Trespass.
However, her true sin was that she would Trespass again,
even though she would again be punished.

She brushed her long blonde hair over the rough wool
jerkin she wore. Lately, her breasts had grown full, and it
would not be a good idea to display her sexual matura-
tion before the Mother. Such was Flesh, and these were
distractions to the true callings of her Order.

She knelt. "It is Sofia, Mother. I have come as you have
requested."

The Mother was all wrapped in white robes, of different fabrics and textures. She seemed now nothing so much
as an unfolded lily, beautiful and serene. Her face was
pale, folded up with the gauze and gently lined with age.
But when her eyes opened to regard the Disciple, they shone
with a pure intense blue, that was pure, but quintessen-
tially human.

"Sofia," she said. "Sofia de Christabel. You must excuse me, I still have the stuff of my meditations about me.
I must pause for a moment to focus." Mother closed her
eyes. She took a deep breath. Then she opened them again.
"Thank you for your prompt obedience. I will not dissem-
ble with you, Sofia. I have learned of your recent activities."

"Ah. Perhaps that kiss I gave William behind the rose
bushes!" said Sofia. "I am heartily sorry, Mother. My flesh
is weak. I shall take more cold baths."

Mother regarded her and those blue eyes twinkled with

amusement. "Oh, you are clever. Your dalliances with male lips, your sighs and caresses are beside the point, Sofia. That, is not your Trespass. And you well know it."

Sofia bent her head contritely.

"You are a lively young thing. You possess much that is fresh and vibrant about the Flesh, and that is part of your potent magic, your spirit's animated counterpart. She leaned forward and her alb seemed to grow big with wind, fluttering about her as though she were some angel showing its wings. Then, the vestment flattened and grew dark, and the cincture about her waist appeared to glow a soft, ruminating umber.

"However," said the Priestess Mother. "You have Trespassed."

The words hung heavy in the air, like dust motes that had once danced in a ray of light from a stained-glass window suddenly turned into rocks. They seemed to drop heavily upon her head.

Sofia Christabel's first inclination was to deny. However, she checked herself. Even as a small child, it had not taken her long to discover that she lived in the Halls of Knowledge and Truth. If the Mother merely suspected her Trespass, then she would not present the fact in this manner. In such a case, she knew, to deny would dig herself in deeper. But more, deep down, she wanted to tell the Truth. There was a delight in being caught, a thrill . . . because only in this manner could she share what she had learned in the Trespass.

"Yes, Mother."

"Would you care to detail the nature of the Trespass?" Sofia nodded. "I will show you."

She lifted herself back on her haunches, easily standing up with a dancer's grace, bouncing on the balls of her feet.

Mother closed her eyes and faded into standing position, even more graceful. The amice around her shoulders glittered a momentary azure.

"This way," said Sofia.

She walked down a row of books and then turned down into a center aisle. The entrance was bent, the wood of the shelving wizened, but well polished. Past tome and volume, past manuscripts of vellum and papyrus, she led the Mother. At the end of the aisle was the end wall, the limestone abutment of the earth into the Library. It was cool to the touch as she fingered protrusions of rocks. She twisted one Jutting ridge, and there was a rumble, as though the earth below were clearing its throat. The rock wall pushed inward, and after waiting just long enough to allow room for entry, Sofia stepped into this new cavern annex to the Library.

There were no candles or lanterns on the rough limestone walls here, but those walls held luminescent jewels that shone like phosphorescence in the sea. A tunnel stretched back into the unknown earth. Upon the walls of this antechamber verging upon the chthonian were shelves and upon these shelves were more books.

Mother nodded. "How did you find this place, Sofia?"

"I just felt it."

"And you and your friends came in and looked within the books, yes?"

"Yes, Mother. Only they didn't seem to understand them. I think the boys were looking for naughty pictures."

The Mother smiled despite herself. "But you returned alone. And you read."

"Yes, Mother."

"And what did you read? What did you discover?"

Sofia shivered as a chill touched her spine. She looked away from the Mother.

"Things."

"Things? What things. Come. Tell me, Sofia." The voice was stern, and perhaps demanding, but not blaming.

Sofia looked up at the volumes that lay upon the shelves. Their leather smelled like love, and she again experienced the thrill that she felt as the soft material parted beneath her hands and the light of her aromatic candle fell upon the words so oddly inscribed on the pages. She again felt the touch of the magic glasses upon the bridge of her nose that translated the languages thereon.

"There are aeons upon aeons, Mother," she said. "And ages upon the ages. There is beauty beyond telling in the Illumination beyond, but each of the worlds between the Light and Dark reflects and refracts differently. Oh, the joy, Mother . . . The adventures that have occurred . . . The adventures that will come. Bravery and valor, cowardice and fear, glory and hosannas . . . Oh, the wonder before . . . The awe ever after." Her voice was soft with reverence and yet filled with excitement. She turned to the Mother. "And best of all, Mother . . . We embody all that there is of Light and Dark. Now. Here. If we but look within at what we hold within."

The Mother was thoughtfully silent for a moment. She lifted her fingertips, and light flowed and danced amongst the spines of the books. Sparks and dazzles danced a moment. Then her hand returned to knit with the other hand in a prayerful stance.

After a moment, she sighed. "You are the One," she said.

"One, Mother?" Sofia looked up, and she saw a single tear sliding down the pale roseate of Mother's cheek.

"Come."

"I am to be punished, then?" said Sofia with trepidation.

"No. Your Trespass . . . Well, your Trespass was in the name of your nature, Sofia. Which is boundless thirst for Truth and Knowledge."

Sofia clasped Mother's hand. She felt a flood of warmth and love and belonging. The tears that came hot on her face were not from relief that there would be no punishment here; but that she was loved and understood.

"No need for words now, child. There will be plenty of time for words later. But come with me." Mother pulled her behind her. "In the spectral moment, the time is right for assimilation and comprehension."

Sofia did not protest. She followed the Mother as she led her back through the opening in the wall. Behind them there was a grating as the opening closed again. The Mother hurried along at a speedy clip, which surprised Sofia. With her strength, she was able to keep up easily, but she was astonished at the sedentary Priestess' swiftness.

They hurried back through the library, into the foyer and down a hall. Guardian gargoyles glared down, stone-faced, at their torchlit passage. They passed through Chapel and then Sanctuary. When Sofia saw where they were headed, she balked.

"Mother! The Chamber! Even I would not be so defiant of sacredness to Trespass there!"

The Mother turned and her voice was soft but reassuring. "There is no Trespass for one such as you in the Bridal Chamber, child."

At a large door of oak, elaborately carved in runes and figurettes that not even her magical glasses could translate, the Mother stopped. She rummaged through her liturgical vestments, producing a jingling set of keys. Into a brass keyhole, she inserted the long key. Tumblers turned. She pushed on the door, and ancient hinges squeaked as the door opened. Beyond was a room all of smooth marble. As Sofia followed the Mother into the room, she felt warm air, fragrant with attar of rose, touch her face. At the end of a narrow room was an altar, and upon this altar a single flame burned upon a podium—a flame that illumined all of the room. A flame that gave off a pure and golden radiance, without even a suggestion of smoke.

Sofia managed words. "You are taking me to the Bridal Chamber. Am I to be married?"

The Mother laughed softly. The sound was like golden bells. It relieved the weight of the moment. She had heard Mother's laugh before, but after all this tension, the sound was particularly welcome. "No, of course not, child. The term is merely symbolic. Those of us who follow the Path are all wed to the Illumination. Herein lies the distillation of that ceremony." She went forward to the altar. Upon one side was a silvery linen cloth. She knelt and unfurled the cloth. Upon the cloth stretched a pile of smooth, round, polished stones of various colors. Carefully, the Mother selected one of these. It was a soft carnelian, with a trace of azure upon its edge. "Have you your SpellPouch with you, Sofia?"

"Of course!"

The Mother looked at her soberly. "There is much special learning ahead for one such as you, Sofia. You have a unique place here in Alexandria. Already we have noted your abilities in the military arts. Your courage shines indeed. However, there may come a time when you will have need of this Stone. It will be the first gift that I give you . . . but the last that you will use in this life. Will you accept this stone and its responsibilities."

"Responsibilities, Mother?"

"Yes, Sofia. For there are powers that would see what we hold here snuffed out."

"But how is that possible? The Aeons and the Holy are Eternal!"

"The universes wax and wane, Sofia. But only through the powers of light can this equilibrium be preserved. But here, child. Open your purse."

The SpellPouch was a leather purse the size of two large men's fists. It hung on the belt that encircled Sofia's waist. She swung it around and opened it. Inside was a thimble, a set of jacks, and a gopher's paw.

Delicately, the Mother placed the stone amongst this collection. "Thus with the Beginning I give you the End. Do you accept it, Sofia Christabel?"

"Yes, Mother."

"I pray you have the courage to use it, should it be needed," said the Mother.

Sofia lifted herself up proudly to her full height. She felt the burning, swelling joy of purpose and mission. "Of course. In my soldiering I have sworn to uphold the cause of the Illumination! I certainly shall not back down now!"

"Beware pride, Sofia. You do not guard or stand for individuality. You stand for the universal!"

"Of course, of course!" she said almost impatiently. "Tell me, Mother. Tell me what I must do. I will have the courage! I swear!"

And so the Mother told the child, and the child became a child no more.

After the explosion of dark, Sofia found herself sprawled amongst the bodies of her dead soldiers.

Standing a few paces away, like an upthrust of obsidian, was Archon Kyra. "Stand up! Stand up, Sofia de Christabel. We duel now. I have heard your legends. I would test you myself. Screw up your courage. We duel alone. I will not seek the aid of the Powers that I serve. I seek merely to grind you into the ground and claim sweet and total victory."

Anger swept through Sofia. Livid anger gave her strength and she pushed herself up easily despite the weight of her armor, her long sword thrust defiantly at this Dark Minister.

The Archon waggled her own sword haughtily. "Come on, then, fool. Come on! This is your chance! This is your chance to save your precious bundle of books. Your blessed Alexandria!" The woman giggled. "You and me, Soapy Cripple!"

That name! How had the fiend discovered the name with which the boyish tormentors of her youth had mocked her! The very touch of those syllables upon her ears drove her toward fury—

She raised the sword again, and eager bloodlust flashed in the Archon's eyes. But then Sofia lowered her weapon. She took a deep, cleansing breath.

The Archon frowned. "Fool! Where is your valor! Where is your pride! Were all the tales merely lies, then?"

Sofia de Christabel looked out upon the dark waves of the boxorks staring down at this confrontation.

"I have no pride. I only pray for courage. This is no honest match, Archon. But you cannot take what is not given you. You cannot take what I now take away from you."

Quashing the raw, hard fear that vibrated at the very core of her being, Sofia de Christabel drew out the smooth carnelian spellstone. She rubbed it over the blade of her sword swiftly and then in a fluid, continuous motion she placed it into her mouth and swallowed it.

Then, she flung the sword about, put the hilt upon the ground, and placed the tip up under the lower rim of her breastplate.

Incredulity filled the Archon's face. "What . . . What in the name of—"

The sword began to glow, and it was a white glow, the color of infinity and Illumination. "You will not kill me, Archon. You will not burn my city!"

And she pushed down with all her might upon the glowing sword, pushing the blade up into her beating heart. Her body hung there for a moment as though suspended not merely in space but in time itself—and then, limp, it fell down to the ground. Just another dead body amongst the masses.

A great rumble swelled amongst the masses of the boxorks, at first the questioning, baffled sound and then a fearful muttering.

Archon Kyra raced back to her horse and leaped upon

it. She reined the steed about and faced her army, reaching up toward the sky with the tip of her sword.

"Silence! Silence, wormspawn! Our fear is their strength!" The woman's oratory was at the top of her lungs' capacity. "The fact before us is simple! The great Guardian was a coward! A coward, I tell you! She had not even the courage to stand up to me in single combat." She swung her mount around and changed the direction in which her sword was pointed. "The city is ours now, to do with as we wish. Its great army has been defeated. Praise be to the Demiurge!"

The rumbling turned to a swell of scratchy bass voices, gargling out their versions of praise to their Dark Creator. Obscene titters and laughter began to join the throng, and the splashing and thrashing of *mash'queth*, the drugged ale of which the creatures were so fond, joined in the din.

Then a crackly voice rang out: "Look!" it cried. "Look!"

Kyra Archon turned around to see what was the matter, still feeling ebullient with this total victory. Her glee stopped immediately, and she gasped. She reined her horse back and retreated, and then looked back at the bizarre sight.

About the fallen body of her foe, Sofia de Christabel a nimbus of light was forming. This light at first was a roil of the rainbow, shifting and stirring about the bloody form as though awakening from some sleep. Then it cleared and grew in strength to become a searing, brilliant light that seemed to build and build in power and focus. Instinctively, Archon Kyra flung her arms up to shield her face.

"Cover your eyes! Cover your eyes!" she cried out, but her voice was nearly drowned out by the hum of throbbing power that pulsed from the fallen body of her foe. Then, the light focused yet again and a fountain, like the straightest pillar of the most magnificent temple ever assembled shot forth to the sky. It punched through the brooding overhang. Clouds shriveled away from it, and a cerulean blue sky filled with sun shone down.

Then, building yet again in power and volume this Light, like some cylindrical tornado, began to spin. Its base began to move, and where once the body of Sofia de Christabel had lain, there was but a glassy surface, like a pool of crystal. The spinning tube of light gained momentum, and spun off through the valley of Dusk, to the mountains of Myrrhrock, toward the Valley of Nyall where the city of Alexandria lay. Helpless, Kyra Archon watched as the cylinder grew and grew to hurricane size. Its sound was of a dozen hurricanes, a roaring maelstrom of power and purpose.

Then, past the Mountains, it stopped. It expanded. It whirled and it danced, building and building.

"Down!" cried Kyra Archon. "Get down!"

She pulled her mount down to the ground and covered herself with the bodies of the dead as light unlike any light seen before on this land exploded in the mountains beyond. A cascade of brilliance flooded hill and valley and mountain alike, dancing into total white and beyond. The ground shook as though it was turning end over end, hurled through the cosmos toward some final reckoning.

Then, the trembling stilled. When Kyra Archon no longer felt the pressure of the light upon her eyelids, she ventured forth a glimpse up from the piles of bodies in which she had hidden. All clouds were gone now, and a western sun shone down brilliantly. Birdsong from nearby forests touched the air, and the bodies of the army of Alexandria seemed all wrapped in alabaster, showing no blood at all.

Even as the Archon watched, these fallen statues grew whiter, lighter, translucent like wraiths. Then, with interiors asparkle, they faded, faded, faded away as though melting not into the gory earth, but the air and sky itself.

Some of the boxorks had been blinded. These were summarily executed, and then the Dark Army continued, unhampered on its way. Through hill and dale they traveled, and found not blasted heath but grass and flowers and spring where there had once been autumn.

Finally, the rank and file of the army found itself in the valley of Nyall. It was Kyra Archon who crested the ridge first, and looked down. Where there once had been a city and a castle and a palace . . . and a library . . . *the* library . . . of Alexandria, there was now only a grassy field, filled with poppies and small dogwood trees. Mad with fury, the Archon drove her spurs into the flanks of her steed. She tore down the slope, and the horse's hooves dug up great gashes in the green. Amongst a bed of flowers, she halted and dismounted.

"It is not over, Sofia de Christabel!" she shouted, metallic gauntlet shaking in the air. "It will never be over!"

A boxork general cautiously approached the commander. "I do not understand, my Liege Archon. The city . . . the library . . . They are gone from this existence. Is this not as good as destruction itself? Are we not again in control of the Real and the Now?" Its voice was the bastard of a growl and a smirk of victory.

"Maybe for now. And maybe for tomorrow," murmured the Archon. She leaned over and picked a large daisy. "Here, beast. Here now is one of its books. This is what the villains have done! The books are in the dust and the leaves, the oceans and the grass. They are hiding, and yet I see them . . . I see them . . ." She crushed the flower to a pulp. "How can you destroy the sea and the sky, the wind and the sand? Hmm. Tell me, General. Tell me."

With a snarl of disgust, the Archon swiveled and addressed the universe with a challenging bellow. "We will keep your ilk at bay. But you must incarnate again, Sofia, just as I must die . . . But then, somehow, I swear. By all of the power that holds together this Pride, this Will. I shall slaughter all the progeny you care to send into this world . . . Just as my children will slaughter you when again you incarnate. This is not the end, Sofia!" she shrieked. "Do you hear me? This is not the end!"

The lightning and thunder of the voice shook the valley with the promise of future storms beyond imagining.

AIRS ABOVE THE GROUND
by Janet Pack

Originally a native of Independence, Missouri, Janet Pack now resides in the village of Williams Bay, Wisconsin, in a slightly haunted farmhouse with cats Tabirika Onyx, Syrannis Moonstone, and Baron Figaro di Shannivere. Her extensive rock collection adorns her living room. Janet's two dozen plus short stories, interviews, and nonfiction articles have been published by DAW, ACE, Harper-Collins, Thorndike Press, FASA, Xerox Corp., *At the Lake* magazine, and TSR/Wizards of the Coast. Her musical compositions can be found in Weis and Hickman's *The Death Gate Cycle,* and in Dragonlance sourcebooks. Janet works as the manager's assistant at Shadowlawn Stoneware Pottery in Delavan, WI, and, when needed, at the University of Chicago's Yerkes Observatory in Williams Bay. During free moments she sings, reads, embroiders, walks, cooks, watches good movies, plays with her companions, and does as little housework as possible.

LORD PHIRZEN VERITH shook his grizzled head at his daughter, who was showing off with her colt again.

Somehow he couldn't help watching as Lady Sherelan
brought her compact, muscular mount out of a beautifully
controlled rampant in the middle of the horse camp's training ring.

"Now what good's that going to do?" he bellowed in a
voice sandpapered by years of battlefield commands
through the dust of several warriors getting used to new
mounts. "You can't use that maneuver in battle. It leaves
his underside exposed."

"Not for long," she yelled back. Sherelan's impressive
mottled gray lashed out with both forefeet before coming
to ground. He shook his black mane as if he'd enjoyed the
challenging action of standing balanced on his haunches
for the space of fifty heartbeats, and curvetted. The girl
smiled and patted his arched neck, obviously enjoying the
feel of Wind's powerful muscles beneath her hand.

"You never know, Father," she called. "It or one of the
other special things I've invented to teach him might save
my life or someone else's someday." She reined her mount
closer to the old man. "A horse and rider should be a team
in battle. That's what you've always said. Wind and I are
more than that."

Looking at the young woman on her magnificent moon-
dust-and-midnight horse, the lame veteran agreed. Both on
the small side, they were graceful and quick, with surprising reservoirs of energy and strength. Only the gods knew
where she'd discovered the colt. Verith had been in the old
king's cavalry for many years, and had never seen a match
for the deep-chested, dainty-footed animal that owned
enough heart and determination to try flying at his daughter's command.

He'd never thought Sherelan had aptitude toward magic

until seeing her work with the colt. Their pairing made him think her fingers vibrated something unique through the braided reins. Wind's intelligence eclipsed that of any horse the soldier had encountered in his long life: the intent, curious brown gaze mirrored Sherelan's own. Colt and rider missed little between them. It was almost as if they shared a common soul.

Never comfortable with things he couldn't touch or see, Verith shivered in the soft summer air. "Save me your girlish notions," he grumbled, looking at his offspring fondly across his battle-decimated nose. "Now step down for your sword lesson."

"Wait. Look what else he can do," Sherelan called, whirling Wind away. When the center of the ring was clear of drilling cavalry, she gave the horse an invisible command that set his sure black hooves dancing in the packed dirt. "Have you ever seen anything like this?"

Wind bunched powerful hindquarters, lofting them both into the air. He seemed to balance horizontally on the whispering zephyrs of Garrelian's high plains for a long moment, then kicked hard with his back legs and dropped back into the hoof-patterned ring. Before the soldier could catch his breath at the unprecedented maneuver, horse and rider became airborne again, holding the impressive flight even longer. Touching ground with all fours, Wind reared into an upward stretch at a whispered word from his human partner. Settling onto his haunches, the equine hopped three times, demonstrating strength and excellent balance before returning his forefeet to earth.

"Very pretty, very impressive, my dear young lady," her father applauded as the horse nodded his own approval. "But don't show the young king you've been wasting pre-

cious time with such nonsense instead of helping train the
new cavalry horses. Don't forget, he expects us at Corelese in three weeks with the Fifth Cavalry and two squads
of archers in tow. If the treaty talks fail, he'll need every
man we have."

Lord Verith's face hardened, watching the girl as she
racked the horse obliquely toward him on an inside lead.
He didn't allow the fancy dressage step to detour his
thought. "Border raiding by those greedy Kolbarans must
be stopped. If Lord Niezt's diplomacy won't do it, the army
will have to by force." He pointed a square, scarred finger
at her. "And before we march, I'm going to perfect that
lopsided sword stroke of yours."

Sherelan slipped off the saddle and bounced to the
ground, long sorrel braids escaping their knot to settle in
two horsetails on her shoulders. Just entering her nineteenth
year, she reminded the lame old veteran of a kimshar cat,
always vibrating with barely contained energy and curios-
ity. Her father hoped that ruling the demesne he'd leave to
her in a few years would never leech away such vitality.

"Will you allow me in a skirmish this time?"

Verith didn't want to consider his daughter in battle. The
thought made him tremble inwardly. Sherelan had become
even more precious to him after his wife had died from a
terrible quick illness several years ago. The young Lady
Verith was a compact, pretty prize any enemy would sacrifice much to win. Another year or two and she'd gain the
grace to be truly beautiful. Along with being a superb horse-
woman, Sherelan handled a sword well. She also owned a
sharp mind, grasping field strategy with understanding
which staggered most of the young king's advisers. Phirzen
felt proud to claim he'd helped mold her into a real per-

son, not just another showy landed lady worth only the coin of her looks.

It was a wonder young King Zanaris had asked for Sherelan specifically to help her father train this last batch of horses—the ruler normally ignored competent women and forbade them places in his council. Was that her magic again? Verith would very much like his daughter to take his council seat when he became tired of the incessant haggling. That time was fast approaching. He sighed. Unless the king's mind changed, however, it seemed unlikely that Sherelan could succeed him, and that would be a great waste. The aging lord didn't pretend to know the reasons behind some of his monarch's more peculiar decisions.

"No, Daughter," her father said gently. "You're my only heir. You'll watch from afar, probably along the edge of the Dultharr Heights along with the rest of Fifth Cavalry, and only fight if absolutely necessary."

"You've got to let me in a battle one of these days!" Sherelan's face stiffened with pique, making her almond eyes narrow and her full lips straighten. She kicked a rock, sending it skittering out of the horse ring. For long moments it seemed that her temper might conquer sense, lashing out with words sharp as a well-honed blade. With pride, Verith watched his lessons take hold as his offspring gained control of her anger with a rein of caution and a deep breath. Not like her incendiary mother Lady Linat, who had never comprehended the advantage of curbing temper with rationality.

Sherelan settled herself and regarded him again, running Wind's reins through her fingers. "You're right, neither you nor the king have to let me fight," she said softly. "But someday soon I hope you do."

"My opinion opposes yours," Verith stated, "for reasons you understand. If King Zanaris orders you in, or if something happens your talents can positively affect, I'll not protest. You can serve as the Fifth's messenger, though. Get your sword, we'll work on that stroke."

"Race you to the weapons," she teased, pointing to the rack where they rested the length of the training ring away.

"Only if you loan me your horse, Daughter," the lord grinned.

Wind lowered his head, looked at the old man sagely, and whuffled through his long dappled nose.

King Zanaris' Fifth Cavalry advisers met to review their strategy the night before marching to Corelese. Sherelan, dressed in a messenger's leather leggings and blue tunic, sat beside her father on one side of the map table while Lord Deveris harangued from the other.

"So we can't take the most direct route through Neurphy, and it's the only way we'll get this many men there in three days. Any alternatives? I think not."

"Of course there are alternatives, Lord Deveris." Lady Verith's voice fell with deceptive tameness on the adviser's ears. There was assurance behind her tone belying her lack of years. "As my father says, there are always alternatives. What if we headed toward Ythris?"

"Absurd!" spat Deveris, echoed by Lord Ehlyan.

"Then look." Sherelan leaned forward and traced a path above the map with a long finger. "On this track, we go through Thisket toward Mycuria on the eastern border until we turn toward River Choom, which is only a few hours away at that point. It's the best route. And there are likely to be a few Kolbaran spies along that road. If we discover them, all the better."

"Who among the king's crack force is willing to follow the strategies of a female stripling?" sneered Deveris.

"I am." Lord Besket's opinion was echoed by a handful of lesser commanders. From outside the tent, Wind added a whinny.

"And I," stated Lord Verith.

"Of course he stands by his daughter," Lord Ehlyan said.

"You know me better than that," chided the old cavalryman. "I wouldn't unless the plan made sense. She's right, that's the best route. I'll take the voices I heard earlier as affirmatives for Lady Verith's plan. Any disagreement?"

Deveris grumbled, "You've heard mine." Ehylan and a few of his underlings agreed.

Phirzen slapped a hand on his chair arm, rising to close the meeting. "So be it. We march on the morrow for Thisket."

Followed closely by the colt, father and daughter walked to their respective tents together in moonlight so bright it threw shadows. "Does it ever end?" Sherelan sighed.

"You're a talented young lady," returned her father softly, understanding her subject without explanation. "The men trust you. Deveris would lead them straight into an ambush, and they know it. You'll always have detractors who speak more from jealousy than anything else."

"It shouldn't make a difference, but it does," said Sherelan as Wind put his head comfortingly over her shoulder. The girl's fingers rested gently on his sensitive muzzle. Magic of the most profound kind, that which never has to be spoken, almost sparkled between them as she rested her cheek against that of the horse. "One of these days, I'd like to be appreciated by more than you and Wind."

"You already are, girl," said the cavalryman. "You heard those voices supporting you tonight. Lord Besket's men would follow him straight into the coldest hell. They know their good leaders. If it comes to battle and I fall, the Fifth may elect you commander despite your age. Deveris will never get the position, and he knows it. Ehlyan's in the same state."

Sherelan's smile increased the moon's brilliance. Pulling away from the colt, she rose on tiptoe to kiss her father's cheek above his short white beard. "You always make me feel better. Remember to put a pillow under your bad leg before you sleep. Good night, Father. See you at dawn."

"My dear daughter," he whispered into her hair before she pulled away. He watched Sherelan disappear into her tent and the horse post himself sentry before the flap before ducking into his. He had no fear of man or beast crossing her threshold with her horse standing guard. Magic again? Perhaps. Shrugging, he prepared for bed.

The Fifth Cavalry marched the next morning. Hair braided back from her face and hidden beneath her bright blue messenger's cap, dark eyes shining with excitement in the dawn light, Sherelan looked very young. Riding lightly in her saddle at the apex of the column next to her father's right stirrup, she controlled her flashy colt seemingly without movement, hands low on the reins, knees balanced delicately on the leather lying against the animal's warm barrel. As a messenger last year between the cavalry on maneuvers and the King's Council, the lady had learned to hide two flat-hilted daggers within her tunic against unforeseen circumstances.

She remained gracious toward Lords Deveris and Ehlyan when the column's scouts captured three Kolbaran spies along their track within that day and the morning of the next. Turning toward Corelese and the Choom, the Fifth Cavalry picked up another trio of the enemy. The commanders took turns prodding them for information as they traveled.

On the third day, the horsemen and archers of the Fifth marched past Corelese. Lord Verith, Sherelan, and three squads of the Fifth's best soldiers labored up the narrow trail to the Dultharr Heights, a set of two plateaus separating Kolbara and Garrelian. The highest granite table belonged to Kolbara; Garrelian claimed the plains below where River Choom flowed. The middle height, which pushed into the sea of grass like a narrow ship, was considered neutral, and therefore had been used for hundreds of years as the site for treaty negotiations.

"King Zanaris has been here for two days with only a minimum of guards and three negotiators," panted Phirzen to his daughter as they topped the ridge to the first Height. "I hope things are well."

"There's Talishar, his horse, over by the treaty tents," Sherelan replied. A number of chargers stood there, hip-shot and ground tethered, attended by a soldier. "Wait. Where are Lord Niezt's, Lord Rethwyn's, and Lord Fondul's? I recognize only the king's mount. And aren't there far too many soldiers backing the Kolbaran tent to be an honor guard?" Chills chased up her back, prickling the hair at her nape. "This isn't good."

"Something's wrong." The old lord's face turned grim. "Deveris, Ehylan, Besket, Kratar, bring your commanders," he snapped. "Deploy the rest of your forces as planned," he told them as they gathered. "We've got a bad situation here. Approaching it will be tricky. Any move on our part, and it will look like Garrelian broke the truce and began the war."

"Lord Verith," said Sherelan, drawing herself to her full height and grasping her mount's reins tightly. "You have a messenger. In this instance, I can take three men with me and find out exactly what's going on. If the Kolbarans deny me access to King Zanaris, we must assume the worst."

Eyes the color of oak leaves in winter studied his daughter, trying not to show fear for her. Phirzen finally sighed and nodded. "In this instance, I see no better way. My lords, do you agree?" Nods answered. "Keep bringing up the troops. I smell a battle."

He bent toward Sherelan. "Be careful, my daughter. If you can give us a raised fist indicating you need help, do so. We'll be at your side as fast as horses can move. If not . . ."

"If not, we'll do our best. I'll take Kothes, Ammren, and Thrend." Three warriors who had excellent fighting skills. "I'll need an official message, too." She stood beside her colt scratching his neck while Lord Verith delegated tasks. The details were finished in short order: Sherelan folded the sealed and beribboned message into her pouch, and her father sent them off with the customary slap on her boot. She led her unarmed trio forward at a sedate pace.

Wind arched his neck and played his nervousness into a high trot, front hooves almost contacting his chest at each step. They were paces away from the tent flying the Garrelian colors of blue, green, gold, and white when a rough accented voice cried "Halt!"

"I have messages for King Zanaris of Garrelian," announced Lady Verith, hoping her voice didn't tremble. "It is imperative that I see the king."

"The king has asked not to be disturbed during the talks," a smoother voice answered as a man ducked from beneath the tent's entrance. Obviously a lord, Sherelan judged, and a fighter as well by his stance.

"Then I'll give the documents I carry to Lord Niezt," she insisted. "Or Lord Fondul. If they're not available, Lord Rethwyn will do. It's my right as a messenger to pass the documents I carry to one of them, if not the king."

"Very well," the nobleman acquiesced. "Leave your cadre without. Come on, come on," he barked impatiently as she dismounted. "King Zanaris has little time for trivialities."

She pushed beneath the flap, losing vision for a moment in the gloom. Lady Verith blinked, and focused on eyes fired with hope. Zanaris' eyes. He sat on a chair to one side of the tent, hands and feet tied. There was no sign of Lord Niezt or Lord Fondul.

A heavy hand descended on her shoulder. Sherelan reacted without thinking: she tore the long daggers from within her tunic, tossed one into the king's lap, and whirled on the Kolbaran behind her before he had a chance to draw his sword. "Wind!" she screamed, stabbing through the enemy's torso and retrieving the bloody dagger. The wall of the tent shredded beneath the onslaught from her colt's hooves as Zanaris sawed at his bonds.

The soldier from outside replaced the Kolbaran lord, stepping toward her with weapon ready and an ugly smile. Lady Verith feinted and ducked as Wind shouldered past her and struck out with a connecting forehoof that shat-

tered bone. Leaping for the stirrup on the off side, Sherelan gained her saddle and gestured to the king.

"Up behind me, and hold on tight."

Grinning, Zanaris picked up the fallen Kolbaran's sword,
used her stirrup, and settled behind her. Sherelan sent the
colt bolting from the tent.

They didn't get far. Too many Kolbarans stood between
them and the Garrelian lines. Although the Fifth surged forward to engage the enemy, she couldn't see safety for the
king in that direction. Wind danced in place, champing his
bit.

"There's only one way left to Garrelian lines, Majesty,"
Sherelan called over her shoulder. "It's the hardest path."

"Take it," the young king encouraged. "You have my
trust."

Lady Verith immediately reined the colt a quarter turn
to the left, setting him straight at a thin line of Kolbaran
swordsmen guarding the escape route considered impossible. The king whooped and connected weapons with the
first enemy as Wind kicked out behind and sent another
tumbling. Zanaris' chest collided hard with Sherelan's back.
The lady hissed in frustration, turning their mount in a tight
circle as Kolbarans mobbed them. Her dagger connected
with a face and another sword, the impact hard enough to
flip it from her grasp.

She leaned next to the colt's neck, concentrating on steering him away from danger. Wind jumped, kicking behind,
landed, and reared front. That bought them some space.
With a knee signal, Lady Verith urged him to run. The mottled horse needed little encouragement. A few strides, and
a tremendous leap took them over the foot soldiers' heads.

All they had to do now was outrun the few horsed enemy

and a dozen archers chasing them with arrows. Wind's mane whipped her face. Just a little farther, a little farther . . .

"Gods!" exploded the king, realizing where they headed.

"Wind, prince of horses, fly!" screamed Sherelan as the rocky promontory sheered into the precipitous drop to the grasslands below.

The colt hit the angle at a run and shifted for footholds, front hooves stretched for speed, haunches springing forward, then compressing until his hocks and rump raked the rocks and scrubby bushes of the decline. The back of Sherelan's cap touched King Zanaris' chest as she strove to help balance their acute angle and make the ride easier for her mount. She prayed to every god she could think of that her stirrup leathers wouldn't snap. Failure of one strip of hide only as wide as her two fingers would send them into a careening roll from which none of them could rise.

Constantly pumping muscles in fast irregular motions was easy on neither horse nor riders. Sherelan encouraged their mount with whispers she couldn't hear. His ears flicked back and forward again.

Stretching farther, the colt almost put nose between his forelegs at the knees. Jeopardy claimed their insecure balance. With a snort preluding heroic effort, the horse threw back his head and slid, by some magic regaining equilibrium.

Sherelan had slipped forward, head tucked between tense shoulders, the king's body at her back. Wind's crest banged against her face as he recovered. She felt rather than heard the *crack!* as something gave way within her nose. Pain caused her a moment's blankness; the lady lolled right and fouled their newfound center. She felt the colt trying to compensate, without luck. His hooves slipped too far.

"Messenger!" The king's arm forced her upright. Marshaling her will and drawing strength from the magnificent beast laboring beneath them, she ignored the hot blood streaming across her cheek. Her movement restored just enough verticality to stop their sideways plunge. Employing a heart-stopping wrench, Wind won back his footing and plunged on.

Their descent of the Dultharr Heights took centuries and seconds. As the slope eased into grasslands, Wind stretched into a run. Leaning low beside his neck, urging him with her hands far forward on the reins, Lady Verith sent her companion pelting toward the safety of the Garrelian army as Kolbaran arrows thunked into the ground around them.

"Steady. You're among friends here."

"Gently there. Easy, easy." Warriors of the Fifth surrounded them as the colt slowed and finally halted, dancing a little on his front feet and blowing heavily. Sherelan's back cooled suddenly as the king slipped to the ground.

"My gratitude, Messenger," he said, reaching to help her down. "A braver ride I've never seen. Your name?"

She couldn't force words past her teeth. Lady Verith slid clumsily from the saddle and knelt in the thick grass. With bruised and aching fingers, she groped in her pouch for the container of healing ointment she always carried.

"What are you doing, Messenger?" The king stood behind her. Fingers trembling, she scooped out the balm and began applying it to Wind's blood-crusted legs.

"Fifth cavalry cares for horses . . . after . . . after . . ." She couldn't push the rest of the words through her abraded throat. Wind's soft muzzle and warm breath against her cheek were the last things she felt. Dropping the ointment, Sherelan sprawled senseless against his front hooves.

"Healer here, quick!" shouted Zanaris, reaching beneath the colt for her inert body. Balancing her torso against his chest, amazement overwhelmed his face.

"By the gods," he said to the soldiers pressing around them. "This warrior is a woman!"

"Of course, Majesty," replied a veteran proudly. "That's our Lady Verith."

"Wind," she muttered, stirring from the depths of unconsciousness, filled by a foreboding bordered in blood and neglect regarding her equine friend. "Wind!"

Sherelan struggled upright on the cot, suddenly knowing exactly what her father meant by one of his favorite phrases: "After a battle, you hurt to the marrow of your bones." Only one eye opened; the other was swollen shut from her broken nose. Her hands were bruised and tight with swelling, legs felt trembly and puffed around the knees, and the ache in her shoulders was well past agony.

But her worry about the colt wouldn't abate. Gritting her teeth, she pushed back the blanket and slowly, slowly sat up.

"Disobeying my healer's orders, Lady Verith? He said rest."

Shadow and glare shone suddenly. Sherelan recognized the voice, and squinted.

"Your Majesty!" Her feet were firm on the sheepskin rug as she rose and attempted a bow, but her knees betrayed her. Sherelan pitched forward.

Strong arms caught her, forced her to sit on the cot. "That's the second time I've picked you up in three days, Lady," he chided gently. "We're going to have to stop this, or there will be rumors."

"I have to see Wind." She didn't recognize her own voice: it was much too nasal and gravelly.

"Ah, your horse." He rose, striding to the side of the tent. "That's easily arranged. He wouldn't stay in the horse pickets. Pawed them down or chewed through the rope three times."

Sunlight flooded in again as he drew back the sidewall. Outside a mottled gray-and-black head turned. The horse snorted, shuffling sorefooted inside.

"Wind, dear Wind, what have I done to you?" Sherelan gazed at her mount's swollen and scabbed legs, tears sliding hot down her face. She hid them against the short marled hair on his chest. "I asked so very much of you, and you gave almost all of your great heart." The horse put his nose against her neck, nibbling gently beneath her tangled braids.

The young king watched the unusual exchange with a puzzled look. "I've not seen anything to match this," he murmured, embarrassed and fascinated by the closeness and obvious understanding between human and equine. He'd swear the horse had just forgiven Lady Verith everything. How did one reach this kind of communication? Did it hold with other people as well? "Uh, if there's room for another in this conversation. . . ?"

"Forgive me, Your Majesty." Sherelan slid away from Wind and swiped at her sighted eye with the blanket. The rapport between human and horse didn't fade. If anything, it increased. "I was so worried about him. I had horrible dreams about neglecting Wind, and he doesn't deserve that."

"He had the best of care, just as you did, my Lady." He gestured. "My own tent, my own healer for you. Lord

Verith tended your horse. In fact, he wouldn't let anyone else approach the colt, not even me."

"Thank you, Sire," she said faintly, leaning her head against her companion's shoulder.

"None are needed. It's partial payment of the great debt I owe you." Zanaris settled down, one booted foot tucked beneath him, on the end of the cot. "As soon as we prevailed on the Heights against the Kolbarans, I sent for your father. He was distraught after watching us disappear down that cliff." The king's dark blue gaze leveled at her from beneath expressive brows, a small smile stretching the inside corners of his beard. "That will remain one of the more memorable moments of my life. By the way, your father and the Fifth have put together some rather remarkable stories about you. There are more than a dozen versions of your coming to my rescue. And the Kolbarans who survived your horse's intriguing maneuvers thought you and Wind the personification of their demon god Zakt." One hand rose from his lap to gesture, as if needing air. The horse regarded him watchfully.

"In just the few hours I've known you, Lady Verith, you've taught me a valuable lesson. I will never underestimate a lady again."

"I'm a horse trainer, Sire. Assistant to my father, and in your service." Sherelan looked down at her hands, one side of her mouth almost sketching a smile. Zanaris stared, finding the gesture oddly attractive even on her swollen face. "I regret this meeting shows neither myself nor my horse at our best."

"That will soon pass. I look forward to seeing you without this mask." He reached out a finger toward one blackened eye, but a warning stomp from the horse stopped him.

He looked at Wind, startled by the impertinent command, then rose.

"Your horse reminds me of my manners, as well as several favors I crave." The king bowed. "My Lady Verith, I hope you're generous enough to grant those."

"Favors?" Sherelan asked, mystified. "What favors?"

"In a moment. Can you dress?" He pointed to a pile of folded clothing on a camp chair and strode to the flap. "I'll return for you shortly."

Sherelan struggled to stand, then fought her way out of her torn and soiled battle rags into the pretty linen dress that had probably belonged of late to a noblewoman of Corelese. Soft leather slippers completed the outfit. She gave up on the lacings: Wind could not help her clumsy fingers with the holes and knots. Backed by the colt, she limped across rugs threatening to trip her feet.

"Ah, good timing." The king appeared again, facing Wind. "I'd like to present your lady rider and you to some admirers. With your permission."

The horse snorted and tossed his head.

"My lacings . . ." began Sherelan with a hopeless gesture, holding the back of the gown together with aching fingers.

"Of course. I have occasionally done this for my mother, who's a very practical woman. Your pardon, Lady Verith." The young king stepped behind her, catching up the strings and running them through the proper holes, all the while subjected to a head-to-toe snuffling examination by Wind. "Now, everything's proper. My Lady." Zanaris moved beside her and offered a hand. Trembling, Sherelan put hers atop his as Zanaris threw back the tent flap.

A roar ascended from the army when they appeared,

loudest in the front ranks where the men of the Fifth Cavalry stood. The king settled Sherelan in a camp chair surrounded by thick wooly pelts as Wind shouldered through the small opening to stand behind her.

"I present to you the accolades of my army, whom you warned in good time to save many lives, as well as that of your king. I regret deeply the loss of Lords Niezt, Fondul, and Rethwyn, who gave their lives for our cause." Zanaris stood in silent tribute to the dead a moment, then reached into a cherrywood box brought forward by proud Lord Verith. He drew out a heavy medallion of silver and gold. "Lady Sherelan Verith, I am pleased to present you with the Garrelian Sigil, our highest honor." His lips curved upward as he laid the rich red velvet ribbon gently around Sherelan's neck. "There is one for each of you, and with it comes the gratitude of your country and your king."

He turned to his men after similarly adorning Wind. "I want you to know this is the first time such an honor has ever been conferred on a horse. In fact, I'm dubbing this conflict the Verith-Wind Rout."

"My dear daughter," whispered her father in Sherelan's ear as Zanaris handed her a cup of wine twin to his. Garrelian's young monarch lifted it in salutation and drank.

Sherelan sipped. It was deep purple-red, heady and rich, with a delightful peppery finish. Her head spun a little. The cot and the darkness of sleep called to her exhausted body. "Your Majesty," she prodded, fearing a third collapse, "you had another favor to ask?"

The young king sobered instantly, handing his wine to the unsmiling Lord Ehlyan. "Thank you for returning my attention to necessary matters, my Lady. This request is somewhat personal."

She stiffened. She felt Wind stiffen. The indrawn breaths from the army almost sucked dust off the Dultharr Heights above them.

"I have ridden horses most of my life, as have the men behind me," began Zanaris, confronting Sherelan, the colt, and Lord Verith within his gaze. He shrugged. "Yet I have no inkling where you came by your extraordinary colt, nor notion of his breeding. Will you tell me?"

The lady nodded. "I bought him as a tiny thing of six months, all black legs and eyes, in the horse market at Syrristan. The seller didn't know the gem he owned, and sold him for a single steel." She reached up and scratched Wind's chin. "He comes from the breed of Lippensmere. They're renowned for stamina, courage, strength, and intelligence. In fact, there's a legend where they're bred that a warrior's spirit is called to inhabit each foal born. A horse of this breed typically gives its heart and soul to its rider. That person must be able to repay in kind. It's a—a marriage of spirits. Sometimes individuals wanting foals must wait months for the correct animal. There's as much thought going into partnering these wonderful animals as into their breeding."

"A mystery solved," breathed Lord Verith. "No wonder Wind and my daughter share magic."

"May I say, Lady Verith, that you'll have to acquire a most understanding husband," the king said shrewdly. "Since you're already wed to your mount."

Sherelan smiled, nodding. "And your second favor?"

Zanaris' gaze dropped to the curly furs beneath her chair. When he finally raised them again, his expression and tone had become formal.

"It has three parts. First, will you do me the honor of

sitting on my council? I am always in need of sagacious heads such as yours. Second, will you choose me such a horse as yours, and train us both to do those acrobatics that saved us time and again on the battlefield? The animal proved as much a warrior as any human today. What do you call those exotic jumps and turns?"

Sherelan laughed, a gritty sound bubbling with happiness. "Yes, Majesty, I'll sit on your council, find you a Lippensmere, and instruct you in the Airs," she said. "That is, as long as I can have time off to visit my father."

"Perhaps I will come to the kingcity with you, child," Lord Verith beamed, patting her shoulder.

"After experiencing such splendid maneuvers, I'd call them the Airs above the Ground. And you all are witness to the king's word on this agreement," Zanaris cried, whirling to the army. Their cheers rose sunward.

The king turned and knelt at Sherelan's feet. Embarrassed, she held out a hand to prevent him, but her father's touch held her in place. "I know you're tired and need rest, Lady, but I have just one more small request. On behalf of my men."

Lady Verith laid her head against Wind's nose, almost too spent to hold it up. "What is it?"

"Teach us." The chant began in the ranks of the Fifth Cavalry, and soon resounded all the way to the youngest of pages far in the back lines. "Teach us. Teach us! *Teach us!*"

Sherelan stood and smiled, her hand raised for silence. It was long in coming. "Choose ten commanders with the brightest, strongest horses. Wind and I'll begin with them in the morning despite our aches. Garrelian will soon have the best cavalry in the world!"

The army broke formation, mobbing their heroes and their monarch in celebration of their victory over Kolbara. Supported on one arm by her father, on the other by King Zanaris, and backed by her noble steed Wind, Sherelan began planning how to teach the Airs Above the Ground to the Fifth Cavalry of Garrelian.

DEMON HUNTER
by Pauline E. Dungate

Pauline E. Dungate lives in Birmingham, England, and is a teacher at the Birmingham Museum and Art Gallery. Her stories have appeared in such anthologies as *Merlin, The Skin of the Soul* and *Narrow Houses.* She has also written numerous reviews and articles under the name Pauline Morgan. Her other interests include gardening, cooking, ferret keeping, and truck driving.

DURGA rested one hand on the head of the lion as she watched the spiral of dust dwindle across the scrubland. At its heart, leading a party of *rajput* warriors, was the demon Kesin. She had hunted him for two years and had at last found his hiding place. She had to flush him out before she could engage him in battle, or the forces they would unleash would devastate the town. Kesin might not worry about the lives cut short, but in her aspect of Parvati, she was creator. The mortals were in her care.

Kesin threw the reins of his gaudily clad steed to a hovering servant and strode up the steps to the palace entrance. He glared at the low-caste *bhangi* woman sweeping the treads and causing twists of dust to swirl unnaturally around her feet. She dropped her gaze and stilled the movements until he was past, but he sensed eyes watching him. He had been watched ever since he had killed the traitor, Bikramsingh, in the forest four days ago.

Once in the shadows at the top of the steps, Kesin looked back. The sweeper had her back to him and the rajput troops were already moving away toward the stables. None of the people in the square below appeared to linger and a lone pigeon pecking at fallen rice grains flapped away as a potter staggered past laden with earthenware gourds.

The rajput warriors who flanked the entrance and stood at intervals along the corridors within the palace remained motionless as he passed from the heat fierce sunlight to the chill of the marbled passages. The city on the plain was less comfortable than the forests he had lately left.

Word had gone before him. His party would have been seen long before they reached the city's walls. The raja rose from his cushioned throne as Kesin entered the long audience chamber and waved away the woman who knelt at his feet holding an ewer of water.

Kesin prostrated himself at the base of the dais but rose quickly at a word from the raja, who descended partway to meet him.

"Well?" the prince demanded.

"It is done." Kesin untied the bloody bundle that was slung at his waist. He laid it on the steps and unwound the cloth.

The raja bent to study the severed head that tumbled free, smiling. "Are you sure it is he? This looks too old."

"From his own mouth."

"It is good. Have it impaled before the temple of Shiva and proclaim that the slayer of my father's wife is brought to justice." He lowered his voice a little. "Criminals need to know that even twenty years is not long enough to escape my hand, or thine. Burn it after five days."

Kesin grinned. "Yes, Lord."

The prince turned away, dismissing Kesin who backed out of the hall. As the doors were closed, he tossed the head to the nearest guard.

"You heard the raja's orders. See to it."

The man caught the grisly object awkwardly. Supposedly deaf and blind to all that went on in the raja's presence, Kesin knew that the news would be round the barracks by nightfall. He had often stood the same duty when Bikramsingh led the old raja's personal guard.

A dark-skinned beggar-woman was sitting cross-legged by his gate when he returned to his home. Her hair and torso were grayed with dust, her eyes downcast and her alms bowl before her.

"Get rid of her," he said to the group of warriors who lounged in the forecourt. These were members of the raja's elite whom he had assigned for his own protection. Rank had privileges, he thought smugly.

Three of the men leaped to their feet, drawing curved swords from their belts as they did so. Kesin watched from within as they shouted at the woman, prodding her with the tips of their blades, careful not to touch her in case she should contaminate them. Her bowl was kicked down the street, spilling the rice someone had placed there. She climbed slowly to her feet, her hair falling lank and greasy over her face. They continued to shout and wave their swords at her as she stooped to pick up the bowl. She scooped the rice from the dust. One soldier struck her with the flat of his blade. She gazed at him through the strands of hair as if marking him. He took a step backward, fearful.

The others tired of their sport as she retreated, hobbling down the street.

The entertainment over, Kesin passed through the cool entrance to his house and entered the inner courtyard. Only the most favored were permitted houses with their own wells. His was small but shadowed by a neem tree, the leaves of which remained fresh in the heat as its roots tapped the source of the well's water.

A woman scurried across to draw water for him the moment he stepped into the courtyard while another brought him a leaf of honey-sweet cakes. The strings of beads that they wore over their naked torsos chimed musically with their movements. Kesin chose his servants for their grace.

He took the bucket as it appeared at the lip of the well and upended it over his head. Green slime cascaded down his hair and face.

Kesin roared.

The woman dropped the bucket back into the well. The honey-cakes scattered in the dust. Both hauled it to the top again and peered inside. One dipped her hand in the water and raised it to her lips.

"This water is clean," she said timidly, obviously expecting to be blamed.

Kesin examined it for himself before using it to wash the muck from his body. Then he dropped his clothing in a filthy heap by the well and strode into the shade of his house.

Kesin stirred only slightly when the woman, Shabana, left his bed. It was almost light, and she would be returning to the temple before the sun rose fully. Though any of his body servants would willingly have slept with him, he preferred the courtesan, perhaps because he had to charm her and she was not available at his whim. Shabana had been given to the temple as a child and could command high prices to permit clients to worship through her. Normally they visited her. Because of his rank, she came to Kesin, but he had to make some effort to please her or she would tire of him before he was ready to discard her favors for another.

Outside the arched window a pair of doves cooed to each other, welcoming the dawn. Disturbed by their sounds, Kesin rolled over, his arm resting in the cooling depression Shabana had vacated. He opened his eyes to gauge the hour from the brightness of the chamber. His fingers touched an unfamiliar length of silk. A sash perhaps. The growing light revealed its scarlet color. He didn't remember Shabana wearing it.

"It isn't mine," Shabana said when he tried to return it.

They stood in a courtyard of the temple where Shabana danced for the pleasure of the gods. The ornately carved building rose behind them with its arched entrances to the inner shrines.

"Then I will give it to you." Kesin had noticed how her fingers had lingered on the silk when he held it out.

Shabana shook her head. "Better to give it to the Goddess," she said.

"Which one?" Kesin said, smiling.

"Parvati, the mother, of course."

Kesin shivered as Shabana led him into the presence of the triple goddess. The stone images of her incarnations stood on three sides of the stupa. Kali the destroyer leered

at him malignantly, her necklace of skulls rattling and grinning eyelessly at him. Durga, many-armed for war, looked
coldly on him, though Shabana had said that she ought to
be his partroness. But gentle Parvati smiled benevolently
as on an errant child.

Shabana took the sash to lay it over the wrist of the
Parvati's outstretched arm. Kesin felt as if Kali's eyes were
burning into his back. He snatched at the silk and crossed
the shrine to stand before the demon-slayer.

"Red suits her better," Kesin said, tossing the cloth at
the foot of the image. It drifted down to lie across the
throat of the demon her raised foot rested on.

"What did you do that for?" Shabana followed him into
the sunlight.

Kesin shrugged. He didn't really know himself. "It isn't
wise to neglect the harsher aspects of the Goddess," he
said.

"What do you mean?"

He wasn't listening. He was staring at the bronze statue
that stood just inside the gateway leading to the street. He
hadn't noticed it when he entered as it stood within the
shadow of the wall. He was sure he hadn't seen it in the
temple grounds before, but he hesitated to ask Shabana
how long it had been there. Instead, he turned to her with
a smile.

"I hope you will dance for me again," he said. "Soon."

As he left the courtyard, he ran his hand down the head
and across the back of the bronze lion. For a moment the
cold metal seemed to change to soft, warm fur. His pace increased in his eagerness to mingle with the populace abroad
on this thoroughfare. He glanced back, half-expecting to see
the lion's gaze following him. He breathed easier when it

wasn't, berating himself for allowing the atmosphere within the temple to affect his senses.

Kesin struggled for breath. Something soft and yielding dragged at his windpipe. Was molded to it. He tried to prize it away, but his nails failed to catch at the edges. He heard his own breath rasping. Mingled with another sound. A purring. Coming closer. A pad, like that of a large animal, pressed on his chest. The tips of extended claws pricked his skin.

As he struggled, his hands brushed soft fur. He felt carrion-warm air caress his face.

Then red washed the darkness.

He was awoken by one of the servant girls bringing him a jug of lasse prepared from soured milk mixed with cold well water and flavored with cinnamon and salt. His throat felt tender as though he had spent a day shouting. His fingers probed at the spot and encountered silk. The red silk sash was looped about his neck, its ends weighted.

"Guards!" he roared and went into a spasm of coughing. It exacerbated the rawness.

"Drink this, Master," the girl said, offering him the jug.

Kesin snatched it from her and gulped down the liquid, the creaminess easing his throat a little.

Two warriors charged into the room, their swords drawn.

"Someone has been here," Kesin croaked at them. "Find him."

"Yes, Lord." They disappeared again.

Kesin twisted the rumal in his hands. He doubted they'd find any sign. And he wondered what the purpose was. From the way the cloth had been wound about his neck, killing would have been easy. Frightening him would gain nothing—if it could be done.

"There were lion prints in the dust beneath your window," the warriors reported.

"Nothing else?"

"No, Lord."

"Where did it get in?" he asked.

"The tracks only appear there."

"I want the patrols doubled at night. Anyone found asleep goes back to the ranks."

"Yes, Lord."

"There was a bronze lion there two days ago," Kesin told Shabana. He'd had business in the temple precincts and had taken the opportunity to speak with the courtesan. At this time of day the complex was busy with petitioners bringing gifts of intercession to the deities or thanksgiving for favors considered granted. Women in particular sought Parvati's help.

A handful of guards patrolled though it was rare for them to have to act—most thieves respected the gods. And murder was best done in dark alleys. The inevitable beggars sat on the steps of the main temple waiting patiently for alms—a handful of millet, a portion of boiled rice.

Shabana shook her head. "You are mistaken, Lord. The only lion is the one Durga rides. That is made of stone, like the rest of her image."

Disturbed, Kesin left the temple complex, choosing one of the other gates.

Normally as he walked through the streets, two rajput warriors trailed him, a ritual but largely unnecessary, guard of honor. Now they seemed to have deserted him, perhaps fooled by his departure in an unexpected direction.

Kesin walked quickly. He was less familiar with this part of the city and he intended to circle round the temple and regain the thoroughfare that took him to his home. As he turned between the houses he lost the sound of the usual bustle. The gaps between buildings were narrower, and cooler in the shade they created.

An old man squatting on a step spat betel juice into the dust and disappeared inside his house as Kesin approached. The strings of beads hung in the doorway to discourage the ever-present flies from entering jingled softly as Kesin passed.

He turned into another street expecting to see it widen out ahead. Instead, it was just like the last. A dog urinated against a wall. The only sounds were Kesin's footsteps and the buzzing of insects as they homed in on the patch of wet earth.

At the next corner he paused to get his bearings. In the silence vacated by his feet he heard a distant pad, pad. It sounded too loud for a dog and not sharp enough to be a mule. A sacred cow wandering through this maze would be heralded by the chiming of its bell.

He began to walk quickly, listening intently for the padding that seemed to shadow him.

He turned into another street. It was little more than a narrow alley between the backs of houses where garbage was thrown. As his attention was behind him, he didn't see her at first.

She walked toward him out of the shadows. Her long, black hair fell to her waist, the strands lifting slightly in a faint breeze. There was a dagger in the top of her red *gha-*

gra, which was tied tightly against her dark skin leaving her breasts bare. In her hands was a rumal and at her heels, a lion.

"I remember you," she said.

Kesin had a momentary vision of this girl standing barefoot in the water beside Bikramsingh's headless body. She had uttered similar words before she had turned and run. This time it was Kesin who retreated. He backed away, wondering how she could have arrived in the city so soon.

He backed to the end of the alley, yelled once, and ran.

Round the next corner the maze disgorged him into the busy thoroughfare before the temple of the triple goddess. Here was noise, color, and bright, hot sunlight.

Kesin looked back. An old man spat betel juice into the dust.

Kesin found it difficult to settle. Twice he had checked that the guards were alert, but he wasn't sure that that was enough. If the lion were mortal it would have been seen in the streets and hunted down. He did not believe it was. And the girl. He had seen her—he was certain now—sweeping the steps of the palace when he returned with Bikramsingh's head. And begging outside his gate. But that was impossible. Unless she was not human. Kesin remembered the feel of the red scarf tightening about his throat when there was no-one to hold it. Except the hand of the Goddess, the enemy of his kind. He didn't eat what his serving-women brought him but paced restlessly from room to room. He called for lamps to be lit in all of them.

The household quieted as all except Kesin slept. The flames guttered and died as the wicks smokily consumed the last drops of oil. Dawn lightened the sky.

Kesin entered his sleeping chamber. A lump was silhouetted against the window slit. He held the last lamp out toward it. It illuminated the head yellowly. The distorted, rotting features of Bikramsingh grinned at him.

"Tomorrow," it said and rolled from its perch on the narrow sill.

Kesin leaped for the slit, determined to catch whoever had spoken. The courtyard was deserted.

The empty eye-sockets seemed to follow him as he backed across the room. The demon slayer was here. She had shown she could touch him. Durga was playing with him. He needed space to fight her. To win, he needed to choose the place of the encounter.

The coming of dawn saw the demon climbing into the mountains. He followed the stream as it twisted up the wooded ravine. In his present form, Kesin was a handsome man, turbaned and dressed in richly embroidered clothes which were now dusty and travel-worn. He was armed with both a sword and a spear. He carried shield, breastplate, and helmet in a bundle at his back. He sniffed the air. His enemy was out there and coming closer.

Kesin called up a storm, a hurricane that plucked trees from the ground and disturbed boulders. He hurled it at her. She turned it aside. She quenched, too, the fire that snaked through the forest at his bidding. He was close to the safety of Patala, but she was tenacious and he would retreat no farther. He had no intention of allowing her entrance to the demons' underground realm so that she could cause mayhem and bring her slaughtering kin. Before the next sunrise, one of them would be lodged with Yama.

Kesin looked up at the mountainside. In places, weather

had shattered the vertical walls sending swathes of scree
scything through the vegetation. Such a spur jutted out into
the valley a short way ahead. There, he decided, he would
set his ambush.

He picked his ground and waited.

Durga had long since discarded the illusion of human
form. Her black skin glistened as the humidity increased
with the rising sun. Warily, she threaded her way through
the trees in the ravine. She knew she was close behind the
demon. Kesin was cunning and powerful.

In two of her hands she held her sword and shield. The
third grasped a bow, ready strung, while her free hand rested
on the head of the huge lion she rode. Sunlight glinted on
her bronze helm and was reflected from the white bone of
the skulls that made up her necklace. They clinked with
the rolling stride of the animal beneath her.

Durga was weary. The turning of the storm had drained
a lot of the strength she had borrowed from Indra—but the
making of it must have equally weakened Kesin.

She had entered the valley soon after the light had first
touched the mountains and knew that somewhere within it
her enemy waited. At some point, Kesin would turn and
fight. She sensed it would be soon. He would not want to
lead her into his homeland though the demons, by their
numbers, would quickly overpower her. But once she passed
through the entrance it would not close and others, Indra
perhaps, could follow. The carnage amongst the dwellers
in Patala would be great. If the great God Varuna permitted it to go that far.

A stream threaded between boulders in the valley bottom. The great lion bowed its head to drink. Durga listened

to the wood. Birds sang and in the distance a monkey howled; all seemed normal. Durga slid from the beast's back, certain that it would warn her of the approach of any danger, and scooped up a handful of icy water.

Over her curled fingers she saw a figure seated in the shadows of the trees on the opposite bank. Shy pigeons accepted grain from his outstretched hands. When Durga raised her head to see him more fully, he wasn't there, only a bird pecking at the ground. It rose in fright at her sudden movement. A shiver of apprehension ran down her spine.

Remounting, Durga continued on her way, conscious of the passing time. The sun had reached the zenith and was poised for its descent toward night.

The valley narrowed, the stream twisting between spurs thrust like tentative fingers from the mountains. Ahead, a rockfall had cut a swath through the vegetation. Loose scree prevented anything rooting there.

Durga thought she glimpsed movement amongst the precariously balanced boulders. A light touch and a murmured word turned the lion from the path. He bounded upward, his pads scarcely touching the stones, shifting without dislodging them. Not a pebble fell to alert Kesin of their coming, the lion's color blending with the rock.

The goddess nocked an arrow to her bow. She saw Kesin now. He was on a level with her, crouched with his shoulder against a boulder near the top of the slide. He glanced up as the arrow hissed toward him and moved slightly. It splintered harmlessly against the rock. The second and third, loosed in rapid succession, disintegrated into a shower of sparks.

Kesin hurled his spear at the lion before drawing his

sword. The lion turned aside and Durga reached out. Her fingers touched the haft. The spear stopped in mid-flight, dropped to the ground, and the snake it had become slithered away between the stones.

The demon roared as Durga threw herself from the lion's back, her shield raised to ward off his blows. He staggered back under the onslaught of her sword and dagger. The shale beneath his feet shifted. The boulder, already unstable tottered beneath his weight and began to roll. The scree around it followed, gathering speed as it plunged down the slope. Unable to keep their balance, both combatants were swept along with the avalanche. She glimpsed the lion surfing the pebbles before the rush overwhelmed it, its bloodied body carried out of sight into the trees at the foot of the slope.

Durga brushed the stones from her limbs and rose to her feet, bruised but unharmed. Her shield, still strapped to her arm, had taken the brunt of the fall. It was battered but still serviceable. Her dagger was still gripped in another hand but her sword was a few paces away, wedged between the stones. As she reached for it, Kesin's blade sliced through the air and her fingers. Cursing her stupidity, she whirled, switching her dagger to the uninjured right hand as she did so.

The demon had resumed his natural form. His skin was bright red, his eyes, iris and sclera, an unnatural blue. He grinned, fangs protruding from an overlarge mouth. Muttering under his breath, he rushed at her, his squat body nimble on the bowed, muscular legs.

Her shield took his blows. Durga felt the shock vibrating to her shoulder. Behind her, she heard the grating of stone on stone. As the sound rose to a scream, she flung herself sideways. More of the hillside slipped downward. A few rocks struck her, leaving bloody trails, but most flew past to splinter on Kesin's armor. She twisted, stabbing at his feet, and slicing his calf before he leaped aside. She tore one of the skulls from her necklace. Crushing it between her fingers, Durga flung the pieces skyward. Dark clouds began to gather over the gorge, obscuring the sun and lit internally with sheets of blue fire.

Demon and deva circled each other warily, Kesin glancing uneasily at the sky whenever he dared. Suddenly Durga snatched off her helm and hurled it away. She raised an open palm heavenward, made a fist, and jerked her arm downward. The lightning followed, drawn to Kesin's bronze headpiece. For a moment he was enveloped in blue flame. He rushed Durga. She dodged. His sword struck her shield. It blazed, then shattered. Durga was thrown back as the fire died. Both stood still, stunned by the shock.

Durga recovered first. Throwing down the remains of her shield, she dived for her wedged sword and yanked. It jerked free in time to parry Kesin's next stroke.

They fought now in silence, exchanging blow for blow. Kesin's shield and greater weight were balanced by Durga's extra hands and longer reach. She noticed he tended to favor the leg she had cut; she kept her injured hand tucked in her waistband. It hampered her movements slightly. She dared not slacken her concentration to throw up another illusion lest he slip under her guard. Yet Durga knew she had to trick her way past the darting blade before the sun set. Kesin's strength increased with the declining daylight, reaching a peak in the first four seconds of twilight. Her own strength was waning.

She edged backward toward the trees, the demon following. Both were breathing heavily. Durga's legs and her sword arm ached, the stumps of her missing fingers itched. She dodged behind a slender trunk. Kesin hacked it down. Sweat and blood from various scratches ran down their bodies.

Durga put another tree between them, and watched it fall. A little farther and there would be shadows she could hide in. She fingered a skull in her necklace. She feinted, retreated, and vanished. She waited until Kesin's blade bit into the trunk, then dropped the ornament. She faded into grayness. Kesin struck at the dark after-image. She attacked from the side, her dagger sliding up between his ribs before his shield smashed into her face. Dazed, she fell back, leaving the knife in his chest, limiting the blood flow. The copper in the metal began its slow spread of poison.

A grinning Kesin thrust at her body. She rolled and came to her feet, shaking the stars out of her head. She loosed the sash from about her waist. The ends were weighted and it hung easily across two of her palms. She parried with the sword, feeling her knees give slightly. He played furiously now; each stroke seemingly stronger, more sure than the last. She was again forced to retreat.

Backed against a fallen trunk, Durga's eyes narrowed. Her sword engaged his, hilt locked to hilt. The sash lashed out, the weighted end snaking around his neck. Kesin threw down the shield to wrench at the cloth that tightened about his throat. She could feel his strength waxing as the sun touched the distant horizon. There were only moments left. Jerking at the sash she launched herself at his throat. Her teeth sank into his neck, meeting.

He gripped her hair. The sword blades slid along each

other. The weight on her arm lessened as they fell apart. She felt the pommel strike the base of her skull as she attempted to suck the life from him. He struck again. Distantly she heard an owl calling.

Yama, Lord of the Dead, watched the demon limp up the slope, the head tied by its hair to his belt banging against his thigh. He was followed by the two smaller demons that had sprung from his spilt blood. The remains of Durga's body lay twisted at Yama's feet. The lion padded out from between the trees. Its ears were torn and its coat matted with dried blood from a gash in one flank. Its feet left red pawmarks on the stones. It sniffed the body of its mistress, then looked at Yama before passing on up the hillside, following the demons' trail.

Yama cast his noose. The loop sank into the torso of the dead goddess. He tugged gently and Durga's soul-form rose from it, the rope loosely about her neck.

"I am honored that you have come for me personally, Lord Yama," she said.

"I regret it was not the demon," Yama said. "They are much more fun."

"I share your disappointment."

Yama chuckled, a deep, sonorous sound. "Nevertheless, I welcome the company of an intelligent guest."

Yama held out his hand. Durga took it and followed him.

SUSPENDED ANIMATION
by Nina Kiriki Hoffman

Nina Kiriki Hoffman has been writing for almost twenty years and has sold almost two hundred stories, two short story collections, novels—*The Thread That Binds the Bones, The Silent Strength of Stones, A Red Heart of Memories, Past the Size of Dreaming,* and *Child of an Ancient City,* a young adult novel with Tad Williams—a *Star Trek* novel with Kristine Kathryn Rusch and Dean Wesley Smith—*Star Trek Voyager 15: Echoes*—three *R. L. Stine's Ghosts of Fear Street* books, and one *Sweet Valley Junior High* book. She has cats.

I LIVE to battle, when I live at all. Most of the time I spend in a sleep that is not death, but the sleep of dreams. I sleep in my mystery stone in my boy's pocket.

The boy mastered me. We were young when he did it. We have grown and changed. I change while he watches, and he changes while I sleep. In this way, I am always known to him, and he is always strange to me.

I am my master's best warrior. He calls on me most often. He loves all those he has mastered and placed in the mystery stones, but I think he loves me the best.

He shakes me from dream-heavy sleep. "Klikattack!

Time to fight!" I know it is my master's voice, but it has changed. Still, I obey. I will always obey my master's voice. In lightning form I rush from my stone. I land, as solid shapes and traps me, on my four feet on soft damp earth. Scents of spring, of grass half-dream still, soft as unshape, the few first flowers, the wet that softens tree hides, they are all around, and sun flashes from my needles and warms my yellow skin. Water flows over rocks somewhere near, and birds call.

A few feet away my opponent stands, its back arched, its round yellow eyes wide. Each of its four feet has many long, twisted fingers, and below its small black nose twitches a long mustache, the ends curling and uncurling.

Dru-eyed. I have fought one before, but it was in a smaller, less dangerous form. As was I.

Sparkles spin in the depths of its eyes, draw my gaze. I feel weak and helpless; my strength seeps from me.

"Don't look at its eyes!" cries my master.

Though everything in me strives to obey my master, I cannot look away. I have already fallen prey to the dru-eyed's first attack—soul-suck.

"Close your eyes!" my master cries.

This I can do. Immediately the drain on me ceases. I feel my energy return.

"Remember who you are!" my master murmurs, and I shake myself into my shape. I remember my powers.

It has been a long time since my master summoned me. His voice has changed, deepened and furred. I have not had time to look at him yet, but his voice comes from a higher place in the air.

"Dru-eyed! Tangle attack!" cries a stranger's voice.

"Klik! Needle-throw!"

I do not open my eyes. The dru-eyed used its soul-suck attack on me without a cue from its master; I won't give it that chance again. I know where it was, and sense movement in the air as it leaps closer to follow its master's order and reaches toward me with mustache and fingers.

I lift my broad flat tail and slap it forward, loose eight of my longest, sharpest dagger needles.

The dru-eyed shrieks. Its cry rises and wavers, but does not stop.

I open my eyes.

It is only half a foot away. All of my needles struck it with enough force to drive deep. One went into its right eye.

This is not a proper fight. It is a disgrace. I am not deep enough in battle rage to enjoy my opponent's pain. This defeat was too easy; the dru-eyed's cry scrapes at my heart and makes me regret my own power.

Shame swamps me.

I am never supposed to feel this way. My master must be wise and call on me only when I can face opponents whose skill and techniques match my own.

The dru-eyed could have beat me if its master had better technique. It should have shielded against needle attack from the beginning, and it should have used its soul attack not to suck my power but to convince me I had none.

I hate an unequal fight.

"Dru!" cries the other master. "We concede! Dru!" She runs, weeping, to her fighter, drops beside it, touches its head. It whimpers and licks her hand. "What's the treatment for this attack?"

My master kneels next to me. He strokes his hand from my head along my back; I tighten and lower my needles so none of the barbs spear his flesh. His palm is warm on my skin. I love the moments when he soothes me out of battlemode.

This time is different. I didn't fight long enough to reach divine madness. I don't deserve this care.

I glance at my master. He is not a boy anymore, but has transformed into a man.

Fear pierces me. My master caught me when he was small; I was the second fighter-beast he caught. Since then he has called me forth in all kinds of places to face all manner of other fighters and their masters.

Always, the other masters were children.

We almost never see adults. Adults don't wander the world pitting their fighters against other people's fighters.

And yet the dru-eyed's master is a grown woman.

"We need to take it to the fighter clinic," my master says.

"Klak," I say. "Klik klak klak."

"There's something you can do to help?" asks my master in his new deep voice. "Klik, help the dru-eyed."

He does not know the right command; we have never studied it. He understands me well enough to give me a command which contains the command I want.

Turn to energy, I tell my spent needles. The needles in the dru-eyed flash as they return to energy form and then to me.

Now the dru-eyed can at least close its weeping, wounded eye. The woman gathers it to her chest, embraces it now that she doesn't have to worry about my needles attacking her.

"Wow," says my master. "I didn't know it could do that. Thanks, Klik."

"Thank you, Klik," the woman says, her voice faint. She rises.

My master lifts me, too. Last time he summoned me I was half his size, and he would never have been able to lift me, but now he is big and strong and half a stranger. Only the warmth of his chest is the same, and the bond we forged when first he mastered me.

I glance around. We are in a clearing in a wood, the trees leaf-shorn and shadow-colored. The stream murmurs. The ground here is trodden into a circle, like other dueling grounds where we have fought.

No one watched this match. There was no director.

We do not fight in private very often.

My master stoops and lifts two packs from the ground, one his and the other strange to me. He slings them both over one shoulder; he still holds me against his chest with his other arm. He follows the woman on the path through the wood, but he does not send me back into my mystery stone.

I am glad. I keep my needles sheathed and soft and cling to the warmth of his embrace. Almost always I go back into my stone immediately after battle. This time I fear sleep. Has my master transformed beyond his need for me?

One hears rumors.

Sometimes in dreams we stone-trapped meet each other. Whispers pass among us. Some of us are sent into our mystery stones and never emerge again. Those still dream, but the dream colors fade over time.

If my master commands anything, I will do it. That's the promise we made each other.

We take a trail that leads into a village. Houses here are not like others I have seen. All the walls are built of wood, and carved animals and plants wind their way around the baseboards. The road is beaten earth. No wheels have rutted it. Along the edges of planter-boxes where herbs sprout in untamed tangles, girls sit, clouds of brown, black, and gray wool in their laps. They spin thread on drop spindles and murmur to each other as we go by. Men and boys are on some of the steep roofs, patching thatch.

A tall woman comes to her open front door, hands a carved wooden poison-toad to a little boy playing on the front step. The little boy cries out in delight. "Toadie! Time to fight!" he says, and faces the toad toward us. "Look! A klikattack! There's your opponent!"

My neck needles bristle. They are the ones with stun power.

"Shhh," says my master.

I know I cannot fight a toy. Still, I respond to a battle cry when I hear one. My master pats my needles down. He pricks his finger on the tip of one before I can lower it. "Ow! Klik! My hand...." Before his hand goes completely numb, he reaches into his pocket and pulls out my mystery stone. "Home, Klik," he says.

The stone sucks me back inside of it, and I fall, unwilling, back into the sleep of dreams.

Have I just fought my final battle? A ridiculous battle against a weak opponent?

I would rather die than finish my fighting life this way.

I dream the battle of my final transformation.

My master and I did not know we faced a transformed mustybyte. Their three forms look very like each other—their brown bodies are long and lean, with narrow tails furred at the tips in black, and their faces are narrow and pointed; they gain a little in size with each transformation, and their colors sometimes darken. From one mustybyte to the next, though, there is much color variation, and in the winter some turn white except for their black tailtips.

I faced my opponent across the dueling ground. It hunched its back and lifted a lip to show me its array of teeth. Musties have several different bites; the variety increases with each transformation. They can select different poisons to go into their hollow fangs.

"Ready? Set! Go!" said the director. In the stands, children screamed with delight.

"Klik! Stun needle!" yelled my master.

"Musty! Evade! Sick scent!" yelled the other master.

As I flung my stun needles, the musty danced away and turned its tail to me. It shot a faint blue cloud of stink from its anal glands.

"Klik! Tail fan!"

I fanned the noxious cloud away with my tail before I breathed it.

"Musty! Stagger nip, now!"

The musty closed with me before I could evade it. It nipped my nose and danced away.

"Klik! Blinders!"

The bite stung. Confusion filled my head. I flipped my front legs, casting small crystal needles that could blind or confuse an opponent if they hit anywhere in its face, but I didn't know where my opponent was. My needles thwipped uselessly into the dueling ground.

"Klik! All ball!"

"Musty! Sick bite! Now!"

The musty dashed in from a direction I didn't expect.

I was trying to roll into a ball, my best defensive position, where all my soft parts were hidden and an opponent faced needles in every direction, but my tail kept flapping around. The wine of the musty's stagger nip flowed through me, convincing me that my limbs were beyond my control.

"Dagger needle! To the left! Now!" cried my master.

I flailed my tail and managed to loose six dagger needles. They went off to the right.

The musty nipped the underside of my tail and flipped me over. It sank its fangs into my vulnerable stomach. Searing pain flowed into me from the bite.

Please call me home, I thought. In my mystery stone, I could recuperate, sleep, dream. Forget this defeat.

"Klik!" cried my master. His voice was ragged with despair. "Pleasure needle! Bind needle!"

As long as the musty had its fangs in me, it was trapped. Pain still flowed from its bite, shimmering along my nerves and beating through my head. Even the tips of my needles hurt.

I tried to move my back leg. My front leg twitched instead. *All right. Try to move the front leg.*

And then . . .

Then I shot six pleasure needles from my back leg into the musty's flank.

It screamed. It stopped biting my stomach and curled up beside me. Its cry changed to a mewl of joy as the poisons from my needles stimulated its pleasure centers.

I knew I was going to die. No fighter beast was armed with lethal poisons for these duels; only hunters were bred to kill. Everything in me hurt so badly, though, that I couldn't imagine living past that bite.

I twitched my other hind leg and cast bind needles at the musty. The needles bound its front legs to its back legs.

I might die, but I had disabled my opponent first.

"The klikattack is the winner!" cried the fight director.

"Klik," my master said, and ran to me.

My limbs and tail still twitched with a mix of musty poisons. Colored flowers of fire exploded across my vision. "Klik klak klak," I whispered to my master. *Don't touch me. I might hurt you by mistake.*

"Klik." His voice was so sad. "I have to get you to the clinic."

I felt a deep wrenching within, starting with my stomach. Shudders shook me. My needles clattered against each other.

Death. Beautiful death. Death in battle.

Every part of me twitched and trembled. Hot fire poured into my heart, and my heart beat burning out to all my edges. I shook and shuddered.

I remembered when I had felt like this before.

"Klik!"

Heat consumed me, burned me to ash.

Heat gave birth to me.

I rose up. My paws had sprouted longer talons. My needles were longer, thicker, glossier in the sunlight. I felt new strength and size and power. I had diamond needles now on my shoulders, and stitch needles around the edge of my tail.

"Klik," whispered my master.

Fire had burned pain and hurt out of me. I ran to my master, tamed my needles old and new so that they would not hurt him. He sat on the ground. When I rose on my hind legs, I was as tall as he was, sitting. I had grown! He hugged me, and I hugged me back. Together we had done this. Transformation. Only the hardest-fought battles wrought transformation.

The glow of victory hazed us.

Sometimes I dream my battle of transformation. Sometimes I dream the battle where I hurt the dru-eyed and was sent home because I threatened a toy toad. Sometimes I dream the day when I found my master. I had staggered from my mother's den to play in the spring sunshine. I heard a hiss, turned, found a gludor stalking me. I flipped needles at it, but they were baby needles, soft and not sharp. It spat a web at me. The web dropped over me and pulled tight until I had to ball up. I cried and struggled, but I could not escape.

Then my master came. "You're mine, little klik. You're mine," he said. He was hardly more than a baby himself. He washed the gludor web from me and stroked me all over and fed me something new and tasty. His "mine" clicked into my consciousness and became law.

I loved him.

I dream our battles. I dream the stormy night on the mountain when he took refuge in an abandoned temple and the ghosts scared him so much he summoned some of us for company. It was strange to come from my stone and not fight.

I dream.

The colors fade.

This is what happens when masters transform into adults. I hoped my master never would.

"Klik. Come forth."

It is not my master's voice, yet it summons me.

How can that be?

I lie so deep in dreams I cannot at first shake them off.

"Klik. Come forth."

I swim to the top of the dream sea. I find the lens of my mystery stone and thrust myself through it into the waking world.

"Klik!" The voice is high and childish. One note of it is the same as my master's. Otherwise it could talk to my mystery stone forever and not call me.

I land four-footed on a dusty stone floor. Light seeps through grimy slits of windows, and the air is close and stale. I look for my opponent.

I see only a child.

She is younger than my master was when he caught me. Her skin is earth-brown, and she has coils of dark curls on her head. She wears a dirty shirt and dusty dark shorts. Eyes green as spring stare at me.

"Klik," she says.

I shake out my needles. I have been gone so long I have forgotten what it feels like to stretch. Power crackles through me. My needles clatter and harden. Diamonds and daggers, pleasures and poisons, stuns and blinders and the little darts of sleep.

Where is my master? There is no one to command me, no one to fight.

"Klik. You're mine. You're mine," she says.

I belong only to my master. He won me in combat. Who is this child? Perhaps I should put her to sleep. Maybe I can find my master and he can tell me what has happened. I cannot return to my mystery stone without his command.

I don't wish to return. Even stale air is better than the air of dreams.

"Klik klik klak klik?" *How can I be yours?*

"You were my father's," says the child. "Won't you be mine?"

I can only be won in battle.

No one fights to win me. My master has forgotten me. In dreams I can fight my best battles over and over.

In dreams I fight my final battle over and over, wound the dru who should never have faced me, drown in shame for having harmed something helpless.

"Klik." I creep closer to the child.

"Klik," she echoes. She holds out a hand.

If I choose to, I can send her to sleep, to pleasure, to sickness. I can bind her, blind her, stun her, steal my stone and run away. Own myself.

Act from shame. Sometimes shame is my nature.

If I turn rogue, the hunters will find and kill me.

A fight with a hunter would be a fine final battle. Any hunter they send against me must be a worthy opponent. Hunters fight to the death.

She strokes my head, my back. I gentle my needles.

"Klik. You're mine," she whispers.

The click of mastery hovers over me. I am strong enough now to resist it if I choose. Or accept it. With this child as my master, will I fight better battles?

A few dagger needles bristle on my tail.

Her palm is warm on my head.

SPIRIT WARRIOR
by Kristin Schwengel

Kristin Schwengel's work has appeared in the anthologies *Sword of Ice and Other Stories*, *Black Cats and Broken Mirrors*, and *Legends: Tales from the Eternal Archives*. She lives in Kenosha, Wisconsin, and works in a bookstore. She says, "My life is surrounded by books; I'm either selling them, reading them, or writing for them. Who could ask for anything more?"

"HAS anybody seen Maya?" Karen asked, sticking her head inside the staff break room.

"Last I saw her, she was in the hall on the second floor," Liz, one of the new interns, volunteered. "By the way, Karen, we were wondering . . ."

"She was restless all last night," Karen interrupted. "You know what that usually means." Her eyes slid around the room and locked with Dr. Pearson's.

"Robert," they said with one breath.

Karen's head disappeared and Dr. Pearson hurried through the door after her. Curious, Liz followed.

Karen was the first into Robert Metgar's room, however, and she knew it was too late when she walked in. Maya was sitting on Robert's chest, her bronze-and-brown striped tail waving the slightest bit, staring at the young man's face. The expression he wore was the most content Karen had ever seen on him.

"What the hell is going on here?" Liz muttered.

Karen turned to look at her, lifting her eyebrows in question.

"I think of it as Maya providing comfort in the last moments, so no one dies alone. How would you see it?"

"But Robert was doing so well yesterday . . . we even took him off the autocall system," Liz protested as she picked up the patient charts and glanced through them.

"In a cancer care facility that is mostly filled with terminal patients, 'doing well' is a relative thing," Karen said, her voice dry. Liz glowered at her.

"Weren't there always legends about cats stealing people's breath?" Liz challenged, her voice sharp.

"Ignorant superstition," Karen snapped. "We live in an age of science now, if you hadn't noticed. Studies have shown that the presence of pets in nursing homes and other care facilities like ours increases the morale and sometimes even the health of the residents."

Liz glared at Karen and would have spoken, but Dr. Pearson interrupted, reaching for the charts that Liz clutched.

"Enough of this silly argument," he said, jotting down a few notes. "Maya has been here longer than any of us, and has been an invaluable presence. Liz, Karen is right. You may not like her or her cat, but you can hardly claim that that is the look of a man murdered by a breath-stealing beast." He gestured at the bed, where aides had begun the process of tending to the young man's body.

Liz shook her head in frustration but remained silent as she left the room.

Karen stood a while longer, watching the efficient team at work. Maya had jumped off the bed and stood next to her, head tilted to the side as she, too, watched the flurry of activity.

Before the sheet was lowered for the final time and the gurney was whisked away, Karen got a final glimpse of the young man's face. A wry half-smile lit her features. The Mathers Center had finally brought Robert Metgar peace.

"The healers of their own people have proved inadequate," the translator murmured to Pedemiu and Arameya, "and so they have asked to be brought to the temple of Per-Bastet, to the Sun Healer of Bast. They beg that you tend to their needs," he continued, gesturing at the group of battle-wounded men. Dark eyes beneath blood-soaked bandages watched with trepidation as the temple's representatives looked over the cluster of litters and pallets.

"We cannot attempt—" Pedemiu began, but Arameya spoke as well, her voice rolling over that of the *wabau*-priest.

"Bring them with me," Arameya commanded, a sharp look quelling the protests of Pedemiu and the other *wabau*. "Bastet will succor all who come to her."

"But, Lady-who-is-not," Pedemiu hissed at her, "we pray to Bast's great father Re to destroy these people. These are men who have killed our kin."

"And our men have killed theirs," Arameya returned, gesturing to one of her assistants to lead the party of injured to the House of Healing that stood to the side of the temple. When the strangers were out of earshot, she turned back to Pedemiu.

"I heal in the service of Bast, though I am a woman and cannot serve as *wabau*. My talent for Healing is a gift from the sacred Cat, and I will use it as I must." One of the bronze-spotted temple cats rubbed along her legs, purring, its striped tail winding between them, and she looked down at it. "Pedemiu," she continued, "he-whom-the-cat-gave, you of all should know the necessity of using wisely the blessings of the goddess."

Shamed at the reminder of the gift of his very life, the *wabau* glanced to the ground. His mother proving infertile, his parents had offered gifts and prayers to Bast, and he had been the sacred Cat's response. In gratitude, he offered himself into the service of Her temple for three months of each year, his wife and his duties as a scribe set aside while he resided within the temple enclosure. Pedemiu whispered a quick prayer of thanks to Bast, lest she think him insensible of her blessing, eyeing the cat that nestled at Arameya's feet. "They are still our enemies," he muttered aloud.

"This war is none of their doing. They are merely men, the servants obeying orders of one greater than they. Blame the great ones if you dare, but do not punish the servants," she added, her voice kind. She turned and followed the procession of the wounded to the Chambers of Healing.

Maya paced the hallway, following Karen on her rounds, sniffing at each door. She paused a long time outside one room, her tail lashing back and forth, then moved on.

"Come on, Maya, time to eat and go to sleep!" Karen called from the stairwell, holding the door open for the cat to follow her. Maya padded down the stairs after the woman who had taken the role of her keeper.

Back in the kitchen that connected the hospital with the rooms occupied by the staff, Karen sprinkled some cat food into Maya's dish and set it on the floor. She took another moment to refill Maya's water before opening the freezer and throwing a box dinner into the microwave. This was her first opportunity to eat sitting down since breakfast, more than fifteen hours ago. She yawned, watching Maya delicately crunch her food.

"How come you stay around these dying people, huh?" she asked the cat. Maya lifted her head and blinked at her, then returned to her dish. The microwave beeped, and Karen pulled out her own dinner. Peeling the film off the plastic tray, she smiled wryly. "We sure eat gourmet around here, don't we, Maya?" The cat, finished with her supper, ignored her, pushing through the cat door and leaving Karen to her solitary macaroni and cheese. Karen was so tired, she didn't even notice that Maya had gone back into the hospital side rather than through the kitchen to the staff residences.

Maya slunk along the dim hallway, keeping to the shadows thrown by the dim fluorescent lights. The room she wanted was on the first floor, and she sniffed at the doorway a long time before pushing against the door. It gave just enough for her to slip inside, then closed with a soft brushing noise.

"It's you, isn't it, Maya," said a weak voice from the bed. Maya purred, and the voice continued. "They think we don't know about you . . ." A coughing fit racked the woman's body, and she lay still after it passed, conserving what little energy she had. With a quick leap, Maya jumped to the bed and lay by the woman's side, nestling her head under the bony hand. The frail fingers clenched over the cat's dark-tipped ears, and the woman smiled. For a long time, the two lay silent, building strength for what they both knew was coming.

Late into the afternoon, Arameya worked with the apprentices to heal the strangers. Between treatments, she stepped out into the sun, chanting and drawing Re's strength and heat into herself before returning to the wounded. Her energies were drained rapidly, for it was she alone who had the skill and the Gift to place her hands on each man's forehead and hear his *ká*, his spirit-form, telling her what had escaped the foreign shaman's notice. While her assistants cut and sewed and bandaged, Arameya brought the strength of Re into each man, helping his body to heal.

When she removed her hands from the last man's forehead, she could no longer stand without aid. Leaning heavily on one of the students, she returned to the courtyard of the temple complex, waving the boy away and sinking to the ground. Sitting cross-legged in the center of the bricked sunburst pattern, she faced the sun, absorbing the power of Re as he approached the horizon to journey through the underworld.

An unfamiliar noise interrupted her trance, and Arameya opened her eyes, glancing around her. The shadows had lengthened, and the copper disk of Re had just started to dip below the earth. The sound that had disturbed her came again and she gasped, turning to the trees in the north of the courtyard where the shadows were darkest.

One shadow moved forward, blackness trailing behind it. The dry rustle of scales undulating across the stones played a low harmony to the hissing voice that reached her ears.

"I come to do battle with you once more, little thing."

"I have fought you and won many times over this day." Arameya struggled to keep her voice steady, her mind and heart racing. Never before had the creature of night and death been so bold as to appear to her, or anyone in the temple. She wondered at its strength, that it came from the realm of the underworld to war for the souls of humankind directly. *Re, who nightly slays this viper that dawn may come again, give me the strength of the lioness to fight the serpent of darkness, enemy of light and life*, she prayed, her eyes focused sharply on the murky shape. She tilted her cheek to catch the warmth of the sun upon it, a slight smile dancing across her features.

The shadow in front of her became less ephemeral, the sun glinting off white fangs and horned eye ridges. Dark scales shimmered in the dusky glow of Re. A forked tongue flicked toward her, testing its surroundings. A chill that had nothing to do with the setting sun passed over Arameya's skin, raising the fine hairs on her arms and prickling her scalp beneath the wig that covered her ritually clean-shaven head. The darkness seemed thicker, more oppressive, as though the creature she stood against was swallowing the air around her. The wedge-shaped head tilted, human eyes in the reptilian body watching her with contemptuous amusement.

"You have never yet faced me in my true form. It is time you learned that you cannot keep everyone from my clutches forever, healer. Sooner or later all must come to me, including yourself."

"Or be guided beyond you," Arameya snarled. "You cannot lay claim to those whose souls are not found wanting when balanced with the feather of Truth." The night was coming fast, but she reached desperately toward the setting sun, pulling the red-gold rays toward her for strength.

"You should have heeded the will of your *wabau*, small thing. The victims of my little war are too much for you. You are the last of your kind, for no others can speak with the *ká*, and soon you, too, shall be mine."

The long tail made a swishing half-curve across the stones and the night wind surrounded Arameya's throat, closing off her breath. She wrapped her fingers around the sun pendant she wore, and the pressure against her eased. Arameya tightened her grip on the amulet, feeling the points of the sunburst digging into her flesh. She was indeed the last of the Sun Healers of Bastet, for all the others had died in the last moon-cycles as though struck by a plague— and she must survive to finish the training of the apprentices.

The dark shadow laughed, a dry sound like leaves brushing across the stone courtyard.

The last rays of the sun vanished in the distance and Arameya drew herself to her full height, murmuring quick chants for Re's protection. The pendant under her fingers throbbed with heat, sending its stored fire through her body. Light shimmered in her eyes even as the darkness pressed around her, choking off her whispered voice.

Panic surged through her. She would have moaned at her weakness, if she had been able to use her voice against the stifling night air. A soft pressure at her ankles startled her and she glanced down, afraid to see that dark-scaled tail winding around her legs. The large temple cat stood beside her, hissing at the darkness. Comforted by the presence of an earthly Bast, she looked to the sky in thanksgiving.

Arameya began to laugh silently. Reaching up, her hand caught the light of a single ray of moonlight, the reflected glory of Re, and she clung to the silver rope, pulling the mirrored fire down into herself. The silver glow filled her, sending a chill fire into her blood. She clutched the fire to her chest for long moments, then allowed it to blaze forth in her hands. Her breath came easier as the dark receded.

The devouring serpent hissed, slithering back from her cold flame. She advanced, the spitting cat at her side, forcing the creature of eternal night out of the courtyard and through the temple gate.

Standing just within the gate, she raised her hand once more, drawing the light down through her body and into her other hand, which rested on the gatepost beside her. Silver bands twined forth from her hand into the wooden posts, chasing each other through the wood until the gate was framed with snakes of light. Arameya slid her hand down the rough wood, scraping through the skin of her palm and releasing thick drops of her blood that mingled red with silver, twisting around the gateposts.

"Apap, serpent of darkness and enemy of life, you shall not enter here," she said to the darkness, her voice echoing with command. "This place is secured against you by blood and by the light of Re."

The dark viper hissed at her, promising vengeance but unable to cross the barrier she had created.

Arameya turned and walked with labored steps back to her sleeping room in the House of Healing, the cat dancing before her. Once inside her room, she collapsed onto her pallet, not even bothering to undress. The cat curled beside her, and she absently ran her hand along the curve of its spine.

Before her exhausted body led her into a sleep filled with visions of snakes, her drained mind wondered how long the protection, a spell of last resort, could hold off the dark.

Maya's back arched and she hissed, pulling her head away from the woman when he came into the room. He laughed.

"Little thing, after all these years, you still think you can stop me?"

The years have weakened you, have made you dependent on death to survive. But you shall not have her.

"If the greatness of science cannot keep her alive, surely you cannot, little thing," he said, responding to her thought-speech with a hissing voice.

Her soul belongs to others.

The woman coughed again, shaking and twitching in the narrow bed. The machine behind her went wild with beeping, sending its mechanical alarm forth to call the night staff to the fight. Maya's battle was already enjoined. The shadow slithered around the room, but she kept her eyes on him, refusing to leave her charge unprotected by her glowing stare. He laughed again as the hospital staff rushed in, checking dials and monitors and calling orders. They were used to Maya's presence, if disconcerted by it. His they were unaware of. Maya's ears flattened and she hissed again as he moved closer to the bed. The glow of her eyes stopped him, and he looked down at her in surprise.

"Even in your inadequate form, you are more than I had

thought, little thing," he said, grudgingly acknowledging her power, "but I shall still win."

Maya placed a dainty oval paw on the woman's now-motionless hand, drawing forth her spirit, then hopped off the bed before one of the staffers pushed her off.

The creature of darkness lashed its tail, and a shadowed doorway opened in the wall. The lights of the room illuminated the beginnings of a tunnel, the entrance to the realm of the dead.

"Now you must pass me," he hissed, "and I guarantee you shall not pass free."

You will not have her, Maya repeated. She led the woman's spirit forward. As they approached him and the threshold, the touch of the spirit-realms changed her, bringing out her true spirit-form. She took the woman's hand in hers, reaching out with her other hand raised in supplication to the realms beyond her enemy's control. A warm glow lit the three of them in answer to her silent question.

"She is mine!" he hissed, turning his wedge-shaped head from the light and calling up his own battle forces, dark shades that barked accusations and spat venomous indictments. "She has surrendered her soul to me in her actions, in the deeds of her body and of her heart."

Whatever she has done, you will not touch her. She must speak before the judges and her heart will be weighed in the balance with the feather of Truth. Devourer, you should not claim your feast too soon, lest punishment befall even you.

He glowered at her, his eyes yellow slits. He shifted his body, tensing to dart forward and strike at her, but she stood her ground. The glow of light grew stronger, and with its expanse his demons shrank behind him, not daring to reach forward and sink their fangs and talons into the woman's spirit.

Maya turned to the woman beside her. *I can go no farther into the spirit-realms. Harsiesis, protector of the dead, will guide you. Heed his voice and this one shall have no power over you.* She released the spirit's hand and stepped back.

The woman glanced over at the dark shades, quailing in fear, then turned and eyed the light with longing. Uncertainty passed over her as the taunts of the demons reached her ears.

"You are wrong, unnatural, evil, bad, wrong, wrong, wrong . . ." The voices echoed words she had heard all her life, and she put her hands to her ears to block them, her face anguished.

The creature of darkness smiled and slithered forward, scales glinting in the light.

Moving back from the spirit-realms, Maya watched the battle of emotions play across the woman's face. Fear and hope warred within her spirit, and Maya took her final step to tip the scales.

She meowed, the sound half question and half command.

Bathed in the golden light of his father Re, the figure of Horus-son-of-Isis became clear in the doorway beyond the shadows, one hand already held out to the woman.

The freed soul turned to the light, a rush of joy on her face, and moved into it without another glance at the demons of shadow. The spirit of darkness hissed in frustration and turned upon Maya, but she was safely away from the ghostly doorway, back in her earthly form.

She lashed her tail across the wall and the Gateway

closed, leaving her in a room surrounded by doctors and nurses who now realized that all that they could do had not been enough.

Arameya reached out her hand to the East in supplication, murmuring the ritual prayers of the Sun Healers. She faced the South, West, and North in turn, calling for the four winds to add their strength to hers. She lifted her head in the middle of the circle she had traced in the sand, her eyes closed and her arms spread wide. She turned once more in the same sunwise direction, this time asking for the Blessing of Re on the Healing she would attempt. The warmth of the sun caressed her and she gathered it in, closing her hands around the rays and hugging them to her body. She stood with her head bowed for a long moment, quieting the fire energies within her before she went back into the low hut. Amenptah, her companion on this journey and most talented apprentice, followed her.

Sickness was a dark oppression in the shelter, thick in the incense around her, choking and drowning the strength of the light she brought within her. She touched her hand to her sun amulet, drawing power from it, and walked to the sickbed.

The young man was weak, barely able to turn his head to her, but still he stiffened when she leaned over the pallet. She murmured soothing words to him in her own tongue. He understood their intent, at least, for the suspicion in his eyes faded.

Arameya knelt on the floor next to him, one hand on her sun pendant. She placed her other hand on his forehead and wordlessly asked his spirit-eye, the eye of his *ká*, to show her what ailed him. Amenptah did the same, his fingers nearly touching hers as both sat in silence. Her stomach clenched once, then again, and the pain moved deeper in her belly, settling low and gnawing at her insides before it faded and disappeared. Arameya frowned and glanced over at her assistant, who shook his head slightly. She sighed, gesturing for him to join the Nubian healer, and returned her attention to the sick young man. The pain she felt was more than a matter of the boy having eaten something foul, for that pain should have passed through his body as the food did, and the Nubian healer had indicated to her that it had been weeks since the youth had been healthy.

She lifted her hand from the boy's forehead, taking her ivory wand from her healer's kit, and began to trace his body. Holding the wand a finger's-breadth above the skin, she followed the path of the *metw*, the vessels that carried energy and the fluids of life, through his body, down his arms, then across his torso and legs. The wand twitched in her hand every time she passed it over a certain place on his swollen abdomen. With a bit of kohl, she marked the spot, then turned back to her pouch of medicines.

The young man watched as she removed a few herbs and ground them into a paste, which she spread around the glyph on his skin. Other herbs she stirred into a cup of water, handing it to him. She began to speak, but the word in his language for drink escaped her mind, and at last she mimed a drinking motion. The other healer leaped forward, sniffing and then tasting the mixture before nodding to the boy, murmuring in their guttural language too swiftly for her to follow. The young man drank, and soon drowsiness took him. Reaching up, she closed his eyes and made certain he slept before she took out the tiny dagger. She thrust it into the fire to bless it with the flames of Re, then drew it carefully along the mark on his abdomen, cutting layer by layer into the boy's flesh.

A worm emerged from the slit she made, gorged and fat on the young man's blood. She sprinkled it with salt and cast it into the fire, watching to make sure it was completely destroyed before she took out her needle and thread and closed the wound, sprinkling it with more herbs beneath the bandage.

The Nubian leaned forward to inspect her work, nodding and speaking what she believed were thanks and approbation. Helpless before the speed of his words, she held up her hands before her, and he was silent.

Arameya's broken knowledge of his language was still adequate to instruct him on the care of the sewn wound, for this was something he knew well, though he could not speak with the *ká*. She accepted his slowly-spoken thanks, replacing her herbs from the store he laid before her, and agreed to spend the night in the village before beginning the long journey back to Per-Bastet. She had no wish to find herself and her apprentice alone with darkness in the desert.

Karen leaned back in her bed and smiled, relaxing for the first time in what felt like forever. She reached down and stroked Maya, running her fingers along the cat's dorsal stripe, a dual string of dark brown spots from the back of her head to the beginning of her tail.

"You're a strange-looking thing, you know that?" she murmured. "Spotted body, striped legs and tail. Couldn't make up your mind which to be, so you had to be both, huh? You're big, too, bigger even than the half-wild cat I used to feed when I was a girl." Karen scratched her under the chin, then moved lower, her fingers tracing the spot on the collarbone that looked like an exploded star. She was just beginning to scratch the cat's pale underbelly when Maya tilted her head as though hearing something and hissed.

Digging her claws through the blankets into Karen's thigh, Maya leaped off the bed and padded out the door.

"Well, that'll teach me to show you affection!" Karen called after her before turning back to her book.

Maya raced through the corridors, her long hind legs propelling her. She lost precious time jumping at the elevator buttons, finally triggering the one for the third floor.

Long minutes later, she pushed her way into the little girl's room, her back arched and her fur standing on end.

Tanya lay sleeping, her breathing short and tight. The other creature on the bed, however, held all of Maya's attention.

Its coils resting along the foot of the bed, the serpent's head danced, swaying closer and closer to Tanya's face.

Maya crept to the bed, stalking in silence, always behind the visual range of those sharp eyes. When she was as close as she dared, she gathered herself, bunching her muscles beneath her, and sprang onto the bed.

A spitting, clawing fury, Maya landed on top of the snake's coils. She sank her claws beneath the scales just behind the head, using her weight to push it to the mattress, away from the young girl's still form.

The serpent lashed out, trying to dislodge her from its back. The struggle landed both of them on the floor.

Maya disengaged, leaping back on the bed. Positioning

herself in front of Tanya, she eyed the snake, her ears flattened in anger.

It is not her time. You grow greedy in a world of death.

The serpent of darkness hissed at her, its head darting forward, fangs glinting. Maya stood still, batting the head aside at the last second, her claws leaving thin cuts in the scales.

The snake turned away from the bed, slithering along the wall and opening the doorway to the spirit-realms.

"You cannot control me, little thing. Nor can you starve me."

Maya snarled at him, tensing her hindquarters.

If there is no soul whose time it is, the Gateway will not remain open. She jumped off the bed, dashing toward the shadow on the wall. The serpent shifted to intercept her, but she leaped and twisted to the side in midair, landing in front of the dark opening.

The snake darted back to the bed she left unguarded.

Maya hissed, lashing her tail across the wall. The Gateway closed, as she had declared it would.

"I don't need to be in the realms of the dead to devour their souls," the serpent hissed, turning its head once to look at Maya in triumph before it began to slither up the bedposts.

Maya sprang forward, landing on the bed just as the snake's head edged once more toward Tanya.

Her eyes amber slits, she watched the serpent, her claws and teeth meeting his every attempt to approach the little girl.

Without the food of a soul, the serpent began to grow weary. It shot forward less and less often, bobbing its head a shorter distance each time it began to dance.

Maya moved forward, becoming more aggressive as her opponent weakened. With a flurry of quick blows, she once again drove the snake off the bed.

Before she could jump back to the floor, however, the serpent acknowledged the standoff and slithered away. Once more it opened the doorway to the afterworld, this time to slip through the shadows itself, returning to the realms of spirit from which it had come.

Maya watched the wall for long minutes, alert until she was sure that the creature of death would not return. Then she turned back to the little girl and lay down in the curve of the child's body.

A tube-scarred arm curled around the cat, a small hand nestled in the furry sunburst beneath her neck, and Tanya smiled in her sleep.

Arameya glanced nervously at the sky. She raised her hand to shield her eyes, staring north across the sand-spotted plains. She could just make out the shadow of Per-Bastet, at least half a day's travel away. She had badly misjudged both the distance and her own strength. Re was more than half-done with his descent and only an hour or two of light remained to her.

She took a sip of water from the small pottery jar she carried, stoppering it with a piece of wood to keep the flies out. Not for the first time, nor yet the last, she regretted the independent spirit that had led her to leave Naytahut the previous day with just her apprentice, refusing the escort and servants that Kamose would have provided to her. The journey should have been a simple one, not even a day spent rafting down the still, shallow waters of the river in ebb.

She and Amenptah should have arrived in Per-Bastet
that same day, poling their boat along the eastern fork of
the mighty river. But Amenptah had been struck by a vi-
olent fever yesterday afternoon, and they had landed so
that she could tend him. Before he grew too weak, he had
managed to walk with her nearly to the edge of the desert,
away from the night creatures of the river, but had died
just before dawn. His *ká* had refused to speak to her, and
all her efforts had been for naught. When his life had all
but escaped him, he had begun to speak in fevered ram-
blings until death had choked his voice. The last thing
Arameya had heard had been, "Apa-" and she shuddered
to think that he could have been trying to warn her.

Unable to treat his body properly, and even more unable to transport it to the temple, she had dragged it farther into the desert and wrapped it in his linen garment as
best she could. Using a flat, wide stone, she had dug a
shallow grave for him. Buried in the sand, his body would
be preserved and recognized by his *ká* when it returned.

The boat had proved far too heavy for her to launch
after the effort of the burial, and she was afraid to spend
a night on the desert to regain her strength. She had forded
the river and had spent most of the day following close
to the green waters. Only as Re had begun his descent and
she began to fear nightfall had she left the river, cutting
short the curve that led to Per-Bastet by crossing the shifting plain.

Now night approached, and she would not reach the
temple before dark. She hurried her steps, hoping to close
the distance further. If she did not camp on the sands for
the night, she would arrive at the temple only a few hours
after full dark.

A wind swirled around her, chilling the sweat that dampened her brow. The sound of scales brushing along the shifting sands echoed in her ears. Arameya stopped, whirling about, but saw only the soft shadows of the grasses in the setting sun. She glanced at the blazing orange disk of Re in the west and began to move north again. The winds of night continued around her, casting sand viciously in her eyes, even though she ran across grassy earth. She held the gauzy linen of her sleeve before her face and continued. The winds caught at the fabric, snapping it against her cheeks until tears welled in her eyes from the stinging pain.

She leaned forward into the wind that threatened to push her back the way she had come. The rustling grew louder, blending with a sibilant laughter. From the corner of her eye, she saw the last sliver of sun disappear beneath the horizon.

The wind she struggled against died, and she fell to her knees, landing in the middle of one of the sandy patches that dotted the plains during the dry season. Silence echoed loud in her ears.

Casting wary eyes about her, Arameya stood, one hand finding its way to the amulet that hung around her neck.

"Now it is truly you and I, little healer," the shadow murmured, rising up from the sand before her. Resting on the coils of its tail, its body danced, bringing the head to stand just above her own.

"Apap, serpent of darkness." Arameya glanced to the night sky. Cold stars winked at her in the blackness, and her heart sank.

The enemy of Re followed her gaze, and the hissing laugh rolled over her, making her skin crawl.

"Not even the cat's-eye of the moon to help you this night, little healer."

Arameya gripped her amulet, feeling the warmth of the sunburst spreading through her body.

"I have fought you before," she said. "The gentle cat has claws to slay the asp."

With a twisting movement of his great scaled tail, Apap overturned the healer's pack at her feet, scattering its contents around them. Another flick of the tail, and the night winds had buried all beneath the shifting sand.

"You have never truly fought me. You have faced me and my servants with Re at your hand. Alone, you are nothing. I have slain all the others of your kind, so that the gifts of the Sun Healers will be forgotten."

"The apprentices know all that I do," Arameya snapped. "To slay the teacher does not destroy the knowledge."

"They are blind fools, and will not last long. The only one that could ever hear the *ká* has already died," the serpent responded, and spat something at her feet.

Arameya picked up the object that glinted in the sand before her. She knew it by touch—the amulet of Re that she herself had placed beneath the linen garment this morning when she buried Amenptah.

"Jackals feast upon his flesh this night."

"His *ká* will know him not," Arameya murmured to herself, her thumb tracing the raised pattern on the amulet. "He will wander forever."

"His *ká* I have already devoured," the serpent taunted.

Arameya bared her teeth in fury, her mind racing. Clenching her own amulet in her left hand and that of Amenptah in her right, she muttered a hasty prayer-spell.

"Re, banisher of darkness, grant your daughter

strength." She felt the heat of power rippling across her shoulders as the sun-energy flowed from her amulet into the other. When it became too hot to hold, she cast Amenptah's sunburst at the serpent, aiming just below the head.

With a hiss, Apap swayed to the side, but not before a point of the bespelled sunburst sliced beneath its scales. The cut glowed gold, growing in size as the power of Re drained from the amulet into the magical wound, which began to bleed. Hissing, the serpent jerked and twitched in pain, casting its head about until it found what it sought. A lash of the mighty tail crushed the amulet, which had still glowed faintly in the sand. The gold color faded from the cut on the snake's body, and the bleeding stopped.

The serpent turned back to Arameya, glittering eyes locked with hers as it began its undulating dance. With each slap of the great tail against the sand, the winds surrounding Arameya grew fiercer. They stole her breath, pressing against her chest and throat. Even a whispered spell was beyond her, for the gusts hurled sand that stung her nostrils and choked her voice.

She gripped her amulet of Re, drawing the energy out of it just to stay alive. The serpent smiled in triumph.

"Soon I shall feast upon your *ká*," it hissed, "and the jackals shall bare your bones as they have those of all your kind."

Blood ran from Arameya's fingers onto the pendant she clutched in her hand, but she tightened her grasp even more.

The amulet snapped in half in her hand, its power all but spent. Arameya sagged to the ground, shaking. The winds died and the giant serpent leaned over her, fangs glinting in the starlight.

"You shall not have my *ká*," she gasped around her swollen tongue. "I shall continue to fight you, Apap, serpent of darkness, enemy of Re." She pulled the last of the power from the broken amulet, her mind reaching across the plains.

She caught the touch of a living mind and threw her *ká* toward it, hoping against hope that the *ká* would take root in this new body and give it a spirit's own eternal life span. The empty husk that had been Arameya, last of the Sun Healers of Bast, crumpled to the earth.

The serpent hissed in frustration, unable to follow the flight of her *ká*, and turned to slither across the sands for easier prey. Before it left, it lashed its tail in contempt, casting sand into the spiritless corpse's face. Jackals barked in the near distance.

Across the plains, one of the temple's sacred cats turned and trotted back to the red granite temple, returning to her place in the Chambers of Healing.

Author's Note: I have departed from what we know of daily life in ancient Egypt at two major points in this story. One is in the exact role of Arameya: women were not priests, and medicine was primarily the domain of the priesthood. Women did, however, serve as assistants in a number of temple rituals, so it is not impossible to believe that a woman, especially one with a near-magical gift for healing, would carve a niche for herself within the temple. The second is in my version of the god Apap, which is an amalgam of two myths. Apap was the serpent of darkness who fought with Re each night, trying to prevent the sun from rising in the morning. I have combined him with another creature, the Devourer, to whom were thrown the souls of the dead that were found wanting when balanced in the scales of truth. Any other liberties and errors are entirely my own.

CONSCRIPT
by Jody Lynn Nye

Jody Lynn Nye lists her main career activity as "spoiling cats." She lives northwest of Chicago with two of the above and her husband, author and packager Bill Fawcett. She has written twenty-two books, including four contemporary fantasies (the *Mythology 101* series), three SF novels, four novels in collaboration with Anne McCaffrey, including *The Ship Who Won*, a humorous anthology about mothers, *Don't Forget Your Spacesuit, Dear!*, and over fifty short stories. Her latest book is *The Grand Tour*, third in her new fantasy epic series, *The Dreamland*.

"FIRST-TIMERS!" barked the officer, when the marching troops had paused for a midday meal. Timmen Carver and his sister Anjeli Weaver reported, stepping into the line alongside the other new recruits. They were among ten who had been scooped up as the army passed through their small forest village of Riverstone, now half a day's marching behind them to the west.

"The heralds will have told you why we are gathering forces. Treigol is on the move again. Their current line of march shows them to be a threat to the border town of

Beacon. The wizards of the Circle of Power of Crigol have called you, as is their right as your liege lords, to aid them in preventing an invasion of our eastern border. They have provided appropriate gear for each of you."

Timmen, a strongly built man of average height with bright blue eyes and hair the color of faded ink, listened with dismay. He knew all about the history of the Sundered Lands, thanks to wandering peddlers who brought news of the world into the small village along with their wares. Five hundred and three years had passed since the One Kingdom had been split into five smaller and two larger realms, Crigol and Treigol. Each of the fragmented states was always trying to increase its domain, through negotiation, trick or, he sighed heavily, conquest.

Privately he didn't want to go to war. He would far rather have stayed home. This kind of thing, wars between wizards, was none of his business. Timmen was content with a simple life. He had recently married the beautiful Chara, daughter of the village priest. He ran a successful trade in carpentry and wood-carving, which he loved. It was a growth industry, his old dad had said, laughing a bit in the creaky way he had. Timmen wanted to come home safely from war so he could finish the rood panels for Riverstone's tiny Church of the All-Mother and the All-Father. He was only twenty. Surely a little more time might have passed before he must risk death far away from those he loved. Anjeli, a slim girl of eighteen who looked just like him except for the differences in gender, was excited over the prospects of travel and battle. When the quartermaster distributed sacks of armor and weapons to them, she whistled at the contents in admiration.

"Don't do that," he said, glancing around in alarm. "It's ill-omened to whistle."

"You'll have to become used to magic," she said flippantly. "We're going to battle wizards, after all. Look at all this! It's beautiful!" She turned over the round-crowned helmet, the gauntlets and boots, the heap of slack body mail, all plated with bright silver to repel enchantment. In spite of himself, he admired the workmanship. Each link was sealed shut, and the weave was as tight as linen. Timmen picked up his mail shirt and held it against himself. It would fit. For a moment he wondered how they had known his size, then scoffed at himself. They were wizards, weren't they? They knew everything about him. How old he was, how tall . . . he wondered if they knew what he was thinking, too. He'd better school his mind, then. Just in case they did, he thought hard how grateful he was to have such fine arms to carry into the field in their service.

He admitted that the wizards of the Circle of Power were preparing their troops well. Metal weapons were the only kind that could defeat the mystical forces of the enemy, and only metal armor could withstand their spells.

"Never use a wooden weapon or anything made of a material that once lived, like horn or leather," the old ones of Riverstone had warned him, when he was preparing to go. "Else the killed wizards would rise up after you smote them, and take your spirit."

Here were the right kind of weapons: a sword so shiny it hurt to look at it, a belt dagger and a spear, all metal, though the handles were wrapped with leather so they wouldn't slip out of his fist. He held the sword in one hand and swung it back and forth with ease. Like the mail

shirt, it looked to have been made for him. A talented
archer, Anjeli had a bow made of horn and wood and a
quiver of metal arrows. She crowed over her new pos-
sessions.

"Aren't you excited?" she asked, strapping on the quiver
and holding up the bow to sight along its length. "You
may get to see a battle of wizards!"

"I don't see why it should make any difference to me,"
Timmen said flatly, wishing she'd stop talking about it.

"I wish we could do magic ourselves," Anjeli said, and
her eyes opened wide on a fancy in her own head. "I'd
like to have a loom that ran by itself. Wouldn't you like
a canny knife that could carve scrolls and leaves while
you slept?"

"No!"

Timmen feared magic. He'd never had experience with
anything more mystic than wart-charming. Magic was dangerous. Only wizards were allowed to use it, after many
years of esoteric training. In order to preserve the balance
of nature they came after anyone suspected of practicing.
The hedge witches in the forest around the small village
lived in fear of their lives. It was the same all over the
country. Anyone found to be dabbling in the Unseen was
swept up by the Watch Riders and never seen again.

The officer swore them to the service of the magelords
of Crigol, and in return promised them fealty and aid on
behalf of the Circle of Power. When they had finished
pledging their loyalty, the sword somehow seemed more
familiar and the formerly confusing orders of the officers
easily understood. "We'll go easy on you the first day or
two, to help you get into the rhythm of marching, but after
that you'll have to keep up. Weapons practice daily when

we make camp for the night. Looting is forbidden by penalty of death. You never take a crumb or a copper from anywhere we pass without permission. Pay attention to the rules, and you'll be all right. Now, assignments . . ."

The group was divided into companies. All the foot soldiers from Riverstone were to remain together, as were its archers. Anjeli went off arm in arm with Covana, her dearest friend, and another keen-eyed bowwoman who could shoot the cork off a bottle.

Timmen and his fellows were put under the command of Niall Gander, a second-timer sergeant, a burly, fatherly man with a scarred face and greasy, gray-brown hair. As they marched, Niall let them talk and get to know one another.

"You're putting your life into the hands of the soldiers around you," he said. "This chitchattiness won't be allowed in battle, but I'm easygoing on the road. Stories and songs will help to pass the miles."

As they marched along the well-tramped road through the thick woods, the veterans told the young ones about old campaigns against Treigol, of heroics and magic. Timmen and the others listened raptly.

". . . By the time it was all over," said Stefan Miller, a man whose hair and brows were as white as the flour he ground, "we were the last standing in a field of a thousand dead. The wizards had all fled away."

"A fine tale," Timmen said, shaking his head to bring himself back to the present. "I was there with you, truly."

"So, Timmen Carver, what's it like living in the utter center of nowhere?" Stefan asked.

"Riverstone's the finest place in the world," Timmen said stoutly.

"It's so small I wasn't sure we were stopping," teased Rowni Swynton, an older woman. "Ten houses, maybe?"

"Forty!" Timmen said, leaping to his home's defense.

"Ah, *forty*. You've never hankered for the sights of the big towns, then?"

"Never. I've got all a man needs."

"Ah," Niall said. "So you've a wife and children."

"A wife," Timmen said, with a grin, "but no children yet. We've been trying, though."

His new fellows gave a hearty bark of laughter.

"Trying's the best part of having children," Niall said.

"Are you fighting all the time in a war?" asked a skinny, black-haired boy from the western mill towns.

"There's a lot of time for nothing to do," Rowni said. She had a white streak in her thick red hair from a scalp wound. "That's where the nervous ones lose their way. When you start imagining what is about to happen to you, what the enemy looks like, and whether their lords are as powerful as you fear." She gazed at them from keen hazel eyes under wrinkle-puckered lids.

"The enemy's only human, man and woman, no matter what fancy dress they put on. I've seen wizards die. They've got the power, but they fall and die like the rest of us. You can't put monsters' faces on them. It'll only eat you alive. But after that things happen fast. You don't have time to think."

Not until they'd stopped for the night did Timmen notice the sedan chair slung between two horses at the rear of the gathering force. They'd had one of the feared wizards right behind them all along.

As Timmen and the others watched in awe, the curtains of the box opened. A shadowy figure dressed in a dark blue silk hooded cloak alighted. The figure seemed to have no face, no feet, gliding among the men and turning its empty hood here and there.

"Druimalin, the lord of the western forests," Niall told him in an undertone. "He goes to join his brother and sister wizards at the front. We will be his protection from now until he withdraws. Every one of us must put our lives between his and death."

Timmen was prepared to resent the notion. But loyalty to Druimalin evoked a responsibility to them, too: a duty of care. The wood-carver watched as the silk cloak floated from group to group, dipping its hood a little as it appeared to listen to the sergeants. In the glimmer of their campfire, Timmen spotted a pair of pale hands dart out of the wide sleeves to close briefly over a man's infected foot. Timmen watched the injured man's face unfold like a flower bud from twisted grimace to relief to amazed gratitude. Maybe these wizards were worth protecting after all.

"He'll do," growled a deep voice from deep inside the cloak. To Timmen's astonishment, the hood lifted, and a pair of golden eyes caught the firelight as they bored deep into his. Druimalin was a wizard who spoke to the stars, but he was also a man, who understood pain, and liege-dom.

I could serve you, Timmen thought.

The eyes crinkled slightly at the corners, as if the wizard smiled. Timmen blanched and dropped his gaze to the boots he was cleaning. All-Mother! The man *could* read his thoughts.

*   *   *

Just before sunset six days later they had crossed the river and arrived at the encampment to the southeast of Beacon. Timmen heard it before he saw it, and smelled it long before he arrived. He had never been among more people in his life. He stood for a moment as they crested the last ridge and looked out over the plain. Campfires seemed to be as plentiful as stars in the sky. The buzz of voices was louder than a hive full of bees. The very stink of humanity overwhelmed his senses.

"How many are here?" he asked Niall.

"Nigh on ten thousand. Druimalin's officers say there's more on the other side, bigger and stronger than us. Beacon must not fall," he said. "If Treigol takes the city, it will leave hundreds of miles of countryside vulnerable to raids. But we still hold the bridge. So long as that and the tower stand, the city is still ours."

Timmen followed his pointing finger, and found himself looking at a large round blue dot that looked straight at him like an eye. The light seemed to speak to him.

"Welcome, if you're a friend. Death to intruders." The witchlight's unblinking regard made Timmen quake with fear. Can it tell I am a friend? A lump of ice curdled in his belly. Riverstone felt very far away.

The nightly break for sword practice took on a more urgent tenor. Timmen and his new fellows fought harder, with a gritted-tooth expression showing they were thinking of home and family, just like he was. By morning's first light they would be at war. Timmen took his stance against his sparring partners, but he made the same stupid mistakes over and over again. Niall shouted in his ear while he circled, but the wood-carver couldn't absorb the instructions. They seemed to skid off his brain. Six days

wasn't enough time to make him into a swordsman. He
was astonished to find that he could make all the intricate
attack and defense moves, but never seemed to at the right
time. The drill master made it clear that all he could do
was delay how long it took him to fall. He wasn't alone.
That night every first-timer with him wore a haunted look.

The next morning, in the gray light before dawn, the
forces of Crigol awaited the Treigol army. A third of the
Crigol contingent and five wizards remained behind to defend the bridge that Timmen and the others had just
marched over in the darkness. Another third and five more
magelords were deployed ready upon the battlefield, a
broad valley to the east of the city. Druimalin and eight
other wizards waited on the headlands above the battlefield with the river at their backs, fresh for the second as-
sault. Timmen and the soldiers of Riverstone stood amidst
the honor guard surrounding Druimalin's litter.

"Asked for you particularly," Niall told him, with a glint
in his eyes.

Timmen fidgeted, toying with the hilt of his sword, embarrassed to have drawn the attention of a wizard. He
glanced at the litter. The curtains were closed. His master
must be communing with the All-Mother and All-Father.
Where were the soldiers of Treigol?

They came. At the eastern edge of the gray sky, the
smallest possible dot of yellow appeared. It grew into a
line that widened steadily. Tiny flames surged toward them
in a narrow stream. The enemy forces were carrying
torches. Or perhaps they bore flaming swords. Or Niall
had lied to them, and the Treigol forces were fire-headed

demons. His breath puffed tiny clouds of anxious steam into the cold air. In a moment he'd cut and run.

Then Timmen remembered the words of the Sergeant of Archers. The enemy was only human. He fancied he wasn't an imaginative man, but even he wished the dust of the road that heralded the arrival of the foe would settle so he could see for himself.

The officers began to shout orders, their voices crisp in the cold air.

"Now, remember, spears are your first defense!" Niall shouted. He looked like a spear himself, tall and thin and silver in his mail. He held his sword above his head. "Form a protective wall. None is to pass beyond you. If the enemy closes, draw your sword. If he gets close enough to smell his breath, draw your dagger. Don't let flesh and blood touch yours. Don't drop your shield."

A few of the younger ones, mostly girls, giggled. "Silence in the ranks!" the corporals shouted.

Troops of horsemen clashed first. Each steed wore barding of pure silver painted with the devices of the wizard its knight served. Longbow archers behind Timmen's troop launched flights of arrows into the air to arc down onto the Treigol foot soldiers who marched close behind their horsemen. Missiles from the other side rained upon the Crigol infantry as well. The cries of wounded and dying broke the air along with the sounds of ringing metal. Timmen felt pity for the fallen and wished he could go to their aid. The enemy stopped to re-form, and the arrows falling among their ranks slackened as the Treigol archers moved behind the spear carriers. "How did you stand it?" Timmen asked Goffer, one of the third-timer veterans, a burly grizzled farmer. "The waiting. The first time, I mean."

"Me?" Goffer asked, his eyebrows high. "Personally, I pissed meself. But you don't have to do that." Timmen chuckled, the tension broken.

"I won't, then."

"Look there, boy," Goffer said, nudging Timmen in the ribs. The soldiers of Riverstone huddled around to see.

On the hilltop opposite, scattered pools of blue light grew. He counted twenty, no, thirty wizards on the Treigol side. Timmen felt the skin on the back of his neck prickle, and not just with fear. The air around them crackled with magic as the Crigol wizards readied their own defenses. Violet globes surrounded the covered carriages. Then the sun rose beyond the enemy side, breaking through the light clouds on the horizon. The magelight faded under the onslaught of the Lord of the Day.

"Call that an omen," Rowni said, in her strong, ringing voice. "It'll be a fine day!"

For the first time Timmen could see all around him. They were massed beside a good, packed-stone road that led down into the valley and continued behind them over the bridge. Most was grasslands, apart from a few small copses and plenty of scrub. To the south and north, thick woods bounded the field. The place should have been alive with rabbits at this hour. Instead, it was filled with silver men. Silver and red.

A clap of thunder sounded right over their heads. From a clear sky, ice-blue lightning speared down into the midst of the Treigol infantry, and stitched its way again and again across the army, throwing bodies in every direction. The wild screams of men burned alive in their metal casings reached the force on the headlands. Archers wept for pity. Soldiers like Timmen were grim-faced and silent. The magical attacks had begun. The enemy retaliated with red fire that leaped up out of the ground and consumed whole companies.

"Move out! Move out! For Crigol!"

"For Crigol!" Before Timmen had time to think about it, he and the others were running down the hill. He found himself filled with an unfamiliar bloodlust that seemed to come from nowhere, but there was no time to wonder about it. Niall screamed orders at them to stay in formation around the blue-draped litter. Across the hillside, other wizards and their escorts were descending onto the field of battle. The sounds of metal on metal, thunder of hooves and feet, shouting and screaming deafened them all. In the eighth row Timmen could see only the silver backs of his fellows until, suddenly, a soldier in gleaming armor broke through directly in front of him. The only thing that told him apart from the Crigolian soldiers was that the top of his helmet was shaped into a cone. A Treigolian!

Timmen was too surprised to do anything for a moment. So was the other man. His pause gave Timmen time to gather his thoughts and clap his helm's visor down.

"Crigol!" he shouted. He lowered his spear and charged at the Treigolian. His voice sounded hoarse in his own ears. He realized he must have been screaming war cries with the others all the way down the hill. The other man recovered his wits and drew his sword. With the spear Timmen had the advantage of reach, and knocked the man sideways. The other staggered, then plunged forward, blade outstretched. Alarmed, Timmen dropped his spear and yanked his own sword out of the scabbard hanging on his back. He caught the other's blow on the edge of his blade and flung it away, then jumped forward to chop. For an

eternity, there was no sound but his own breath in his ears.
All his reality was in his arms and his eyes. His shield
seemed to be wizard-led, thrusting forward to turn away
strikes that would have hacked off Timmen's arm or
gouged his side. His sword danced nimbly, cutting in here,
slashing there. Gone was the awkwardness that had plagued
him during weapons practice. It was surprising how light
he felt. The armor, burden of his existence for seven days
and nights, seemed to weigh nothing at all. It was . . .
magic.

In a moment, the blows ceased. Timmen paused for a
moment to gauge his enemy's stance, and realized with a
shock that the man had sunk to his knees. While he watched
in horror, the silver figure sagged sideways to the ground
and lay still like a broken toy, leaking red blood—human
blood—from a dozen wounds. He'd made his first kill.
Timmen felt his gorge rise. He'd taken the life of another
man.

The sounds of battle came surging back. The clanging
and shouting erupted very close to him. Timmen started,
spinning around with sword in hand.

"To Druimalin!" Niall's voice rose beyond a mass of
gleaming bodies struggling together. The litter, suspended
between its two horses, was raised several feet above them.
It swayed alarmingly from side to side as its well-trained
horses danced nervously, but neither screamed nor tried to
flee. Another litter, hung with green, hovered close by.
While Timmen had been killing his man, a Treigolian wizard had gotten within their guard. Druimalin was besieged.

Timmen ran to join Niall and the others. Someone
leaped up as he passed and grabbed him around the neck
from behind. Timmen leaned back, trying to get his right

hand freed so he could reach his dagger. He felt his helmet and gorget slip upward. Cold air rushed over his neck. The touch of skin might follow. Timmen panicked. The enemy must not steal his soul! He twisted away and began to stab furiously, desperately, at the soldier behind him. That soldier fell. More surged in. Timmen found himself with his back against a horse's side. The heavy heave of its belly even under the metal barding felt comforting in the chaos.

The horses began to run. Timmen strode then broke into a trot to keep up with them, blocking blows aimed at the covered sedan chair with arm and shield. Power hot as a bonfire radiated out of the silk tent. Lightnings blasted point-helmeted men apart, leaving the survivors squelching across their bodies in the melee.

When his arm was free, Timmen sheathed his dagger and reached up over his back for his sword. Something caught his arm. He glanced up as he jerked it free. Without Timmen realizing it, the fighters had shifted until they were among branches and scrub at the edge of the southern forest. Ahead, the two litters had pushed into a small glen surrounded by ancient beech trees. Timmen saw Niall battling four point-helmed fighters beside Druimalin's shelter. Timmen rushed to his aid. The pair of them killed or wounded the four, and saw off another three Treigolians. Good thing as they were all of the bodyguard left in sight. Timmen hoped that some of the others had survived and felt a pang of worry for his sister. Then men rushed toward them, drawn to the litters and the prizes they bore.

"No time to congratulate ourselves," Niall said, storming toward a cluster of round-helmed soldiers who were about to be surprised by Treigolians rounding a spinney.

"You lot! Right flank! Right flank, damn you! Keep your eyes open!"

With a deafening rumble the earth opened up in a jagged crack between them. Timmen threw himself toward the nearest bush. His mailed hands scrabbled for a hold on the branches. His legs hung into the chasm. Timmen kicked, trying to find a solid foothold. He didn't see whether Niall had escaped. A silver-booted foot kicked him in the kidneys, trying to knock him off. Groaning in pain, Timmen clung to his lifeline while other Crigolian fighters came to his rescue. As soon as he could, he crawled away from the ravine's edge and hauled himself to his feet.

Their part of the battle had reached a turning point. His side, the round-caps, had succeeded in surrounding the green-sided litter. Men fought standing on the bodies of their fellows, slipped on blood, mud, and fallen weapons while arrows and spells rained down upon them. Timmen heard a crackling sound and dove for cover just in time to avoid a ball of fire that descended from the heavens right onto the spot where he'd been.

When he stood up, the green sedan chair was on its side, crushed. The horses, miraculously unhurt, were kicking to try and right themselves. Most of the litter's defenders and attackers were dead, too, killed by the magical flame. The smell of burned flesh and singed cloth stung his eyes. His left leg pained him. When he looked down, he was horrified to see blood running down from his knee joint.

Just when Timmen rejoiced that the enemy wizard had fallen, a gray-clad figure rose up like a pillar of smoke from the silk-draped compartment. At the end of its right sleeve, it bore a long cane upright, topped by a glowing red jewel. The deep-hooded figure cast about this way and that, not seeming to see Timmen. It halted, sensing what it wanted, and began to pick its way through the carnage toward the sound of screaming horses and thrashing bodies.

Druimalin's litter had fallen, too! The wizard might be dead. Timmen limped and scrambled after the enemy wizard. He must not let Druimalin be killed!

"To me, soldiers of Crigol!" he called hoarsely "Help! Where has everyone gone?" Most were dead. Niall lay dead, too, his uncovered face staring at the sky with an expression of astonishment. The others must have run off in pursuit of the remaining enemy soldiers.

The ghostly figure ahead of him had reached the blue tent-chair. It cast aside the hangings and stood back, apparently pleased by what it beheld. It raised the red-tipped staff high, poised to stab downward. The foot of it was pointed.

"Leave him alone!" Timmen cried. He clapped his hand to his back. His sword was gone! It must have fallen into the chasm. His dagger had been lost, too, and the spear dropped during the first melee. He had his shield, though. "Leave him be!"

He grasped the edge of the shield and cast it clumsily at the enemy wizard. It fell far short of its mark, but the clatter distracted the figure's attention. It turned slowly. Inside the hood, Timmen saw his own face reflected. He gasped with horror.

The enemy wizard cast off its robes, revealing itself to be a giantess, dressed from head to toe in gleaming steel

that was jointed all over like the body of an insect. The
shining faceplate was featureless.

The armor wasn't perfectly intact, though. It must have
been damaged when her litter went down. Her helm was
badly dented on the left side. Timmen also noticed a gap
between the shoulder and breastplates, and another near
the hip. Those openings might not be useful for killing
thrusts, but he could try to keep the wizard at bay until
someone came to his aid. But first he must have a weapon.

Never taking his eyes off the mirror-shiny helm, Timmen tugged first one sword then another from the grips
of dead compatriots. Curses be upon the Cabal for matching weapons magically to each soldier! The first he picked
up was a foot too long and as heavy as an anvil. The next
could have been used for picking his teeth. Even Niall's
sword was wrongly balanced for Timmen. He thought he
heard the wizard chuckle, there was no humor in the sound.
Only one possibility remained. A few yards from the very
feet of his foe was a section of the pole used to support
his leige's sedan chair. It had been snapped off, leaving a
sharp point at either end. He had a feel for wood. He knew
this piece was as strong as his lost spear. If he could get
at it, he could kill with it.

"Now, you move away from him," Timmen ordered the
Treigolian wizard, hoping his voice wasn't trembling. To
appear strong he tried to walk without limping. "Go back,
do you hear! Crigol is not for you!" The magelady held
still and watched him. Perhaps she had been stunned in
the fall. Perhaps he had been. He was taken aback by his
own boldness.

Just before he reached her, she seemed to recover her
own wits. As he dove for the broken piece of wood, she

struck out at him with the sharp point of her staff. Timmen kept rolling, clanking like a bucket falling downhill. He wasn't dodging just physical blows. The wizard had called in the lightning. Small bolts peppered the ground, starting small fires in the grass.

Hold on, Timmen thought. This wasn't fair. Ouch! A filament of blue-white fire touched his left gauntlet. Smoke came out of the wrist end. Timmen beat his hand on the ground, trying to deaden the pain.

It doesn't hurt, he told himself, grabbing for the pole. It doesn't hurt. It doesn't hurt . . . But, oh, it did! He came up on his knees, hand throbbing, but he was clutching the broken piece of wood.

The magelady made to strike him with her glowing staff. The point was sharp enough to stab right through his mail. If it did, the Treigolian wizard could steal his soul. Timmen threw the broken stick up over his head, clumsily warding off her blows. She was educated in the arts of war, but nowhere near as strong as Timmen, who manhandled lintels and panels for a living. He succeeded in knocking the pointed staff away.

Fire-edged demons crawled out of the ground and menaced him with their sharp little teeth, though they couldn't bite through his magic-resistant armor. He kicked them away, but they climbed on him, clinging to his arms, weighing him down, shrieking in tinny voices that stunned his ears. Still on his knees, he struck up at the wizard with the piece of wood. He was risking his soul to use a natural material, but his artist's eye told him the point of the broken stick would just fit into the gap at her shoulder. Even if it didn't kill her, it might slow her down long enough for him to get a metal weapon to finish her off.

The magelady swung her staff in a wide arc up from her feet, and Timmen's helm went flying. While he gaped at her, she brought the stick down on his head. He'd taken a rap on the skull before, but this hurt in a completely different way. Something was being sucked out of him. She was drinking his soul! The demons climbed up and began to claw at his bared neck and face. Strength lent him by fear, Timmen rolled away, and struck out with the broken pole.

Luck, fate or the gods on his side, it pierced through the hole in the magelady's silver armor near her hip. She screamed, the first noise she'd ever made. Timmen wrapped both arms around the stick and drove it deeper with the full weight of his body as she struggled to free herself. Blood spurted, splashing him in the face. He must have pierced the great vessel that ran up through the middle of the body. She dropped to her knees, and brought the red jewel to touch the wound. The red fire flared up.

Timmen's body shook as if he'd been struck by lightning again. He closed his eyes, gritted his teeth and clutched his makeshift spear.

When the jolting ceased, he opened his eyes. All the demons had vanished. The silver insect-body of the Treigolian lay still. The magelady's staff had rolled out of her hand. The jewel had lost its fire. He'd killed her. He'd killed a wizard.

The world had gone quiet all of a sudden. The battle had moved away toward the north. The noises were too far away to penetrate the haze that suddenly enveloped him. His legs trembled.

Timmen sank to hands and knees and crawled to the litter to see if Druimalin lived. Under the sumptuous silk hangings a body in armor lay curled up like a babe in the womb. He pushed aside the enveloping cloak and shoved his hand inside the gorget. A pulse beat in the neck. Timmen thanked the All-Mother and the All-Father, and staggered back toward the camp to get help.

The doctors and field aides came out to meet him when he was still a long way out. They helped him over to a blazing fire. Some took away his armor; others dressed his wounds. The skin of his hand was burned black, and he had dozens of little bite marks on his neck and cheeks.

"The battle went well," the doctor said chattily, winding gauze around the lint pad and poultice he had put on Timmen's leg. "Twelve wizards killed on the two sides, and five thousand men. Druimalin still lives, thanks to you. You're a hero."

Timmen couldn't speak, not even to offer thanks. The aides wrapped him in blankets, talked to him, gave him a cup of soup, and sat with him while he drank it.

In the trees, a bird burst into song. Timmen jumped, dropping the cup. The music was so loud that it pierced to the heart of his being. He'd never heard a sound like that in his life. The aides murmured to one another, seeking to calm him down. Timmen's hands shook as he batted at the others. Everything was too loud, too real. He wanted them all to go away. He bowed over his clenched fists, trying to pull himself together. The next thing he knew, the doctor was standing over him.

"You're in shock," he told Timmen kindly. "You'll be better soon. Your part in the battle is done, young man. It's all over for you."

"Is it?" Timmen asked blankly.

Shortly before sunset they succeeded in driving the depleted invasion force over the eastern hills. Leaving watchers and scouts behind, the rest of the army returned for an evening meal and rest. Word had already spread about Timmen's feat. The others kept asking him for details of how he had defeated a wizard. Timmen put off the questioners. He didn't want to admit he had used a piece of wood. The body was gone, removed by its own people, but someone had brought him the jeweled staff.

"This is yours by right," Louia Blacksmith said proudly, handing it to him. "A tribute to our village."

Timmen was nervous about touching it. But the others expected him to, so he accepted it. His hands stroked the smooth wood. It'd have been a joy to carve, with its fine grain. It had the virtue of sound timber, but he sensed something more than that—a questing. Could it be trying to finish the job begun by its late mistress? Hastily, he wrapped the shaft around with a fold of the blanket, so he wasn't touching it directly. The others looked concerned and puzzled. He could almost hear their unspoken questions. He didn't know what to say to them.

Timmen felt as though the world was suddenly hemming him in. He went off to sit by himself.

There was a service for the dead that evening. They built a pyre for Niall and the other fallen, to free the souls to return to the All-Father. The priest read prayers. The officers came forward to praise those who had fought so well.

"Victory will surely be ours because so many brave hearts beat for Crigol."

Everyone left from Niall's troop looked at Timmen. Timmen stared at the fire and wept like a baby. He knew

Niall and the others weren't in those broken bodies any longer, thank the All-Mother. They'd fought well, and now they were at peace with the High Ones. He couldn't have said why or how he knew, but he did. Timmen went to sleep dreaming of lightning.

He woke long before dawn the next day. His surviving friends from Riverstone were tucked up in bedrolls on the ground around him, dreaming peacefully. He grieved for the two who had died, but at least his sister had been safe on her high ground with the other archers.

Timmen was too restless to go back to sleep. The sensations kept crowding in on him. He'd listened to the others who had been wounded, and knew that what had happened to him was not the same as what had happened to them. He longed for something as easily explained as a shattered leg or a severed hand. He looked up at the sky. The stars were a hundred new colors, and each bursting to tell him about itself. Suddenly, he cast his eyes down in shock. The likes of him should not be hearing the sacred music of the Universe. But he did. He lifted his gaze up again. The constellations seemed to come to life. They were dancing—for him!

It had all happened in that moment, while the wizard died. The magic had sprung out of her and flowed into him. Now it was showing him things, telling him things, like a second voice in his head that he couldn't still.

How horrible to know he wasn't normal anymore. He would go back to Riverstone, to Chara, his father, and his shop, but it would never be like home again. He'd broken the rules, and now he'd no choice but to accept the consequences.

He left the sleeping area and wandered down the hill

onto the moonlit battlefield. The sentries stopped him, recognized him as a hero of the day, and let him pass. Timmen walked, feeling as though he was dreaming. His perspective had changed. Nature was talking to him. He understood the nightbirds' calls. The earth cried out where it was torn up by the hooves of horses. Blood rumbled where it had spilled on the ground, speaking of vengeance, fear, death, and regret. Unsettled spirits flitted.

Timmen felt drawn to the forest's edge, where the wizard had died. No, perhaps it was the trees that called him. He'd always had an affinity for trees. He had a sense of their strength. He'd always seen pictures in wood, could envision how well an image would carve just by looking at the grain. Now he passed among the shadow-dappled boles with new awareness. He could tell which ones were rotten or sound without touching them. They had life of their own. It was fascinating and wonderful to know them as only the Makers knew them.

Timmen was overwhelmed by shame. How had he taken an ax to these magnificent creatures? How dare he take a life at all? From now on he would carve only dead wood.

The fear that had been rising in him for hours burst out among the peaceful wood. Someone was bound to find out what he had done. He would have to defend his action. But was the magic worth fighting for? Oh, indeed it was, but so was his peace of mind. This magic was hungry. It sought war. It wanted him to do battle again the next day, and the day after that. The talent wasn't content to lie still within him, either. It wanted to do things. Of its own volition, his hand pointed down at a clump of dried grass, and the grass burst into flame. Hastily Timmen leaped on it and stamped the fire out, terrified the sentries had seen. He'd have to control himself better.

He knew now that what they'd told him about wizards was a lie. Metal weapons would wound them, but not kill them. Oh, they'd kill the fighters that protected them. Those were ordinary men and women. Wooden weapons would do for the ordinary human, too, but they would also kill the wizards themselves. Natural material acted like . . . like a straw, allowing one combatant to drink the other's life. Which way the drain went depended upon who won. If you lost, your soul was theirs. If you defeated one of them, well, their magic belonged to you.

The mighty ones must have made a pact between them never to allow the use of living material by their soldiers because it could conceivably permit power to go from one of them to a lowly individual, a peasant from a green-field village. Like him. He could probably do great enchantments, a prospect that nearly made him wet himself in fear. How his sister would laugh. He hadn't wanted to go to war among wizards in the first place. He didn't care about magic. And now he was the guardian of what felt like a full barrel of the stuff. What a laugh.

Practicing magic was illegal. If he were caught, he'd never be able to go home. All he held precious was there. Perhaps he should flee now, just keep walking away from the camp forever. Yet the talent refused to listen. It promised him treasure, the stars, a realm as big as all of creation. Timmen sat down on a rock in the moonlit glade, his head in his hands. He'd never completely be at peace again. He'd be fighting new battles forever, but mostly with himself. Anyone who'd tasted wizard's fire was one of them. Now he knew why they were constantly fighting for greater domains. They were driven to it.

To want so much more than you rightfully deserved was wrong. He'd had that hammered into him from a boy. He was a simple man, he told himself. A common man, like all the rest.

That was a lie, too. He wasn't ordinary any longer. He could never go home to Riverstone. He couldn't bring this curse with him. He mustn't sire children, either, lest they betray themselves by a natural act of magic. Poor Chara. Poor him.

He was aware of the approach before the grass behind him rustled.

"Anjeli, you should be asleep."

"I didn't think you could see me yet," she complained. She circled around him and sat down on a rock beside him. Moonlight lit her hair and her cheekbones and nose, but his new power let him see the glowing soul within her. It was pure and strong. "Are you all right?"

"Not really," he said. "I . . . I'm tired."

"Was it exciting watching the battle of wizards fighting up close?" she asked. "We could see the lightning from the hilltop, but there were so many little things going on too far away to see. Bright colors! Shaped fire! Tell me what it was like!"

"I don't want to think about it just now."

She wrapped her arms around her knees and leaned back to stare at the moon. "You'll have to tell your adventures when we get home. You'll be famous. The man who brought down a wizard all by himself!"

"No!" Timmen sprang to his feet. "No. Anjeli, I can't go home."

"Why not?" she asked. "What happened to you? Did she show you a war spell? All-Mother! We'll have magic in our own village! Think of that! Maybe you can teach me what you learned."

"No!" Timmen shouted, throwing his hands out. "I wasn't born a warrior or a wizard. I want nothing to do with either!"

Lightning leaped from his fingertips, plunging across the field and lighting up the night sky. Anjeli's eyes were huge, blue pools of astonishment.

A heartbeat later, the two of them were surrounded by hooded figures staring at Timmen. The Sergeant of Archers appeared and took Anjeli away. Timmen had one last glimpse of her face. Anjeli was weeping. So was he.

Druimalin's golden eyes glinted in the moonlight as he studied Timmen.

"We wondered what became of the wizard's share of the power. My art told me it had not scattered to the winds. Well, well, young man. You're entitled to all she left behind. Naturally you won't have her estates, since they lie deep inside Treigol, though they will belong to you. You will dwell among us. You shall have a castle. Servants."

"I don't want estates!" Timmen said, trying to catch sight of his sister over the cloaked shoulders. "I want to go home." But he knew it was his home no longer.

"Some would call it a reward for bravery," Druimalin said. "But you don't feel so. Why not? You've gained a world for your actions."

I've lost one, he thought, disconsolately. Druimalin's hand fell on his arm, flesh to flesh. No power transferred from him to the senior wizard. It was simply a companionable touch. No, his soul had already been stolen, and all because he didn't listen to those who knew better.

He hoped he'd be able to carve wood where he was going.

FINAL SCORE
by Bradley H. Sinor

Not long ago Brad Sinor ran into someone he hadn't seen for several years. The friend asked if Brad was still writing. Brad's wife, Sue, said, "There's still a pulse. So he's still writing." He has written one novel, *Highlander: The Eye of Dawn*. His short fiction has appeared in the *Merovingen Nights* series, *Time of the Vampires*, *On Crusade: More Tales Of The Knights Templar*, *Lord of the Fantastic*, *Horrors: 365 Scary Stories*, *Merlin*, and *Such a Pretty Face*. This is his third story dealing with Lancelot after the fall of Camelot.

"CAN I get you something, m'lord?"

For a moment Ashe was sitting once again at his favorite table, just to the right of the door at the Bearded Cockerel Tavern. The place was a dump. The thatched roof needed patching, the rafters were cracked and burned, and the ale was heavily watered, but the memory of it was as precious to Ashe as anything. That was a moment he would have given anything to make last.

"M'lord?"

As they all do, the memories faded. Only this time Ashe found himself facing something almost as pleasant; a young woman, dressed in a dark green blouse and brown skirt of a style that would have been at home on any of the tavern wenches at the Bearded Cockerel.

He caught himself about to address her as Cassie, the name of a woman nearly fourteen hundred years dead. But Cassie would never have been wearing a pager on her belt and a button with the inscription **"Goes From Zero to Bitch in 4.5 Seconds."** "I'm sorry. I let my mind wander a bit," he said.

"It's early," she smiled. "So, what can I get for you, m'lord?" The girl was at least not trying to affect a British accent. Most of them came off sounding like something you hear on reruns of *Fawlty Towers*.

She was one of several employees in what had been dubbed The Cross-eyed Tavern, one of over two dozen refreshment tents and booths that were part of the three-day-long Medieval Fair staged by the University of Oklahoma.

In the twenty years since its beginning, the Fair had outgrown its original campus site. Now it was staged at a nearby park, in the shadow of the towering gothic spires of the university's library and Owen Stadium, home of the O.U. Sooners football team.

"I don't feel like coffee this morning, and it seems far too early for anything stronger," said Ashe. "With those restrictions, what would you suggest, m'lady?"

"I take it caffeine is your drug of choice?"

"Exactly."

"Well, then, we do have several very good breakfast teas." She pointed toward a large chalkboard just to the right of the bar.

Ashe scanned the list. Most of them had names like King Charles' Best and Queen Anne's Delight.

"Try the Prince Alfred special. It's really a variation of Earl Gray, heavy with caffeine with a very distinctive blend of cinnamon and some other things. It will definitely wake you up," she said.

"Kind of the Jolt Cola of teas?"

"Exactly!"

Ashe accepted a Styrofoam cup from her. The smell was strong. He had tasted better, much better, but under the circumstances this was far better than he had expected.

The girl watched him for a moment. "Is this your first time?"

"Drinking tea?"

"No, at Med. Fair, silly." She laughed. Ashe smiled at the sound of her laughter. It was a momentary light in the darkness.

"Yes. I've been to some in other places, but that was a long time ago."

"If you want a guide, stop by just after noon. I'll be off work then."

"Who knows, I may be back." said Ashe.

"No maybe about it," smiled the girl.

Ashe sipped his tea as he watched the sea serpent. It wallowed from side to side in an ungainly dance, slowly crisscrossing the small man-made pond. The water was just dirty enough to hide the guide wires that were pulling it, unless someone stood on the stone bridge and watched for more than a few minutes. An odd looking section of rock next to the bridge seemed to be where the motor had been hidden,

It had been the serpent that had brought Ashe to Norman, Oklahoma, and to the Medieval Fair.

He didn't need to pull the much folded sheet of yellow paper out of his wallet. It featured an elaborate pen-and-ink rendering of a sea serpent rearing its head out of the water with the turrets of a castle in the background. Duplicates of it, blown up to poster size, had been spread out all across Norman and surrounding towns announcing the three days of the annual celebration.

He had found the flyer crumpled up in the corner of a room in a certain cheap motel in a Baltimore suburb. But knowing the occupant's obsession, it had been enough.

The serpent, at least, was an attempt at something special. Not a very successful one, especially since the rivets in its metal hide were clearly visible, but an attempt nonetheless. Ashe took another drink. The caffeine left a warm, welcome feeling in his throat.

Below him, half a dozen ducks and a lone goose paddled across the pond, carefully steering clear of the serpent. It would be quite the unexpected surprise if the beast were to accidentally run down one of the birds. Ashe wouldn't have been surprised if that happened.

"You've got to be less cynical, stop expecting the worst, let yourself enjoy life a little bit more. Don't be so afraid to just live."

He could still hear her voice. Hannah Cortez. Half Spanish, half Irish and bloody proud of both sides of her heritage. When he closed his eyes, he could *almost* feel her standing next to him, a gentle touch on his hand, whispered breath along the back of his neck.

"Hannah," he whispered, crushing the Styrofoam cup into pieces, the remaining tepid liquid dripping between his fingers.

Ashe had met her only sixteen months before. It had

been a glorious time, a time when he had been happy. That anyone he loved would die eventually was something he had reluctantly grown used to in the fourteen centuries since he had watched Camelot fall around him. But Hannah had not been taken as a casualty of war or as part of the natural order of things. She had been murdered: cruelly, painfully, slowly.

Now, as he had when he had been a knight of Camelot, when he had been a brother of the Knights Templar and so many other things, it fell to him to find her killer and exact justice.

Ashe let the Styrofoam pieces of his cup fall into the dirt near the bridge.

The Medieval Fair actually covered nearly ten acres. Parking fanned out along the edges of the grounds and then snaked down through the neighborhood, forming an intricate kind of spiderweb along the streets.

The radio had said that there was a better than fifty percent chance of rain, so he had his choice of whole rows in the parking lot. Until the weather cleared, only the hardiest would venture forth. He hoped the man he was looking for would fit that description.

Ashe walked with no destination in mind. The food booths and the artisans' tents had been laid out in no obvious order or logical pattern that he could discern. Right now he just wanted to look and listen and wait.

Later in the morning Ashe stood watching a small man dressed in a vaguely medieval costume made up of the most outlandish combination of colors: purple scarf, orange shirt, a black-feathered cap. The little man was deep in conversation with a fellow wearing what looked like a dark brown tuxedo jacket, jeans, and no shirt.

Ashe smiled. No doubt the two of them thought they were being outlandish, original, standing out from the crowd. He had seen it all before, more times than he could count, and each time watched the would-be rebels blending into an ocean of sameness.

"You are looking far too philosophical for your own good."

Standing almost at Ashe's elbow was the young woman who had waited on him that morning. She was smiling and had exchanged her apron for a beaded vest and matching gypsy-style head scarf.

"Really?" he said.

"Really."

"Well, then, if not philosophical, how should I look?" asked Ashe.

"I'm not sure," she said. "Maybe like you were having fun?"

Ashe chuckled. There was something infectious in the girl's attitude. "Hmm . . . fun? Now what is that?"

"Fun. F . . . U . . . N. Fun. It is definitely something that I think you should have," she said. "And I'm going to make sure you have it. You can't say you weren't warned. I did tell you this morning that I would see you again."

"Well, it seems you were right. If you're that good at predicting things, how are you on the lottery, or maybe the daily double at Fair Meadows Race Track?" he said.

"I might be afraid if I were right and just as afraid if I were wrong," she laughed.

"A wise attitude. One that I think a lot of so-called

seers would have been better off for, had they adopted it," he said.

"You *are* quite the philosopher, m'lord, *quite* the philosopher. I've not heard many of the fellows around here saying things like that. They mainly speak longingly of the glories of war and the prowess they would bring to battle," she said.

Memories of battles without end danced among Ashe's memories: the pain; the stink of blood; the screams of the dying; the utter exhaustion that permeates a soldier, both in the body and soul after a battle.

"The only honor in battle is in having survived. The only glory comes in those tales told by fools and the songs sung by minstrels. A great adventure is what you have when you're telling the tale over a pint and a good meal afterward; when it's happening, you're scared out of your wits and certain that you will die in the next second—if you're thinking at all. Anyone who isn't, is a fool, a fanatic, or a fake," he said.

"You certainly don't sound like the medieval reenactment guys I've been hanging around with," she said.

"Each to their own. It occurs to me, m'lady, that I have not had the honor of knowing your name."

She grinned and curtsied, almost colliding with a boy in a jester's hat. "M'lord, I am Serina de Lyman. I am most pleased to meet you."

Ashe bowed at the waist in the courtly fashion that he had learned in Italy.

"A beautiful name for a beautiful lady. My name is Landon Ashe."

"Actually," she smiled. "It's Serina Smith. I added the last part for the Fair and for medieval reenactment events."

"Nonetheless, it is lovely. So when do you have to be back at work?"

"By pure chance, I'm off for the rest of the afternoon."

"Pure chance, indeed? Since I'm a stranger in town myself, I'm still in need of someone to show me around the fair."

Serina grinned. "I think we can find you a guide."

"That is a most unusual stone in your ring, sir. I don't think I've ever seen one like it before."

Ashe and Serina were standing in front of the large tent of a vendor who dealt in jewelry ranging from lost wax designs to wire wraps to what appeared to be handmade specialty designs. Serina had spotted a small necklace done in a Celtic design around the profile of a bird in flight.

Ashe nodded. The ring was unusual, the stone a piece from the Giant's Dance, and crafted by no less a master than Merlin himself.

"The man who made it was an old friend. He gave it to me for luck."

Ashe couldn't help but smile at that. Over the years he had called Merlin many things; in those first days, when Ashe had been known as Lancelot, that had actually included friend.

"And has it brought you luck, sir?" the jeweler asked.

"I suppose you could say that."

"Well, if you were inclined to part with it, I have an idea it would fetch a pretty penny. The workmanship is so detailed. I'm not sure what kind of stone that is, but it is one that holds the eye."

The thing was, if Ashe did part with it, the effects, especially if he were caught out in the direct sunlight, would be most unpleasant and very painful. He did not like to recall the few times that had happened.

"So, what do you think? Is it me?" Serina held the necklace around her neck. It hung to the edge of her low cut blouse, the silver surface shining against her skin.

"It looks as if he made it with you, and only you, in mind," said Ashe.

"Oh, get off with you now," she laughed.

Serina had turned to the jeweler when Ashe felt someone grabbing his shoulder pulling him sharply around. He found himself facing a man in his early twenties, dressed in a black-and-white musketeer's style costume. The man's buzz cut seemed as out of place as a Grateful Dead T-shirt on a samurai.

"What the hell is going on here?" said the stranger.

"Michael! What do you want now?" yelled Serina. She obviously knew him, and just as obviously did not like him. The young man called Michael ignored her, moving toward Ashe until he was only inches from the other man's face.

"What kind of man are you, trying to put the make on my woman?"

The crowd, sensing a fight about to begin, moved back, clearing a rough circle in front of the booth.

"Michael! I told you last week that we were through. You're only making a fool out of yourself! What does it take to get through that thick skull of yours, a two by four?" Serina said.

"Shut up! I'll deal with you later!"

"If I were you, Michael," Ashe said softly. "*I* would take what the lady says to heart. And I would be wary of how I spoke to her, if *I* were you."

"Are you threatening me? You're not me, and I don't need your advice!" hissed Michael. As he spoke, a dagger dropped out of his sleeve into his hand.

"I'm tired of this macho bull crap!" Serina said. Instead of turning away, she jammed herself between Ashe and Michael.

"Get out of the way, Serina," Michael said. "This is between him and me."

"Wrong answer!" Serina slammed her knee hard into Michael's crotch. His face contorted with the sudden pain, a loud groan rolling out of his mouth. The knife dropped, hitting the side of the counter before it clattered to the ground

He looked at her, pain, surprise, and confusion rolling across his face. He tried to speak, but before he could, Serina punched him hard in the stomach. The impact was enough to send him to his knees. Around them the crowd, who had been yelling encouragement, broke into applause.

"M'lady Serina, it's obvious you don't utter threats," Ashe said. "Remind me never to get you mad at me."

"I don't know why he can't understand that we're through and I never want to see him again," said Serina.

She and Ashe sat on a small boulder near the pond. Around them, the voices that were the Medieval Fair and its participants rose and fell. Serina hadn't spoken for some time, hadn't even looked at Ashe, just watched the ducks and the sea serpent.

It had taken less than half an hour to explain things to the off-duty police officers working security for the Fair. Thanks to more than a dozen witnesses, not to mention

Michael's fairly long police record, Ashe and Serina had been allowed to go with no problem.

"Just because he said he was sorry after I caught him in the sack with two different women at the same time, he thinks I should forgive him."

"Two?"

"Yeah, two," she sighed. "When I walked in on them, the asshole had the gall to suggest that I join them in their little games."

"That just proves what I already knew; Michael is an idiot."

"On that we agree." Serina grabbed Ashe and pulled him tightly to her. Their lips met in a hard passionate kiss, her hands moving up and down his back. Ashe's hands responded, gripping her shoulders tightly.

"My apartment is only a couple of blocks away. Think you can show a girl a good time, mister?"

"I think I can."

"You better."

Ashe gently touched Serina's shoulders. Then he began massaging her shoulders and neck. Serina let out a long sigh as his fingers worked her muscles back and forth.

"You only have about a week to stop that," she murmured.

Ashe smiled and continued to work. Every now and again a sound would give him proof of her approval. Slowly he let his hands begin to work their way from her shoulders, first to her arms, then around her breasts. He cupped one, then the other, moving in slow regular motions. He began to kiss her neck and then moved gently along her shoulder.

"Oh, yes," Serina murmured. She turned, facing him, pushing her breasts hard against his chest.

Ashe felt his fangs sliding into place. He touched them to her wrist, her breasts and then her neck.

"Ah, m'lady," he said softly

As he drank deeply from Serina, Ashe's hands worked swiftly, slipping her blouse off her shoulders, and then her skirt flowed to pool around her ankles. Her own hands had begun to pull Ashe's clothing off of him.

"I want you," she murmured into his ear.

The party, hosted by the local chapter of the medieval reenactment organization that Serina belonged to, was being held in a loft that covered half a city block in downtown Norman.

Serina had outfitted Ashe in a knee-length tunic, soft suede boots, cape, hood, and sword. The style was tenth century Welsh with a dash or two of Scottish.

"You look fantastic. It's like you were born to wear this type of clothing."

"Perhaps I did," he said. "In another lifetime, of course."

"Maybe so, m'lord," she said.

Serina had opted not for her tavern wench outfit but for a more elegant fourteenth century Spanish-style gown in green and black. Ashe had noticed her slipping a few things into her belt bag that he definitely didn't remember from that time period, her pager, a roll of breath mints, and a canister of pepper gas.

As Ashe and Serina made their way along the street, they spotted a man in Roman armor standing in deep conversation with a woman in a Russian-style gown. Nearby a Japanese samurai was puffing on a corncob pipe.

"I think this must be the place," Ashe said to Serina.

"I wonder what could have ever given you that idea. Could it have been those two dressed so strangely?" She gestured at a couple of guys standing in front of a theater marquee across the street; wearing football jerseys and shorts.

"Exactly. They're such an anachronism when compared to normal people like us."

"I'm beginning to wonder about you, m'lord," Serina said, smiling.

"Good," said Ashe.

Serina led them up a long outside stairway. Once inside she was recognized almost at once, even as the door herald announced their arrival. "Lady Serina de Lyman and Lord Landon Ashe."

They were no more than twenty feet beyond the door when someone motioned Serina over. Ashe recognized the woman as the other person he had seen at the tavern tent that morning.

"It's my boss," Serina said. "She's supposed to have the shift schedule for the rest of the Fair."

"Go make nice," Ashe told her. "It always helps to have the boss on your side."

"Okay. This may take a few minutes," she sighed. "Could you possibly get us some wine?"

"No problem."

The walls that had once separated the loft into a variety of rooms had been removed. Screens and curtains had been hung to create smaller areas, but not lose the spacious open feeling. At one end there was organized singing and dancing. In another corner a demonstration of fighting techniques. Any number of groups were just standing and talking about everything from the Fair to current politics to the latest fantasy movie.

That was when he heard *the voice*. He had heard it only once before, on Hannah's answering machine, but it was something he could not forget. Standing a dozen feet from him was the tall, square, blond figure whose face matched the Polaroid photo in Ashe's suitcase, the one he had found in the same house as the medieval fair flyer.

The man was a killer. The FBI and a dozen different local police organizations had files on him, by deed but not by name. Eight murders were attributed to him, with another four suspected, all in and around medieval and Renaissance fairs. Ashe had no doubt that there were FBI agents prowling the Fair. He also had no doubt that they would not discover him in a million years, unless he was presented to them on a silver platter.

"I tell you, m'lords and ladies, we are living in the ass end of history, in the dregs. Society today knows nothing, I say again nothing, of the concept of honor and pride. In older, better times men understood things like that. They were ready to die for honor.

"We saw that today, when one of our own was attacked by a clod who knew nothing of honor, truth, or justice. All this scum wanted was a chance to get into the pants of a woman. Then he did not even have the heart to stand and fight himself, he let a woman do it for him!"

The crowds around the man laughed. Ashe had seen these people before, with a hundred different faces in a hundred different places. They courted what seemed new and daring; the minute it bored them, they were gone.

"So there you are!" Serina came up behind him, smiling, with two glasses of wine in her hand. "I had the feeling that you would never find the wine. I was wondering where you had run off to. I hoped I wouldn't find you in the arms of some ravishing wench, because I would have had to cut her tits off if I had."

"I would never risk your wrath, m'lady. Besides, why should I settle for second best when I am with the best," he said. "No, I was just listening to this fellow discoursing on what a terrible age we live in."

Serina looked over toward the crowd. The look on her face told Ashe that she knew the man. "I was hoping *he* wouldn't be here tonight. Though I can't honestly say I'm surprised. He blew into town a couple of months ago and has been trying to wrap the entire barony around his little finger. He disgusts me. Michael and he have become best buddies. Sometimes I think that they're attached at the hip, or maybe in some other organ of the body."

"What's his name?"

"Chalker. Ian Chalker. He sometimes uses the medieval name of Rudolph von Tarquin."

"But we're here to have a good time. Come on, there are some people I want to show you off to."

"Your wish is my command."

Ashe waited in the parking lot. He had left Serina talking to several other ladies, which suited him just fine. What he needed to do now, he needed to do without her.

Holding himself in the shadows, he watched as the square-shaped figure of Chalker came closer. The sounds of the party drifted out open windows, voices and music blending together like a steady heartbeat.

Chalker had a half empty bottle of champagne in one hand, his car keys in the other. Ashe waited until the man had stopped in front of a station wagon. He came out of the darkness, grabbing Chalker and slamming him hard against the car.

Keys and champagne bottle crashed to the ground. Then he pulled Chalker around, to face him. Ashe's hand, now holding a dagger, pushed the edge against Chalker's throat.

"Move and you're dead! Speak without my permission and you're dead! At this moment you may thank whatever dark gods watch over you that I'm allowing you to continue to breathe, even for a little while. Do you understand?" Ashe said.

Chalker nodded.

"Now listen and listen well. I know who you are and I know what you've done. Call yourself Ian Chalker, call yourself Groucho Marx or Stephen King. Call yourself any damn thing you want. I don't care! *I know who you really are!*"

"What are you?" whispered Chalker.

Ashe drove his fist hard into Chalker's stomach. "I told you not to speak unless I said. I don't do second chances. You've had your one strike. Next time I will be ripping your lungs out through your ears.

"But I will answer your question. I am fear. I am death. I am everything that you've ever seen when you stared into a woman's face, every bit of pain and terror you've pulled out of all those dead girls over the years. Now, I think it's time you say something in your own defense. If you can even have the gall to try and have one," Ashe said.

"I don't know what you're talking about," Chalker said. "You're insane. If it's money you want, take it. Take the car. My watch is a Rolex. It'll get you at least a grand from a fence. Just take them and be gone."

Ashe shook his head. "I don't want your money. I don't want your watch; it's as phony as you are. I've come for your life. That's all that I want. In case it interests you, I'm the one who you were talking about earlier. I'm the one you said had no honor, no sense of pride. My pride and my blood have led me to you. Your friend Michael got the beating he deserved, from the woman he had mistreated. I'm here to give you something of the same."

"Then you're street scum, nothing but the lowest form of trash. You have no idea of how a true man fights his battles, otherwise you wouldn't have ambushed me from behind," Chalker said.

Ashe laughed as he watched the man swelling up with pride. It was the same bravado he had seen earlier in the middle of the crowd.

"One does what one has to. You don't know who you are bandying words with about honor and heart, punk. I have forgotten more about true warriors and what it means to fight for honor than you have ever known," said Ashe.

"I'm sure that you know all about honor," Chalker retorted.

Ashe could feel his fangs sliding into place. The beast within him was struggling to get out. In his mind's eye he could see himself ripping Chalker's throat to bloody shreds. The image overlaid one of Hannah, as he had found her that night four months ago, carved into bloody pieces, her skin carefully removed and laid neatly on a white bridal bed.

"I'm going to give you more of a chance than you deserve."

With his last word, Ashe vanished. Chalker sagged back against his car, his breath coming in ragged gasps.

Then Ashe was there again, his form coalescing out of mist, standing only a few inches in front of Chalker.

"Owen Stadium in one hour. If you are a man of honor as you claim, a man better than this decadent age we live in, be there, with your sharpest sword. If you are not, I will hunt you down like the dog that you are and not give you the mercy I would a dumb animal."

Then Ashe was gone.

An almost tomblike silence filled Owen Stadium. As Ashe walked along the sidelines, he knew that not a hundred yards away, beyond the southern wall of the stadium, cars were filling up Norman's main drag, the sounds of their engines like a distant buzz of insects. Here there was only silence, and memories.

Football stadiums had always reminded Ashe of the old Roman arenas in Britain and France. The ones close to his family's ancestral holdings had been in ruins, but those near Camelot had been almost intact. The game itself was just another version of cavalry maneuvers; all the players needed were horses and sabers.

He remembered the long debates with Arthur about refurbishing the arenas. Arthur had wanted them left abandoned, remnants of a pagan past, but Ashe, or Lancelot du Lac, as he had been known then, had proclaimed them perfect for cavalry training. In the end, he had won that argument and given Arthur the best mobile infantry of the time.

From a custom-made case in the back of his van he withdrew a broadsword. It had been designed just for him, made of the finest Toledo steel. The blade was razor sharp, the edge honed with infinite patience and practice.

The weapon was hidden by a long overcoat Ashe carried over his arm. The local police would not be happy if, even during Medieval Fair, someone were caught carrying a sword, especially one like this, away from the event site.

Suggesting that they return to Serina's apartment, Ashe had left her there, asleep, with the implanted idea of a night full of passion to come. He spotted Chalker standing to one side of the home team's bench.

Ashe had discarded his medieval clothing, exchanging them for a black T-shirt, jeans, and a biker's leather jacket. Chalker, on the other hand, had gone to the opposite extreme. He now wore a full shirt of chain mail and a tabard emblazoned with a heraldic house badge. A helmet was tucked under one arm, and a fearsome looking sword rested on the ground.

"I wondered if you would show up," said Chalker.

"Really?" Ashe chuckled. "Since I issued the challenge, you doubted I would be here? That's muddy thinking; gets you in trouble every time."

"Honorless scum such as you have been known to lose their nerve."

"Honorless?"

"I should expect someone like you to know little of honor and to disparage an honorable warrior. It is honor that will guide my blade in a fight," Chalker intoned.

"Speaking of fighting," said Ashe. "Did you come here to fight or to stand here chattering like a magpie all night? I noticed at the party that you seemed very adept at the latter."

The fury in Chalker's eyes blazed as he pulled the helmet over his head. Ashe dropped his jacket and unsheathed his sword.

"I suppose you know you won't walk out of here alive. But before we begin, tell me one thing," said Chalker. "I've never laid eyes on you before tonight. So why?"

"Why? Why do I want your life? Because you are a no good murdering piece of offal that persists in trying to act human. I make no claims to being human myself, but you, sir, are scum. Does the name Hannah Cortez mean anything to you?"

Chalker looked puzzled. "No. Should it?"

Ashe shook his head. "Cleveland. Four months ago. She was tall, with long brown hair, emerald eyes, and an enjoyment of life like none I have ever seen. You should remember her. You should remember them all. You killed her, slowly, painfully."

Chalker grinned. He had sensed an advantage and meant to press it. "Oh, yes. Cleveland. Now I seem to recall her. I made her last for four days. Did you realize that she begged me to kill her. But I did it very slowly, very slowly. I made her last and savored each scream.

"You know, it's an art form. I did her a great honor taking her. She was one of the whores, you know. One of the ones that it is my holy charge to rid the world of!"

With that, Chalker pulled his sword up and went for Ashe. Turning to one side Ashe let the other man's blade pass inches away from its target. Chalker whirled and struck again, this time, Ashe deflected the blow by pushing his blade hard forward.

That his opponent had experience with a sword was obvious. He knew how to land a blow and to counter more than a few moves. Ashe let himself wait, attacking a few times, mostly to learn, to see how Chalker would react. Ashe himself had not stood to blood combat with a sword in nearly five years. There had been no call. But old skills, learned first in the practice fields of France, honed as one of Arthur's commanders and then used over the centuries, had not faded.

Sparks flew with each blow, showering each man in an otherworldly light. Ashe had begun to carefully drive Chalker back when the last thing in the world he expected happened.

Someone fired a shot.

The bullet came from behind Ashe, echoing like a back-firing truck among the empty seats of the stadium. Ashe swung wide and away from Chalker, turning as he moved back toward the stands. The gunman was making no attempt to hide himself.

Standing just behind the metal railing at the fifty-yard line was the same figure he had seen that afternoon, dressed in a black-and-white musketeer's outfit. Michael, Serina's ex-boyfriend, his hands wrapped around the butt of a very large gun.

The second shot struck the turf not a foot from where Ashe stood.

"Looks like if I don't get you," laughed Chalker, "he will."

"Some man of honor you turned out to be, having your lackey ambush me!" said Ashe.

"One does what one can," said Chalker.

"I told you to stay away from her. Serina is mine. She will never belong to anyone else," Michael shouted. "I told you! I saw the two of you together, there in her bed rutting like animals! I warned you! Now you're going to pay."

Michael drew the gun up, assuming a firing stance, but before he could fire, he suddenly lurched forward, crashing into the railing, the gun flying from his hand to crash onto the fifty-yard line below him.

Standing behind him was Serina, a long wooden pole in her hand.

"I told you I'm not your girlfriend any more!" Michael managed to stay on his feet, turning toward Serina. She produced a can of pepper gas and sprayed him directly in the eyes, sending him screaming to the ground.

Ashe turned just as Chalker charged him. He managed to bring his sword up at the last moment, blocking the edge of the other man's blade as it sliced hard toward Ashe.

"You have no chance against me," Chalker's muffled voice said. "My skill has been honed for lifetimes, generations beyond anything that you can do."

"Indeed?" Ashe said.

Chalker struck at him three times in succession, slicing into the leather that wrapped around Ashe's arm.

"Indeed. My soul is an old one. Once I wore the name of Galahad of Camelot! I learned from the masters: Gawain, Arthur, and even Lancelot himself!"

Ashe laughed. The very thought that this "man" could be carrying the soul of Galahad was a repugnant one. He struck hard against Chalker, his sword cutting into the chain mail the man wore.

"You are not Galahad. If your soul were his, he would have killed himself before allowing you to do the things that you have done. I knew Galahad. Galahad was a friend of mine. You're no Galahad!"

"What would you know? You're nothing but street scum, not even fit to clean the stables of Camelot."

"I? I am Lancelot!" With those words Ashe drove his sword down hard, pushing aside the other man's blade, his weapon cutting deep into chain mail and then the flesh of Chalker's stomach. His foe stood there, staring, uncomprehending. Ashe pulled his blade clear and then drove it through Chalker's neck. The bone and flesh clung together for only a moment, then separated. The head lingered where it was for a few seconds, teetering from side to side, before rolling from his shoulders; blood spraying over the green turf.

With a single kick, Ashe kicked the head straight between the goal posts.

"He scores, and the crowd goes wild," he said.

"I hope you take this the right way," Ashe said. "Understand, I am grateful as all hell, but I would like to know just what you were doing there? I expected you to be sound asleep until morning."

Serina laughed. "You're welcome. You should learn to never take anything for granted."

They had left the stadium quickly, retrieving Serina's bicycle and then heading for an alley near the student union where Ashe had parked his van.

"My place," she said.

"Okay, but I'm still waiting for an answer," he said.

"And I'm still waiting for my stomach to stop churning. It isn't often that I see somebody decapitated," she said.

Ashe could understand her reaction. Even through the dim mists of centuries, he could recall the first time that he had ridden to battle with his father's army. His reaction after the fighting was over had been anything but heroic. The sight of Lancelot du Lac throwing up was not one that fit the legend that had come to be associated with the name. But then again, Ashe had never felt like he wanted to fit *that* image anyway.

"I heard what he said to you," she said slowly. "About killing all those women. Was it true?"

"I only wish it weren't." He wasn't sure if the police would be able to connect Chalker with the killings or if this would be listed as some bizarre gang execution.

"And what about Michael?"

"Oh, him?" grinned Ashe. "I don't think we'll have to worry about a thing with Michael."

Ashe had roused Michael and then carefully *suggested* to him that he had not seen any of them that night. Instead, Michael had gone out after the medieval party and gotten plastered, failed miserably when he tried to pick up a couple of coeds, then headed for his own home to sleep it off. If any of the memories ever returned to him, it would be in the form of nightmares that would make no sense.

"Normally, when I implant a suggestion in someone's mind, they do what I require of them." Ashe had now and again encountered those who were immune to his abilities. Thankfully this had been one of those times.

Serina grinned. "You guys think that all you have to do is snap a finger and a girl is in your power. Hello! I've got news for you. I've never been that easy to hypnotize. When you tried to do it, I decided to follow you and see

if I could find out what was going on. Just consider yourself lucky that I did."

"Oh, that I do, m'lady."

"Now, just on the off chance that the police question
you about Chalker's death," Serina said. "Just tell them
that you spent the entire night with me. Besides, you didn't
think that I was through with you? Did you?"

"I wouldn't think of being that presumptuous."

"Of course not."

BARBARIAN
by Bill Fawcett

Bill Fawcett has been a professor, teacher, corporate executive, college dean, game designer, author, agent, and book packager. Bill Fawcett & Associates has packaged over 200 books. He has also designed almost a dozen board games, including Charles Roberts award winners such as *Empire Builder* and *Sanctuary*. He has written or collaborated on several novels, mysteries such as the *Authorized Mycroft Holmes* novels, the *Madame Vernet Investigates* series, *Making Contact, It Seemed Like a Good Idea: Great Historical Fiascos, Hunters and Shooters* and *The Teams*, the last two oral histories of the SEALs in Vietnam.

T HE High Lord Gerwick, Adviser to Kings, Hand of the Emperor, and Chief Magistrate of the Southern Lands, hesitated in the moonless night outside the tavern, unable for a moment to bring himself to enter. He knew he had to go in, but couldn't. Admittedly the Boar's Tusk was one of the least reputable places in the city, and as chief magistrate he had certainly seen enough miscreants who had become drunk there. It was also the favorite of the local mercenaries, the only trained warriors in the city except the city watch. But these men of war often were ill suited to peace. It was likely he had sentenced more than one of the men inside to months of hard labor or worse. The problem was those men had intimidated him even when he sat in judgment over them, surrounded by guards. Now he had no choice but to face them on their own terms. Gerwick wasn't surprised to notice his heart was pounding.

The door the slightly built aristocrat faced was massive and crossed with an iron band. It looked ready to survive a siege, and perhaps was intended for just that. Two centuries earlier, the building had been elegant, but had declined with the neighborhood around it. Now the white brick walls were stained by years of soot and ash and most of the windows were nailed shut with unpainted wood.

He checked that he was still inconspicuously dressed in some rather shabby clothes borrowed from a servant, who, like his "loyal" bodyguards, had run off the night before. Finally taking a shuddering breath, Gerwick let the threatening shadows in the nearby alleys frighten him into the place he had to go.

Inside, it was less filthy than he had expected, but more malodorous and raucously louder than anywhere he had ever been. The magistrate was even more surprised to see two junior officers of the city watch seemingly relaxed in one corner. He wasn't sure if their presence gave him confidence or worried him. They could have been sent there to check on him, but there was no way that they could have known he would come to this tavern. No, they were simply slumming. He would call on them if things went badly.

The air was filled with the odor of unwashed humanity and sour ale. Gerwick almost sneezed and fought the urge as it might attract unwanted attention. The noble had just restored his nerve enough to act when a leather-clad oaf easily twice his weight shoved him aside as he staggered past. The heavily-muscled man took a drunken swing at the head of another equally muscular man sitting at a table near Gerwick, the mug in his ham-sized hand spraying sour ale as it came around. The blow landed with a hollow, metallic ring, and the man who had shoved Gerwick crumpled to the floor. There was a small cheer from those nearby, and then the buzz of conversation returned to normal. No one bothered to move the body, stepping over it as they came and went.

Now that he was inside, Gerwick was unsure as to what to do next. Finally he realized that a few of the drinkers had noticed him standing near the door and were eyeing him. He had to act or leave. Leaving alone was likely to be as fatal as any mistake he could make here.

The bartender hurried over and leaned close as the magistrate placed a silver coin on the wooden plank and covered it with his hand. Watching the coin more than the man, the bartender waited. He knew that Gerwick wanted something, likely information which was any barkeep's stock in trade, and that the coin was its price. Withdrawing his hand and leaving the coin behind, Gerwick spoke slowly, trying to disguise his aristocratic class accent.

"I need to hire a mercenary who would be a trustworthy bodyguard." Even as he asked, the noble wondered why he expected to actually be referred to anyone trustworthy. Still, he had to ask someone.

The barkeep's mouth opened in a big smile as he reached for the five-talon coin. His teeth were rotten, and several were missing. He leaned forward, palming the coin and speaking into Gerwick's ear. His breath was a most noxious combination of garlic, old meat, and something really fetid, likely those teeth. It was all Gerwick could do to not pull away.

"Him, I hear he's a veteran of the Kasha War. Once fought a Bandi by himself and can tell of it," the bartender informed him in a whisper audible to half the room while obviously pointing at a man sitting nearby.

"Sure, he is," the magistrate mumbled turning to glance at the mercenary indicated. He hoped the man really was a veteran, but there was no way to tell. The barkeep's choice looked physically strong enough anyhow. Gerwin rather doubted the second claim, since a typical Bandi was about eight feet long and all claws with acid breath. The reptiles were hunted by companies of men, not one, and even then you expected serious casualties among the hunters. Still, that was quite a reputation, and just what he needed.

Gerwick risked inhaling, now that the barkeep stood a few steps away, and moved toward the man the barkeep had indicated. After a step, the magistrate realized that the man wasn't sitting nearby, but rather against the far wall. The mercenary was so huge he had at first glance seemed closer. The man's arms had to be thicker than the magistrate's legs and all muscle.

As he continued to approach him, the noble realized that the large man was already watching him. Gerwin tried to smile at the chain mail-wearing giant, using his best Imperial Palace party smile. The forced friendliness felt weak even to him, and he gave up the effort as he sat down across the table from the mercenary. The big man had the mark of the Imperial Guard on his armor, and the noble wondered who from the guard had fallen into such hard times that he had to sell his armor to a barbarian. Gerwick was a good magistrate, an expert at judging other men. His life might . . . no, it did depend on his selecting the best bodyguard. He studied the man and his eyes. There was no change of expression, or even any expression at all on the man's face or in his eyes as long moments passed.

There was an awkward silence while Gerwick sat staring at the man, unable to speak and feeling like he should simply leave. But there was a very good chance he would not survive the night if he did that.

"I need a bodyguard," he explained, speaking slowly. "Can you work for me, starting now?"

The man, who even sitting down was still a head taller than the aristocrat, nodded, his face still expressionless. His hair was dark and pulled back and his complexion ruddy and mottled. Over almost black eyes sat thick brows with a hint of gray in them.

Didn't this barbarian speak? Gerwick fought to overcome his awe of the man's obvious physical attributes. He was the magistrate, he told himself, and this was a man he was hiring. It almost worked. What worried the noble was that the mercenary was likely simply big and well muscled, but not very bright, like so many of the men he sentenced every day.

"Can you understand me?" he demanded, almost succeeding in keeping his voice from breaking nervously.

Was that a trace of a smile? Gerwick wasn't sure. The man nodded.

Great. He's slow. Maybe I should ask someone else. "I

am Gerwick, Magistrate," he introduced himself and waited. After a pause he added, "That's a man who sits in judgment of criminals for the Emperor." Perhaps he should look somewhere else or find another barbarian. One that at least had the brains to react to his presence.

Just before the noble was about to stand the large man replied. "Nil."

There was a pause. Nothing? Gerwick realized that the one sound must be his name.

"I can protect you." The mercenary's voice was low and deep.

Gerwick considered. So the barbarian could speak though his accent gave away his foreign origins. Like so many mercenaries, he must be from the more primitive northern lands where muscle and violence ruled. This man was simple enough to be trusted, then, but strong. He would serve. Settling back down, the magistrate was tempted to use a truth spell on the man. But he was reluctant to use magic here; it was too much above the intellect of those in this room and would attract attention he didn't want. It took a keen mind and years of study to cast even the most minor glamour and the actions were unmistakable.

"My problem is," Gerwick explained, trying to keep his words simple, "that tomorrow I will rule against Delos, a man of power in this city, one whose life will be forfeit. He is, unfortunately, also an officer in the city guard. So I can trust none of them to protect me. Two other magistrates disappeared mysteriously the night before bringing this man to justice. Only their charred skeletons were found the morning of trial. He is in prison now, but he was held there the other two times as well. I need you to guard me for this one night. Tomorrow he will be dead, and I'll be safe."

"Fifty talons." The large man actually grinned slightly as he named the figure. It was equal to what Gerwick would earn in a tenday. The noble started to protest, then hesitated. If he lived, it was worth it. If he died, he had no further use for money. It was outrageous, but he had no choice, and there was the very real fear of turning this giant of a man down. Somehow he didn't want to haggle with the man he hoped would keep him alive.

"Agreed."

Now Nil was almost smiling. "Half now."

Gerwick hesitated before passing over the coins. There was nothing to prevent this hulk from taking his money and walking away. The barbarian's head turned as he watched the two guardsmen leave the tavern. "First time here," he grunted.

The guardsmen *had* been waiting for him. Fifty talons suddenly sounded like a bargain. The magistrate winced but nodded his agreement. Pulling out his purse, he tried to be inconspicuous while he picked out the coins, momentarily wondering if his new bodyguard could count to twenty-five. He could feel the greedy eyes of half the room on him. "We must go to my villa and prepare," he insisted as soon as the coins left his hand.

"Meet you there," Nil replied rising up and towering over the aristocrat.

If size mattered, Gerwick was safe. Before he could insist that the man really must accompany him back, the man had stepped past him. There was no use shouting after Nil amid the din of the tavern, and within seconds the big man was out the door.

*   *   *

Gerwick was halfway home, moving nervously down the center of the street and watching every shadow. He was sure the two city guards from the tavern would jump him at any moment. By the time he had returned home, he was ready to collapse. But the servants were gone, and even his familiar villa and beloved garden seemed filled with shadows that hid assassins or worse. It wasn't until the magistrate had settled onto a divan and revived himself with a goblet of Saltarian red that he realized he had never told the barbarian where he lived. With rising panic, he wondered if the man had taken his money and left the city.

The noble opened the door and saw Nil standing outside with a large bag over his shoulder. Babbling with relief the magistrate began to tell Nil how glad he was to have him there and how much faith he had in him.

"Wait," the massive barbarian grunted out as he pushed past the noble. "You stay here," he added as he entered the large garden that covered most of the grounds.

Standing at the door, Gerwick was somewhat stunned. He stood and studied his bodyguard. Who was this barbarian to order *him* around? The man was large, but he was unlikely to do more than bash any assassins. Carrying his bag, the mercenary pushed through carefully pruned bushes. Nil was dressed now in black leather, with only his head and hands bare. Once outside the torchlight emanating from the villa, for all his bulk the man seemed to disappear.

Moving toward the gardens, the noble regained sight of his bodyguard. As he watched Nil bent down and his shoulders tightened as the large man heaved upward, pulling a five-foot-tall bush out by its roots. The noble almost protested. What did this brute think he was doing, creating a fortress out of bushes? *That hulk is ruining my carefully maintained garden.* But he stopped himself. More than a garden was at stake here. The magistrate stood, silently sentencing the traitor Delos to an extra horrible death as several of his prized flowering Argos were similarly uprooted.

Hurrying past the magistrate, Nil burst into the house only to emerge later with the amphora full of water from the cooking area. Placing the large vase on the ground near the entrance to the garden, the barbarian reached into it and washed the dirt off his face.

Trying not to snicker, Gerwick watched Nil clean himself. He couldn't help but wonder if the man was so crude he was unable to bring himself to wash inside a house. Or was he that simple. The noble was filled with doubt, although he kept his face carefully neutral. Did his life really depend on this simpleton?

"More water," Nil demand, looking around as if searching for some in the garden.

"There is no more. That will have to do," Gerwick answered, trying to keep the worry out of his voice. "You look clean," he couldn't help but add.

This got him the strangest look from Nil. Then the barbarian shrugged, half-smiling for an instant.

"Wine, then."

Was he going to get drunk? Wine, when the assassins could arrive any moment? Gerwick was tempted to refuse. But the sheer bulk of the man was intimidating, and the noble reminded himself that no matter how slow the mind, that muscle was all that stood between him and death. Reluctantly, he pointed to the thick-walled storehouse where wines were kept cool.

To his employer's astonishment Nil proceeded to carry one after another of the twenty gallon amphorae out of the stone storehouse and place them around the garden. When he brought out the tenth large jar of wine, the magistrate could stand it no longer.

"You that thirsty?" he probed, hoping to slow down, if not distract the man before he got too drunk to protect him. How much was this giant barbarian planning to drink? There was already a season's supply spread across the fifty-pace-wide garden. With a sigh, Gerwick hoped that drink inspired the mercenary, like the berserk warriors of the frozen wastes.

"Something will be," came the cryptic answer after a short pause.

The magistrate didn't bother to try to understand what that meant. Was the brute speaking of himself in the third person now, like a king? With the last amphora placed, Nil pushed through the bushes. Then the big barbarian disappeared into the shadows for what seemed an eternity. There was only the occasional grunt as assurance the mercenary was still there. The sound of the breeze in the trees and the chitter of the night birds seemed loud and full of portents as Gerwick waited, seemingly alone. He could feel his fears surging. He had banked on the muscles of this one man to stop Delos' assassins. But he might have been a fool, for the man he had hired seemed too slow to do the job, and was also likely more concerned with preparing for a tremendous drunk.

Suddenly, Nil was standing beside him.

"Put these on," the tall man ordered, holding out a bundle of clothes. It took only one whiff to cause the noble to back away. The stench was horrible. They smelled of night soil and decay, like the stuff he paid servants to spread on the plants. If he wanted to smell like that, he could roll in the waste pile. Gerwick refused with an adamant shake of his head.

"There is no time. Strip!" Nil ordered, throwing the clothes against Gerwick. With exaggerated motions, the muscular barbarian turned and washed his own hands clean in the water amphora. "Or die."

The magistrate wasn't sure who would kill him, but suddenly wearing the wretched things seemed a good idea. Gerwick realized he was making a lot of compromises today and none were enhancing his dignity. Now he was taking orders from a barbarian in his own home. Delos would pay for this—if he lived long enough to render his judgment tomorrow, something that was becoming more doubtful.

Gritting his teeth, Gerwick changed as Nil stood nearby, towering over him. After pulling the robe over his head and almost retching, the noble was surprised to hear Nil speak again.

"How did the others die?"

Six words and a full sentence, the magistrate almost said something about his bodyguard becoming talkative, then realized it was probably a bad idea to insult the man he had hired to protect him.

"It appears they were murdered and then the bodies were burned. There were traces of assassins, even a few bodies, and some blood." He paused and then his sense of fairness forced the next from him. "And all their bodyguards died and were burned as well. Three very good men failed to protect the magistrates before me."

Nil nodded, his face once more blank, took away the clothes Gerwick had been wearing, and disappeared deeper into the villa. A short time later the bodyguard emerged with those same old clothes and two of the noble's best outfits.

Seeing the outraged expression on his employer's face, the big man shrugged and said simply, "Bait," and disappeared into the dark.

"It is time," Nil explained, reappearing, leading the noble into the garden. His grip on the smaller man's arm was strong, obviously unbreakable, but somehow stopped just short of hurting.

"Men outside," he offered in explanation as he hustled Gerwick through the garden. He got a glimpse of a huddled figure to one side, jumped nervously toward Nil, then realized the figure was wearing his clothes, the set Nil had been carrying earlier. A few steps later Gerwick's worst fears were confirmed. They were stopping at the midden heap near the back of the garden.

Nil had dug a small hole in the waist-high pile and covered it with a rusty shield. Smiling widely, Nil pointed at the hole and then gestured for silence. With a resigned sigh the Chief Magistrate of the Southern Regions of the greatest empire on the continent climbed into a hole in the center of a pile of rotting food and night wastes. Nil placed the shield over him and then heaped decaying leaves and dung over it. Gerwick raised the shield a few inches and looked out across his garden. As he walked away, Nil gave him another smile over his shoulder, this one much more friendly, almost reassuring.

The magistrate waited, breathing as little of the rancid air in his hole as possible, but looking forward to watching his bodyguard pound the assassins into pulp. He was picturing this satisfying image when the first murderer scuttled over the wall on the north side of the garden. Within seconds another followed, also darkly dressed, each wielded wickedly curved knives.

The third assassin began to clamber over the wall near where Gerwick hid. The noble was surprised to note that the spikes, common on all villa walls, were now missing where the man was climbing in. Close enough that Gerwick could see his wicked grin, the assassin dropped off the wall . . . and let out a sharp scream that ended abruptly.

The magistrate looked for Nil. Neither he nor the man was visible through the narrow slit under the shield. With two more assassins in sight, Gerwick tried to remain very still and waited. He could see the two remaining murderers conversing briefly. One threw a rock into the center of the garden and, when there was no reaction, they split up so that each one was working his way down one side. *They are searching for me*, the noble realized as his heart beat harder and his breath shortened. Gerwick found himself sweating, but he refused to wipe his hands or face on the soiled and malodorous clothes he wore.

The assassins came closer, yet there was still no sign of Nil. They were halfway across the garden and would meet about where he was hidden. Did they know he was here? Was Nil in league with them? The guardsmen had been at the same tavern. Was his sitting in this pile of dung and garbage part of Delos' plan? A final insult to the injury of his death?

Anger fought with fear. Where was that oversized mercenary? It would be just like a barbarian to be off relieving himself at the wrong time.

One of the assassins stopped short and crouched. Gerwick could make out a dark form near the man. Nil! Should he warn him? If he rose or shouted, the other killer would see him for sure.

Before the noble could bring himself to react, the assassin leaped forward, his knife raised, but seemed to stumble a step away from the huddled figure. Then there was only a gurgling death rattle, but that sound was enough to attract the remaining assassin. The man rushed across the open center area and to his fellow's side.

Just as the assassin glanced down at the body, Nil rose behind him, holding a log as thick as Gerwick's leg. The hollow thunk of it striking the leather-helmeted head of the killer actually echoed off the garden walls.

With a worried glance where the first assassin had disappeared, the magistrate stood up and threw off the shield. With quick steps he rushed to congratulate his bodyguard. However the man had done it, he had saved Gerwick. The assassins were dead.

Nil, who had been facing away from the magistrate, spun toward him. There was an expression of panic on the mercenary's face that brought him to an immediate halt.

The big man ran toward the noble and literally lifted him off the ground by his shoulders. Seconds later Gerwick was flying through the air to land with a thud on the manure pile. Gratitude turned to anger. He had the taste of feces in his mouth, and his face was smeared with something that had been rotting for a long time. The barbarian fool had lost himself in the fight. He couldn't tell friend from foe.

Rising to his feet, Gerwick started to bellow angrily, only to be drowned out by the sudden hiss of flames rising from the central area of the garden about halfway between Gerwick and Nil.

The magistrate realized, standing with muck dripping off him, that whatever the assassins had thrown earlier, it had summoned the fire elemental scorching the center of his garden. The monster was not large, perhaps two feet high and vaguely wolf-shaped. But the heat radiating from it was intense. The flaming wolf turned slowly, its head raised as if sniffing the air.

"Down!" Nil bellowed scooping up the amphora he had been washing in. The muscles on the massive mercenary's arms strained as he launched the tall vase full of water toward the fiery assassin.

Gerwick fell and burrowed into the filth and waste, its odor suddenly more protective than offensive. He raised his head just far enough to see the battle between his bodyguard and the elemental.

The first amphora smashed just short of the flame creature and sprayed it. This was instantly followed by a hiss of steam and a throaty roar. The noble thought the roar was from the elemental, but he wasn't sure. Nil was yelling war cries as he strained to throw the large amphorae of wine as quickly as possible.

The elemental took three quick steps toward the barbarian and a gout of flame emerged from its mouth.

The air was full of the smell of sulfur, but not scorched flesh. The big barbarian had dived and rolled away, leaving the fruit tree he had been under charred to ash by the monster's flaming breath.

Almost as quickly, the mercenary was on his feet, throwing vase after vase of wine to burst on or near the elemental. The air was filled with smoke and howls, and the flaming monster retreated a few steps, then a few more. It was visibly weaker now, its flames smaller and flickering.

For a moment the creature stopped and searched the garden once more. It seemed confused and bewildered. Then three amphora burst on it almost as one, and the fire died. With a mournful howl, still full of hate and hunger, the now flameless and ludicrously hairless small wolf staggered a few steps directly toward Gerwick and then fell.

To make sure it was no longer a threat, Nil rushed over and chopped it not once, but three times with the mantall sword he had not even unsheathed until then. With the elemental dead, the big barbarian gave the magistrate a genuinely friendly smile.

Suddenly aware of the filth he had burrowed into, Gerwick rose with what dignity he could manage. It took him another few moments to absorb all he had seen. The assassins had been defeated, not by Nil's size, but without a fight. And it was apparent the barbarian had expected the fire elemental.

"Thank you," the magistrate began, genuinely grateful, He could never have defeated even the human foes. Then in a humbler voice, as he walked slowly toward the big mercenary, "I am embarrassed at how badly I underestimated you."

"It happens all the time," Nil answered, his smile widening. "Actually I encourage it. Gives me an edge . . . though

I am surprised that a magistrate took so long to see past the muscles."

Gerwick would have been embarrassed, but he was too happy to be alive. Instead he answered the mercenary's smile with his own and extended his hand.

BRIGHT BE THE FACE
by Gary A. Braunbeck

Gary A. Braunbeck is the author of the acclaimed collection *Things Left Behind,* as well as the forthcoming collections *Escaping Purgatory* (in collaboration with Alan M. Clark) and the CD-ROM *Sorties, Cathexes, and Personal Effects.* His first solo novel, *The Indifference of Heaven,* was recently released, as was his Dark Matter novel, *In Hollow Houses.* He lives in Columbus, Ohio and has, to date, sold nearly 170 short stories. His fiction, to quote *Publisher's Weekly.* ". . . stirs the mind as it chills the marrow."

"Once a fool was soundly thrashed during the night, and the next day everyone made fun of him. 'You should thank God,' he said, 'that the night was clear; otherwise I would have played such a trick on you!' 'What trick? Tell us!' 'I would have hidden myself.'"
—17th century Russian fable

HIS name was Edward Something-or-Other, and though everyone in the village recognized him on sight, no one really knew much about him, except that he was a large and strong young man who was always willing to do odd jobs for reasonable pay, that he never spoke an ill word against anyone, and that he went off to war one cold and foggy September morning where he eventually saved many of his fellow soldiers from certain death, was given many medals, hailed a hero and great warrior, and came home with no face. But by then he had been gone for so long that no one in the village could remember what he'd looked like before war had broken out.

To say he had no face is a bit of an exaggeration; he had eyes for he could see, and he had eardrums because he could hear but no ears to speak of, just bits of dangling, discolored flesh on the sides of his head. The skin which formed his cheeks had been grafted on from flesh the doctors removed from his thighs, and though he was told that everything would heal over and appear normal Some Day Soon, it still hurt him to walk or smile; walking was something he could not avoid, but not so smiling. His nose was gone, as well; his nostrils were two small skeletal caves that were often blocked and forced him to breathe through his mouth, which in turn dried up his throat and made it difficult—sometimes even impossible—for him to swallow; as a result, he was often hoarse and coughed frequently. Gone also were his teeth, but his jaw remained intact and his gums were firm, making it possible for him to wear dentures. Sometimes, though, when he talked—which he rarely did, due to his hoarseness, and also because his difficulty in swallowing caused him to drool—the dentures would slip a little and click and whomever he was talking with would make sorry work of hiding their amusement.

And so Edward Something-or-Other, heroic warrior and village handyman, began to speak less and less, until, at last, he spoke not at all . . . except to the priest.

Everyone in the village took to calling him only "Soldier Boy," and found much humor in it. Edward Something-or-Other merely nodded his head and went about his business. He took to wearing a bandage on the space where his nose used to be. The bandage reached the back of his head and was kept in place with a safety pin. He covered the lower half of his face with a long gray scarf, which he liked to imagine flowed in the wind behind him as he walked, like in the old photos and drawings he'd seen of the aviators in their planes as they flew over the battlefields of Europe. Perhaps, he fantasized, people would see him walking with his flowing scarf and think to themselves, "This is a heroic-looking fellow, and I know he was in the war and was given many medals. Perhaps he deserves more respect than we have given to him."

But this never happened.

People left him alone, save for those times when a merchant in the village needed something repaired, or hauled away, or a local farmer needed someone to help spread fertilizer. Edward Something-or-Other was the boy for the job; quiet, a bit disturbing in appearance but seemingly pleasant in nature, no job too hard or too dirty or too undignified.

The odd jobs became sparse, so Edward Something-or-Other, under the name "Soldier Boy," became a fighter with a local carnival. He wore a mask and boxing trunks and was said to be able to knock out any and all challengers before the end of Round One. This he did three times a day, six days a week, throughout the spring and summer. He was always careful never to hit any of his opponents in the face for fear he might leave permanent damage; a good, solid blow to the center of the chest usually did it.

"Soldier Boy" was never once knocked down, never lost a fight, and made a great deal of money as a result, though he continued to live as he always had; frugally, in a small and sparse room, continuing to do odd jobs in the village whenever they were offered.

Still, there were times, late at night as he lay in his bed trying to remember what his old face had looked like, when he longed to hear the cheering of the crowds as he fought. There, in the ring—even if it was with the carnival—he was, for a little while, admired and cheered as a hero, and no one cared what he looked like.

But like the scarf and his hopes that gave him the air of a hero, it was only something to cheer him a little before he fell into sleep, a little something to help keep the bad dreams away.

The village grew as more children were born and they, in turn, grew to have families of their own. Every summer people came to cheer "Soldier Boy" as he fought his opponents in the ring at the carnival. He was so tall and strong that tiny children would ask to climb on him as if he were a mountain. Edward enjoyed the children, their laughter, the touch of their warm and affectionate hands on his arms, the way they would hug him.

Those who had been alive when he returned from the war grew old and died; only a few remained, and their memories grew dim and fragmented.

"Who is the big fellow who wears the scarf?" younger villagers would ask.

"I don't quite remember," the older ones would reply. "I think he was a hero in the war or something."

"Why does he hide his face?"

Then they would remember: "Because he doesn't have one. That's 'Soldier Boy.'"

Children stopped wanting to play with him after that.

One morning, after cleaning up a local merchant's basement after heavy rains had caused the sewers to back up, Edward Something-or-Other was drinking a glass of water (being careful to hold the rim of the glass under his scarf) when the merchant asked of him: "Did you see many men die during the war?"

Edward Something-or-Other looked at a space in the air as if it contained a window only he could see through, and beyond this window he seemed to see something that haunted him and made him sadder than he was, and instead of answering the merchant with words, he gave a slow nod of his head, but his eyes betrayed that there was much more to his silence and melancholy than this gesture revealed.

What he did not speak of to the merchant that day, what he dared not tell anyone except the priest, was this: he suspected that he was not supposed to have lived, that he somehow had been accidentally passed over by Death that day on the battlefield when the shells were screaming and the mortars exploding and the mines reducing men to chunks of searing meat.

And he suspected this because of the ghosts.

Now, whether they were actual ghosts, he was not at first certain. He only knew that one night, while he sat in his room reading and listening to his tiny radio, a dog began to howl outside his window. The dog sounded frightened, and so Edward Something-or-Other went outside (taking care to first don the scarf so his face would not alarm anyone who might happen by) and lifted the dog in his strong arms. The animal continued to stare down the darkened street and whine, then snarl, and, at last, bury its head in the crook of Edward's arm.

A procession of figures came out of the darkness, walking without sound, all of them carrying burning candles. As they passed by the opened door of Edward's room, he saw that they were all figures of dead soldiers, many of whom he had stepped or fallen over on the battlefield. Some were missing arms, others legs, and many, like Edward himself, were missing parts of their faces. It was these figures—those missing facial features—who slowed their step as they passed by his doorway and nodded to him like old friends. They spoke to him, whispering promises.

At last one of them—an older man, missing forehead and one eye—broke away from the procession and came toward Edward and gave him a lighted candle.

"Keep this nearby," he said to Edward, "and the next time we pass through this ungrateful place, give it back to me."

And with that, he fell back into the procession of dead soldiers and followed them through the streets of the village, into the darkness of the night to eternity.

Edward took both the candle and the dog inside. He allowed the dog to sleep at the foot of his bed. The candle he placed on his nightstand and let it burn through the night as he slept.

He kept hearing his voice calling the village an "ungrateful place," kept seeing the hatred that was in his eyes as he said it, the disgust in his voice.

Or perhaps that was all part of his dream.

* * *

When he woke the next morning, he saw that sometime during the night the candle had changed into the faceplate of a skull.

The dog at the foot of the bed would not look upon the face. It growled when Edward tried to touch it, then bolted out the door and down the road in the same direction taken by the ghosts.

And it was then Edward Something-or-Other realized that he had been destined to die in battle and not come home with the repulsive remnants of a face.

He went to confession and spoke to the priest. Edward spoke slowly, for his dentures and hoarseness made speech difficult, as did the drooling because he could not swallow at all today. He also spoke in this manner because the priest was now so very old and had trouble hearing.

"Father, they told me that if I were to solve the riddle of the Old Man's Candle, then they would give me back my face."

"Your actual face?" asked the priest.

Edward hesitated a moment before answering. "No, Father, not exactly. One said he would give to me his ears for the sides of my head; another promised me his nose so that I would no longer have to wear this bandage; and yet another said that he would give me his teeth so I wouldn't have to wear these dentures and pretend not to notice when the people laughed at me because sometimes they become loose and click."

"Do you believe them to be ghosts?"

"Yes, Father. I recognized some of them from their bodies on the battlefield."

"This riddle you speak—"

"The Riddle of the Old Man's Candle."

"—yes. Do you know its solution?"

"No. The candle, Father, it . . . it changed during the night."

"How did it change?"

"It became . . . well . . ." Edward reached into his sack and removed the faceplate and showed it to the priest.

"Lord save us," the priest whispered.

"I know what it is, Father," said Edward. "It is the bone of my face as it will appear when it has been healed and made whole again."

The priest gave the faceplate back to Edward, who, feeling embarrassed and humiliated, slipped it quickly back into his bag.

"Do you read your Bible, Edward?"

"Yes, Father."

"Do you remember what Jesus said to the leper who asked that He heal the sores which covered his body?"

"No, Father, I don't."

"Jesus said: 'Heed not the clay countenance that is the flesh, for bright be the face of the soul.'"

Edward said nothing for several moments.

"Edward?"

"Yes, Father?"

"Do you believe that, if these spirits indeed are real, they will keep their word?"

"I'm not sure, but I suspect not."

"Ah—you still believe that you were meant to die in battle?"

"Yes."

The priest then was silent, deep in thought and troubled by what he was about to say. At last, he leaned forward and whispered: "This is what you must do, Edward; take a candle from the altar and I shall bless it for you. Take that candle home and light it and then set it upon the face of the skull which you showed to me. Allow the wax to melt so that it covers the entire face, let it dry and harden, and then set three more candles on it—two on the sides, to represent where your ears should be, and one in the center, to show where your nose once was. Do this, and then wait for the spirits to return to you. Only then should you light the three candles and return it to the old man."

Edward did as the priest instructed.

Autumn passed into Winter, and then came Spring and still the spirits had not returned.

Edward Something-or-Other came to believe deep in his heart that he was not meant to be here.

Summer arrived, and with it the carnival and the rides and the ring and the return of "Soldier Boy"—only now there were not so many to cheer his battles. He fought well but without the energy of years past. He was knocked down once by a young man from another village, but managed to rise and defeat his opponent.

He looked once into the crowd and saw, sitting among the spectators, those spirits whose faces were as incomplete as his own.

He knew they would be coming for him soon.

Summer passed into Autumn and with its passing came the dry, whispering leaves which skittered along the streets during the day and gathered in dark corners at night.

It was on just such a chill and whispering Autumn night that the dog returned to Edward's window, howling.

"How are you, old friend?" asked Edward as he came outside and lifted the dog into his arms. He wore neither the scarf tonight nor the bandage; his face was, for the first time in many decades, exposed fully to the world—but no one was there to see it.

The dog buried its face in the crook of Edward's arm as the procession of the dead came out of the darkness, their candles burning bright.

This time, however, they did not pass Edward's door but began to gather around. The old man who had given Edward the candle stepped forward and smiled, then asked of him: "Do you have the candle which I gave you?"

"Yes," replied Edward, and produced from behind his back the wax-covered faceplate, now decorated with three burning candles.

The old man smiled and took the burning face from Edward, holding it high for the others to see.

"'Bright be the face of the soul,'" said the old man; then, turning to Edward, said: "You have solved my riddle, Edward Howe. You have offered your soul to save your village as you once risked your life to save your fellow soldiers." He handed the burning face back to Edward.

It had been so long since Edward had heard his true last name spoken by anyone that he did not at first recognize it; nor did the words "... save your village" at first register.

"You shall be rewarded," continued the old man, "in two ways: First, we shall not, as we were supposed to do, take you with us."

"So it's true, then," whispered Edward. "I was supposed to die that day?"

"Yes, but no matter now, you shall grow to be a very, very old man, and let us hope that it will be a happy life from this night on. Touch your face, Edward."

He did, and discovered that it was now whole and healed;

ears, cheeks, teeth, nose, skin—it was a normal face, one that he would never again have to hide behind masks or scarves.

"I am whole again," he said, startled by the sound of his voice, its fullness, its richness and timbre. For the first time in decades he pulled in a deep breath through his nose; there was no pain.

"Secondly," said the old man, "you shall now be the only true face in your village."

"What do you—?" But before he could complete the question, there came from a nearby window a scream of singular horror, and soon a woman ran into the street clutching her face. She spun around, eyes wide with terror, and pulled away her hands to reveal that she had no nose, only a smooth, flat area of flesh.

Soon other villagers spilled into the street, all of them missing facial features, some who now had no faces at all, merely blank ovals of flesh where their features should have been.

"No!" cried Edward.

"Why?" asked the old man. "Look at us, Edward Howe. Fallen warriors, all of us. Some of us died in battle, but many of us, like yourself, returned home scarred and disfigured, only to find ourselves mocked outcasts. 'Abomination!' they called us. Well, now, let *them* know how it feels to be the one who is mocked, who is scorned and turned away from, who never again knows the warm touch of a friend, the kiss of a woman's lips upon their own, the feel of a child's loving arms around their necks. We have traveled from village to village to find others just like you, Edward, and they have all accepted our bargain. So many years since the war, and how easily those who never knew battle forget the sacrifices we made for them. Let them know now."

Edward saw the people of his village running, screaming, crying, clutching at their ruined or missing faces, and for a moment, just one moment, a moment he would never forgive himself for, Edward Howe, formerly Edward Something-or-Other and Soldier Boy, felt a brief, bright satisfaction in their pain; but a moment later he realized just how wrong this was and thrust out the burning face. "No. If this is the price of having a normal face restored to me, I do not want it; and if it means that you take my soul and I come with you now, then so be it. Return everything as it was and you can take my soul. I will not fight you. The wars are over. I have no desire to fight again."

The old man took the burning face and an instant later, the villagers found their faces restored to them. None looked in Edward's direction; even if they had, none would have seen the spirits surrounding him.

"So I come with you now?"

The old man shook his head. "Not now, but soon enough. A season or three. Listen to the wind, and you'll hear our approach in the whisper of leaves across the cobblestones. Good-bye, Edward Howe. Enjoy your isolation and grotesquerie."

They left him there, alone save for the dog, and he watched them vanish up the road toward eternity.

His throat was dry and his nostril cavities were blocked. It was time to take some medicine and try to sleep.

The dog followed Edward into his room and slept at the foot of his new master's bed, where he would sleep for the rest of his days. Years later, upon Edward's death, the dog would be found sleeping at the foot of his master's grave and would refuse to move. It would lay there until it, too, passed away, and would be buried alongside its master.

But that was many years away.

The next morning, everyone in the village was talking about the horror of the previous night, wondering what they could have done to offend God so badly that He would punish them in such a way.

"But He did not make the punishment permanent," said one merchant.

"True," replied a cook. "It was as if he were . . . warning us."

"Or reminding us," said the priest.

"Reminding us of what?"

The priest said nothing, only glimpsed for a moment toward the doorway where Edward stood, scarf and bandage in their place, dog at his feet.

Later that day, someone left a fresh-baked apple pie on the sill of Edward's open window.

The next morning, he found a tray with a delicious breakfast waiting outside his door. The odd jobs began to become plentiful again. Sometimes children would stop and ask him about his scarf and bandage.

In their sleep, the villagers would often dream of Edward sacrificing his soul for them so they would never know the loneliness of having a face like his.

They began speaking to him, and, eventually, he began to speak in return. He was invited to attend church socials, to join in a game of cards or come to a village picnic.

Toward the end of his life, he stopped wearing the scarf and bandage. The villagers took to carrying extra handkerchiefs with them so that they might have one should

Edward need it on a day when swallowing was difficult for him.

He took his medals out of their box and put them in a case and that case was put on display in the village hall.

He had many friends in the village who grew to love and respect him.

When Edward passed away quietly in his sleep, the village closed all of its schools and shops for the day so that everyone could attend his funeral. The day was pleasant but slightly overcast and warm.

Near his grave, there was found an oddly-shaped candle holder with three candles in it. Attached to it was a note which read: *Some Burn Too Brightly For Us to Take.*

As it was placed on the lid of Edward's coffin, the sun emerged from behind the clouds and the day became as bright as anyone in the village had ever seen.

There were tears, and later there was the business with Edward's poor dog, but, for generations to come, there was also a tale to pass along to the children; some of it based on fact, some on supposition, some of it on dreams, but it, like its subject, would be remembered, if not forever, then for long enough.

It began: *His name was Edward Something-or-Other and though everyone in the village recognized him on sight, no one really knew much about him, except that he was a large and strong young man who was always willing to do odd jobs for reasonable pay, that he never spoke an ill word against anyone. . . .*

MAKING A NOISE IN
THIS WORLD
by Charles de Lint

Charles de Lint is a full-time writer and musician who presently makes his home in Ottawa, Canada, with his wife Mary Ann Harris, an artist and musician. His latest novel is *Forests of the Heart*. He has a new collection called *Triskell Tales*. His classic novel *Svaha* has just been reprinted. Other recent publications include mass market editions of *Moonlight and Vines,* a third collection of *Newford* stories, and his novel *Someplace to Be Flying*. For more information about his work, visit his website at <http://www.cyberus.ca/~cdl>.

I'M driving up from the city when I spot a flock of crows near the chained gates of the old gravel pit that sits on the left side of the highway, about halfway to the rez. It's that time of the morning when the night's mostly a memory, but the sun's still blinking the sleep from its eyes as it gets ready to shine us into another day.

Me, I'm on my way to bed. I'm wearing gloves and have a take-out coffee in my free hand, a cigarette burning between the tobacco-stained fingers of the one hold-

ing the wheel. A plastic bag full of aerosol paint cans, half
of them empty, rattles on the floor on the passenger's side
every time I hit a bump. Behind me I've left freight cars
painted with thunderbirds and buffalo heads and whatever
other icons I could think up tonight to tell the world that
the Indians have counted another coup, hi-ya-ya-ya. I draw
the line at dream catchers, though I suppose some people
might mistake my spiderwebs for them.

My favorite tonight has become sort of a personal trademark: a big crow, its wings spread wide like the traditional
thunderbird and running the whole length of the boxcar,
but it's got that crow beak you can't mistake and a sly,
kind of laughing look in its eyes. Tonight I painted that
bird fire engine red with black markings. On its belly I
made the old Kickaha sign for *Bín-ji-gú-sân*, the sacred
medicine bag: a snake, with luck lines radiating from its
head and back.

I've been doing that crow ever since I woke one morning from a dream where I was painting graffiti on a 747
at the airport, smiling because this time my bird was really
going to fly. I opened my eyes to hear the crows outside
my window, squawking and gossiping, and there were three
black feathers on the pillow beside me.

Out on the highway now, I ease up on the gas and try
to see what's got these birds up so early.

Crows are sacred on the rez—at least with the Aunts
and the other elders. Most of my generation's just happy
to make it through the day, never mind getting mystical
about it. But I've always liked them. Crows and coyotes.
Like the Aunts say, they're the smart ones. They never had
anything for the white men to take away and they sure do
hold their own against them. Shoot them, poison them, do

your best. You manage to kill one and a couple more'll show up to take its place. If we'd been as wily, we'd never have lost our lands.

It's a cold morning. My hands are still stinging from when I was painting those boxcars, all night long. Though some of that time was spent hiding from the railroad rent-a-cops and warming up outside the freight yard where some hobo skins had them a fire burning in a big metal drum. Half the time the paints just clogged up in the cans. If I'd been in the wind, I doubt they'd have worked at all.

The colors I use are blacks and reds, greens and yellows, oranges and purples. No blues—the sky's already got them. Maybe some of the Aunts' spirit talk's worn off on me, because when I'm trainpainting, I don't want to insult the Grandfather Thunders. Blue's their color, at least among my people.

My tag's "Crow." I was born James Raven, but Aunt Nancy says I've got too much crow in me. No respect for anything, just like my black-winged brothers. And then there's those feathers I found on my pillow that morning. Maybe that's why I pull over. Because in my head, we're kin. Same clan, anyway.

There's times later when maybe I wished I hadn't. I'm still weighing that on a day-to-day basis. But my life's sure on the road to nowhere I could've planned because of that impulse.

The birds don't fly off when I get out of the car, leaving my coffee on the dash. I take a last drag on my cigarette and flick the butt into the snow. Jesus, but it's cold. A *lot* colder here than it was in the freight yards. There I had the cars blocking the wind most of the time. Out here, it comes roaring at me from about as far north as the cold can come. It must be twenty, thirty below out here, factoring in the wind chill.

I start to walk toward where the birds have gathered and I go a little colder still, but this time it's inside, like there's frost on my heart.

They've found themselves a man. A dead skin, just lying here in the snow. I don't know what killed him, but I can make an educated guess considering all he's wearing is a thin, unzipped windbreaker over a T-shirt and chinos. Running shoes on his feet, no socks.

He must've frozen to death.

The crows don't fly off when I approach, which makes me think maybe the dead man's kin, too. That they weren't here to eat him, but to see him on his way, like in the old stories. I crouch down beside him, snow crunching under my knee. I can see now he's been in a fight. I take off my paint-stained gloves and reach for his throat, looking for a pulse, but not expecting to find one. He twitches at my touch. I almost fall over backwards when those frosted eyelashes suddenly crack open and he's looking right at me.

He has pale blue eyes—unusual for a skin. They study me for a moment. I see an alcohol haze just on the other side of their calm, lucid gaze. What strikes me at that moment is that I don't see any pain.

Words creep out of his mouth. "Who . . . who was it that said, 'It is a good day to die'?"

"I don't know," I find myself answering. "Some famous chief, I guess. Sitting Bull, maybe." Then I realize what I'm doing, having a conversation with a dying man. "We've got to get you to a hospital."

"It's bullshit," he says.

I think he's going to lose his hands. They're blue with

the cold. I can't see his feet, but in those thin running shoes, they can't be in much better condition.

"No, you'll be okay," I lie. "The doctors'll have you fixed up in no time."

But he's not talking about the hospital.

"It's never a good day to die," he tells me. "You tell Turk that for me."

My pulse quickens at the name. Everybody on the rez knows Tom McGurk. He's a detective with the NPD that's got this constant hard-on for Indians. He goes out of his way to break our heads, bust the skin hookers, roust the hobo bloods. On the rez they even say he's killed him a few skins, took their scalps like some old Indian hunter, but I know that's bullshit. Something like that, it would've made the papers. Not because it was skins dying, but for the gory details of the story.

"He did this to you?" I ask. "Turk did this?"

Now it doesn't seem so odd, finding this drunk brave dying here in the snow. Cops like to beat on us, and I've heard about this before, how they grab some skin, usually drunk, beat the crap out of him, then drive him twenty miles or so out of town and dump him. Let him walk back to the city if he's up for some more punishment.

But on a night like this . . .

The dying man tries to grab my arm, but his frozen fingers don't work anymore. It's like all he's got is this lump on the end of his arm, hard as a branch, banging against me. It brings a sour taste up my throat.

"My name," he says, "is John Walking Elk. My father was an Oglala Sioux from the Pine Ridge rez and my mother was a Kickaha from just up the road. Don't let me be forgotten."

"I . . . I won't."

"Be a warrior for me."

I figure he wants his revenge on Turk, the one he can't take for himself, and I find myself nodding. Me, who's never won a fight in his life. By the time I realize we have different definitions for the word "warrior," my life's completely changed.

*   *   *

I remember the look on my mom's face the first time I got arrested for vandalism. She didn't know whether to be happy or mad. See, she never had to worry about me drinking or doing drugs. And while she knew that trainpainting was against the law, she understood that I saw it as bringing Beauty into the world.

"At least you're not a drunk like your father's brother was," she finally said.

Uncle Frank was an alcoholic who died in the city, choking on his own puke after an all-night bender. We've no idea what ever happened to my father, Frank's brother. One day we woke up and he was gone, vanished like the promises in all those treaties the chiefs signed.

"But why can't you paint on canvases like other artists do?" she wanted to know.

I don't know where to begin to explain.

Part of it's got to do with the transitory nature of painting freight cars. Nobody can stand there and criticize it the way you can a painting hanging in a gallery or a museum, or even a mural on the side of some building. By the time you realize you're looking at a painting on the side of a boxcar, the locomotive's already pulled that car out of your sight and farther on down the line. All you're left with is the memory of it; what you saw, and what you have to fill in from your own imagination.

Part of it's got to do with the act itself. Sneaking into the freight yards, taking the chance on getting beat up or arrested by the rent-a-cops, having to work so fast. But if you pull it off, you've put a piece of Beauty back into the world, a piece of art that'll go traveling right across the continent. Most artists are lucky to get a show in one gallery. But trainpainters . . . our work's being shown from New York City to L.A. and every place in between.

And I guess part of it's got to do with the self-image you get to carry around inside you. You're an outlaw, like the chiefs of old, making a stand against the big white machine that just rolls across the country, knocking down anything that gets in its way.

So it fills something in my life, but even with the train-painting, I've always felt like there was something miss-ing, and I don't mean my father. Though trainpainting's the only time I feel complete, it's still like I'm doing the right thing, but for the wrong reason. Too much me, not enough everything else that's in the world.

* * *

I'm holding John Walking Elk in my arms when he dies. I'm about to pick him up when this rattle goes through his chest and his head sags away from me, hanging at an un-natural angle. I feel something in that moment, like a breath touching the inside of my skin, passing through me. That's when I know for sure he's gone.

I sit there until the cold starts to work its way through

my coat, then I get a firmer grip on the dead man and stagger back to my car with him. I don't take him back to the
city, report his death to the same authorities that killed him.
Instead, I gather my courage and take him to Jack Whiteduck.

I don't know how much I really buy into the mysteries.
I mean, I like the idea of them, the way you hear about
them in the old stories. Honoring the Creator and the Grandfather Thunders, taking care of this world we've all found
ourselves living in, thinking crows can be kin, being re-
spectful to the spirits, that kind of thing. But it's usually
an intellectual appreciation, not something I feel in my gut.
Like I said, trainpainting's about the only time it's real for
me. Finding Beauty, creating Beauty, painting her face on
the side of a freight car.

But with Jack Whiteduck it's different. He makes you
believe. Makes you see with the heart instead of the eye.
Everybody feels that way about him, though if you ask
most people, they'll just say he makes them nervous. The
corporate braves who run the casino, the kids sniffing glue
and gasoline under the highway bridge and making fun of
the elders, the drunks hitting the bars off the rez . . . press
them hard enough and even they'll admit, yeah, something
about the old man puts a hole in their party that all the
good times run out of.

He makes you remember, though what you're remembering is hard to put into words. Just that things could be
different, I guess. That once our lives were different, and
they could be that way again, if we give the old ways a
chance. White people, they think of us as either the noble
savage, or the drunk in the gutter, puking on their shoes.
They'll come to the powwows, take their pictures and buy

some souvenirs, sample the frybread, maybe try to dance. They'll walk by us in the city, not able to meet our gaze, either because they're scared we'll try to rob them, or hurt them, or they just don't want to accept our misery, don't want to allow that it exists in the same perfect world they live in.

We're one or the other to them, and they don't see a whole lot of range in between. Trouble is, a lot of us see ourselves the same way. Whiteduck doesn't let you. As a people, we were never perfect—nobody is—but there's something about him that tells us we don't have to be losers either.

Whiteduck's not the oldest of the elders on the rez, but he's the one everybody goes to when they've got a problem nobody else can solve.

So I drive out to his cabin, up past Pineback Road, drive in as far as I can, then I get out and walk the rest of the way, carrying John Walking Elk's body in my arms, following the narrow path that leads through the drifts to Whiteduck's cabin. I don't know where I get the strength.

There's a glow spilling out of the windows—a flickering light of some kind. Oil lamp, I'm guessing, or a candle. Whiteduck doesn't have electricity. Doesn't have a phone or running water either. The door opens before I reach it and Whiteduck stands silhouetted against the yellow light like he's expecting me. I feel a pinprick of nervousness settle in between my shoulder blades as I keep walking forward, boots crunching in the snow.

He's not as tall as I remember, but when I think about it, that's always been the case, the few times I've seen him. I guess I build him up in my mind. He's got the broad Kickaha face, but there's no fat on his body. Pushing close to seventy now, his features are a road map of brown wrinkles, surrounding a pair of eyes that are darker than the wings of the crows that pulled me into this in the first place.

"Heard you were coming," he says.

I guess my face reflects my confusion.

"I saw the dead man's spirit pass by on the morning wind," he explains, "and the manitou told me you were bringing his body to me. You did the right thing. After what the whites did to him, they've got no more business with this poor dead skin."

He steps aside to let me go in, and I angle the body so I can get it through the door. Whiteduck indicates that I should lay it out on his bed.

There's not much to the place. A pot-bellied cast-iron stove with a fire burning in it. A wooden table with a couple of chairs, all of them handmade from cedar. A kind of counter running along one wall with a sink in it and a pail underneath to catch the runoff. A chest under the counter that holds his food, I'm guessing, since his clothes are hanging from pegs on the wall above his bed. Bunches of herbs are drying over the counter, tied together with thin strips of leather. In the far corner is a pile of furs, mostly beaver.

The oil lamp's sitting on the table, but moment by moment, it becomes less necessary as the sun keeps rising outside.

"*Mico'mis*," I begin, giving him the honorific, but I don't know where to go with my words past it.

"That's good," he says. "Too many boys your age don't have respect for their elders."

I'd take offense at the designation of "boy"—I'll be

twenty-one in the spring—but compared to him, I guess that's what I am.

"What will you do with the body?" I ask.

"That's not a body," he tells me. "It's a man, got pushed off the wheel before his time. I'm going to make sure his spirit knows where it needs to go next."

"But . . . what will you do with what he's left behind?"

"Maybe a better question would be, what will you do with yourself?"

I remember John Walking Elk's dying words. *Be a warrior for me.*

"I'm going to set things right," I say.

Whiteduck looks at me and all that nervousness that's been hiding somewhere just between my shoulder blades comes flooding through me. I get the feeling he can read my every thought and feeling. I get the feeling he can see the whole of my life laid out, what's been and what's to come, and that he's going to tell me how to live it right. But he only nods.

"There's some things we need to learn for ourselves," he says finally. "But you think on this, James Raven. There's more than one way to be a warrior. You can, and should, fight for the people, but being a warrior also means a way of living. It's something you forge in your heart to make the spirit strong and it doesn't mean you have to go out and kill anything, even when it's vermin that you feel need exterminating. Everything we do comes back to us—goes for whites the same as skins."

I was wrong. He does have advice.

"You're saying I should just let this slide?" I ask. "That Turk gets away with killing another one of us?"

"I'm saying, do what your heart tells you you must do,

no'cicen. Listen to it, not to some old man living by himself in a cabin in the woods."

"But—"

"Now go," he says, firm but not unfriendly. "We both
have tasks ahead of us."

* * *

I leave there feeling confused. Like I said, I'm not a
fighter. Whenever I have gotten into a fight, I got my ass
kicked. But there's something just not right about letting
Turk get away with this. Finding the dying man has lodged
a hot coal of anger in my head, put a shiver of ice through
my heart.

I figure what I need now is a gun, and I know where
to get it.

* * *

"I don't know," Jackson says. "I'm not really in the business of selling weapons. What do you want a gun for anyway?"

That Jackson Red Dog has never been in prison is an
ongoing mystery on the rez. It's an open secret that he has
variously been, and by all accounts still is, a bootlegger, a
drug dealer, a fence, a smuggler, and pretty much anything
else against the law that's on this side of murder and mayhem. "I draw the line at killing people," he's said. "There's
no percentage in it. Today's enemy could be tomorrow's
customer."

He's in his fifties now, a dark-skinned Indian with a
graying ponytail, standing about six-two with a linebacker's

build and hands so big he can hold a cantaloupe the way you or I might hold an apple. He lives on the southern edge of the rez and works out of the back of that general store on the highway, just inside the boundaries of the rez, where he can comfortably do business with our people and anybody willing to drive up from the city.

"I figure it's something I need," I tell him. "You got any that can't be traced?"

He laughs. "You watch too much TV, kid."

"I'm serious," I say. "I've got the money. Cash."

I'd cleaned out my savings account before driving over to the store. I found Jackson in the back as usual, holding court in a smoky room filled with skins his age and older, sitting around a pot-bellied stove, none of them saying much. This is his office, though, come spring, it moves out onto the front porch. When I said I needed to talk to him, he took me outside and lit a cigarette, offered me one.

"How much money?" Jackson asks.

"How much is the gun?" I reply.

I'm not stupid. I tell him what I've got in my pocket—basically enough to cover next month's rent and a couple of cases of beer—and that's what he'll be charging me. He looks me over, then gives me a slow nod.

"Maybe I could put you in touch with a guy that can get you a gun," he says.

Which I translate as, "We can do business."

"Just tell me," he adds. "Who're you planning to kill?"

"Nobody you'd know."

"I know everybody."

All things considered, that's probably true.

"Nobody you'd care about," I tell him.

"That's good enough for me."

There's laughter in his eyes, like he knows more than he's letting on, but I can't figure out what it is.

* * *

The gun's heavy in my pocket as I leave the store and drive south to the city. I don't know any more about handguns than I do fighting, but Jackson offers me some advice as he counts my money.

"You ever shoot one of these before?" he asks.

I shake my head.

"What you've got there's a .38 Smith and Wesson. It's got a kick and to tell you the truth, the barrel's been cut down some and it's had a ramp foresight added. Whoever did the work, wasn't exactly a gunsmith. The sight's off, so even if you were some fancy shot, you'd have trouble with it. Best thing you can do is notch a few crosses on the tips of your bullets and aim for the body. Bullet goes in and makes a tiny hole, comes back out again and takes away half the guy's back."

I feel a little sick, listening to him, but then I think of John Walking Elk dying in the snow, of Turk sitting in his precinct, laughing it off. I wonder how many others he's left to die the way he did Walking Elk. I get to thinking about some of the other drunks I've heard of that were supposed to have died of exposure, nobody quite sure what they were doing out in the middle of nowhere, or how they got there.

"You planning to come out of this alive?" Jackson asks when I'm leaving.

"It's not essential."

He gives me another of those slow nods of his. "That'll

make it easier. You got the time, tell Turk it's been a long time coming."

That stops me in the doorway.

"How'd you know it was Turk?" I ask.

He laughs. "Christ, kid. This is the rez. Everybody here knows your business before you do. What, did you think you were excused?"

I think about that on the drive down to the city, how gossip travels from one end of the rez to the other. It's like my paintings, traveling across the country. I don't plan where they go, how they go, they just go. It's not something you can control.

I'm not worried about anybody up here knowing what I'm planning. I can't think of a single skin who would save Turk's life if they came upon him dying, even if all they had to do was toss him a nickel. I'm just hoping my mom doesn't hear about it too soon. I'd like to explain to her why I'm doing this, but I'm not entirely sure myself, and I know if I go to her before I do it, she'll talk me out of it. And if that doesn't work, she'll sit on me until the impulse goes away.

*   *   *

There are crows lined up on the power lines and leafing the trees for miles down the road. Dozens of them, more than I've ever seen. I know their roost is up around Pineback Road, near Whiteduck's cabin. A rez inside the rez. But they're safe there. Nobody on the rez takes potshots at our black-feathered cousins.

When I come up on the entrance to the gravel pit, I see the crows are still there as well. I stand on the brakes and the car goes slewing toward the ditch. I only just manage to keep it on the road. Then I sit there, looking in my rearview mirror. I see a man standing there among the crows, John Walking Elk, leaning on the gate at the entrance and big as life.

I back up until I'm abreast the gates and look out the passenger window at him. He smiles and gives me a wave. He's still wearing that thin windbreaker, the T-shirt and chinos, the running shoes without socks. The big difference is, he's not dead. He's not even dying.

I light a cigarette with shaking hands and look at him for a long moment before I finally open my door. I walk around the car, the wind knifing through my jacket, but Walking Elk's not even shivering. The weight of the gun in my pocket makes me feel like I'm walking at an angle, tilted over on one side.

"Don't worry," he says when I get near. "You're not losing it. I'm still dead."

And seeing a walking, talking dead man isn't losing it?

"Only why'd you have to go leave me with that shaman?" he adds.

My throat's as dry and thick as it was when I did my first two vision quests. I haven't done the other two yet. Trainpainting distracted me from them.

"I . . . I thought it was the right thing to do," I manage after a long moment.

"I suppose. But he's shaking his rattle and burning smudge sticks, singing the death songs that'll see me on my way. Makes it hard not to go."

I'm feeling a little confused. "And that's a bad thing because. . . ?"

He shrugs. "I'm kind of enjoying this chance to walk around one last time."

I think I understand. Nobody knows what's waiting for us when we die. It's fine to be all stoic and talk about wheels turning and everything, but if it was me, I don't think I'd be in any hurry to go either.

"So you're going to shoot Turk, are you?" the dead man says.

"What, is it written on my forehead or something?"

Walking Elk laughs. "You know the rez . . ."

"Everybody knows everybody else's business."

He nods. "You thinks it's bad on the rez, you should try the spiritworld."

"No thanks."

"You try and kill Turk," he says, "you might be finding out firsthand, whether you want to or not." He gives a slow shake of his head. "I've got to give it to you, though. I don't think I'd have the balls to see it through."

"I don't know that I do either," I admit. "It just seems like a thing I've got to do."

"Won't bring me back," Walking Elk says. "Once the shaman finishes his ceremony, I'll be out of here."

"It's not just for you," I tell him. "It's for the others he might kill."

The dead man only shakes his head at that. "You think it starts and stops with Tom McGurk? Hell, this happens anyplace you got a cold climate and white cops. They just get tired of dealing with us. I had a cousin who died the same way up in Saskatchewan, another in Colorado. And when they haven't got the winter to do their job for them, they find other ways."

"That's why they've got to be held accountable," I say.

"You got some special sight that'll tell you which cop's decent and which isn't?"

I know there are good cops. Hell, Chief Morningstar's brother is a detective with the NPD. But we only ever seem to get to deal with the ones that have a hard-on for us.

I shake my head. "But I know Turk hasn't got any redeeming qualities."

He sighs. "Wish I could have one of those cigarettes of yours."

I shake one out of the pack and light it for him, surprised that he can hold it, that he can suck in the smoke and blow it out again, just like a living man. I wonder if this is like offering tobacco to the manitou.

"How come you're trying to talk me out of this?" I ask him. "You're the one who told me to be a warrior for you."

He blows out another lungful of smoke. "You think killing's what makes a warrior?"

"Now you sound like Whiteduck."

He laughs. "I've been compared to a lot of things, but never a shaman."

"So what is it you want from me?" I ask. "Why'd you ask me to be a warrior for you?"

"You look like a good kid," he says. "I didn't want to see you turn out like me. I want you to be a good man, somebody to make your parents proud. Make yourself proud."

I've no idea what would make my father proud. But my mom, all she wants is for me to get a decent job and stay out of trouble. I can't seem to manage the first and here I am, walking straight into the second. But he's annoying me all the same. Funny how fast you can go from feeling awed to being fed up.

"You don't think I have any pride?" I ask.

"I don't know the first damn thing about you," he says, "except you were decent enough to stop for a dying man."

He takes a last drag and drops his butt in the snow. Studies something behind me, over my shoulder, but I don't turn. He's got a look I recognize—his gaze is turned inward.

"See, someone told me that once," he goes on, his gaze coming back to me, "except I didn't listen. I worked hard, figured I'd earned the right to play hard, too. Trouble is I played too hard. Lost my job. Lost my family. Lost my pride. It's funny how quick you can lose everything and never see it coming."

I think about my uncle Frank, but I don't say anything.

"I guess it was my grandma told me," the dead man says, "how there's no use in bringing hurt into the world. We do that well enough on our own. You meet someone, you try to give them a little life instead. Let them take something positive away from whatever time they spend with you. Makes the world a better place in the short and the long haul."

I nod. "Putting Beauty in the world."

"That's a warrior's way, too. Stand up for what's right. Ya-ha-hey. Make a noise. I can remember powwow dancing, there'd be so many of us out there, following the drumbeat and the singing, you'd swear you could feel the ground tremble and shake underfoot. But these last few years, I've been too drunk to dance and the only noise I make is when I'm puking."

I know what he means about the powwows, that feeling you can't get anywhere else except maybe a sweat and that's a more contemplative kind of a thing. In a powwow it's all rhythm and dancing, everybody individual, but we're all part of something bigger than us at the same time. There's nothing like it in the world.

"Yeah," the dead man says. "We used to be a proud people for good reason. We can still be a proud people, but sometimes our reasons aren't so good anymore. Sometimes it's not for how we stand tall and honor the ancestors and the spirits with grace and beauty. Sometimes it's for how we beat the enemy at their own game."

"You're starting to sound pretty old school for a drunk," I tell him.

He shakes his head, "I'm just repeating things I was told when I was growing up. Things I didn't feel were important enough to pay attention to."

"I pay attention," I say. "At least I try to."

He gives me a considering look. "I'm not saying it's right or wrong, but what part of what you were taught has to do with that gun in your pocket?"

"The part about standing up for ourselves. The part about defending our people."

"I suppose."

"I hear what you're saying," I tell him. "But I still have to go down to the city."

He gives me a nod.

"Sure you do," he says. "Why would you listen to a dead drunk like me?" He chuckles. "And I mean dead in the strictest sense of the word." He pushes away from the gates. "Time I was going. Whiteduck's doing a hell of a job with his singing. I can feel the pull of that someplace else getting stronger and stronger."

I don't know what to say. Good luck? Good-bye?

"Spare another of those smokes?" he asks.

"Sure."

I shake another one free and light it for him. He pats my cheek. The touch of his hand is still cold, but there's movement in all the fingers. It's not like the block of ice that tried to grab my sleeve this morning.

"You're a good kid," he says.

And then he fades away.

I stand there for a long time, looking at the gate, at the crows, feeling the wind on my face, bitter and cold. Then I walk back to my car.

* * *

Before I first started trainpainting, I thought graffiti was just vandalism, a crime that might include a little creativity, but a crime nonetheless. Then one day I was driving back to the rez and I had to wait at a crossing for a freight train to go by. It was the one near Brendon Road, where the tracks go uphill and the freights tend to slow down because of the incline.

So I'm sitting there, bored, a little impatient more than anything else, and suddenly I see all this art going by. Huge murals painted on the sides of the boxcars and all I can do is stare, thinking, where's all that coming from? Who did these amazing paintings?

And then just like that, there's this collision of the synchronicity at seeing those painted cars and this feeling I've had of wanting to do something different with the iconology I grew up with on the rez—you know, like the bead patterns my mom sews on her powwow dresses. I turn my car back around and drive for the freight yards, stopping off at a hardware store along the way.

I felt a kinship to whoever it was that was painting those boxcars, a complete understanding of what they'd done and why they'd done it. And I wanted to send them a message back. I wanted to tell them, I've seen your work and here's my side of the conversation.

That was the day Crow was born and my first thunderbird joined that ongoing hobo gallery that the freights take from city to city, across the country.

*   *   *

It's a long ride down to the city. I leave the crows behind, but the winter comes with me, wind blowing snow down the highway behind my car, howling like the cries of dying buffalo. It's full night by the time I'm in the downtown core. It's so cold, there's nobody out, not even the hookers. I drive until I reach the precinct house where Turk works and park across the street from it. And then I sit there, my hand in my pocket, fingers wrapped around the handle of the gun.

Comes to me, I can't kill a man, not even a man like Turk. Maybe if he was standing right in front of me and we were fighting. Maybe if he was threatening my mom. Maybe I could do it in the heat of the moment. But not like this, waiting to ambush him like in some Hollywood Western.

But I know I've got to do something.

My gaze travels from the precinct house to the stores alongside the street where I'm parked. I don't even hesitate. I reach in the back for a plastic bag full of unused spray cans and I get out of the car to meet that cold wind head on.

I don't know how long I've got, so I work even faster than usual. It's not a boxcar, but the paint goes on the bricks and glass as easy as it does on wooden slats. It doesn't even clog up in the muzzle—maybe the Grandfather Thunders are giving me a helping hand. I do the crow first, thunderbird style, a yellow one to make the black and red words stand out when I write them along the spread of its wings.

TOM McGURK KILLS INDIANS.

I add a roughly-rendered brave with the daubed clay of a ghost dancer masking his features. He's lying faceup to the sky, power lines flowing up out of his head as his spirit leaves his body, a row of crosses behind him—not Christian crosses, but ours, the ones that stand for the four quarters of the world.

HE HAULS THEM OUT OF TOWN, I write in big sloppy letters, AND LEAVES THEM TO DIE IN THE COLD.

I'm starting a monster, a cannibal windigo all white fur and blood, raging in the middle of a winter storm, when a couple of cops stop their squad car abreast of where I parked my own. They're on their way back to the precinct, I guess, ending their shift and look what they've found. I keep spraying the paint, my fingers frozen into a locked position from the cold.

"Okay, Tonto," one of them says. "Drop the can and assume the position."

I couldn't drop the can if I wanted to. I can barely move my fingers. So I keep spraying on the paint until one of them gives me a sucker punch in the kidneys, knocks me down, kicks me as I'm falling. I lose the spray can and it goes rattling across the sidewalk. I lose the gun, too, which I forgot I was carrying.

There's a long moment of silence as we're all three staring at that gun lying there on the pavement.

They really work me over then.

* * *

So as I sit here in county, waiting for my trial, I think back on all of this and find I'm not sorry that I didn't try to shoot Turk. I'm not sorry that I got busted in the middle of vandalizing a building right across the street from the precinct house either. But I do regret not getting rid of the gun first.

The charges against me are vandalism, possession of an unlicensed weapon, carrying a concealed weapon, and resisting arrest. I'll be doing some time, heading up to the pen, but I won't be alone in there. Like Leonard Peltier says on that song he does with Robbie Robertson, "It's the fastest growing rez in the country," and he should know, they've kept him locked up long enough.

But something good came out of all of this. The police didn't have time to get rid of my graffiti before the press showed up. I guess it was a slow news day because pictures of those paintings showed up on the front page of all three of the daily papers, and made the news on every channel. You might think, what's good about that? It's like prime evidence against me. But I'm not denying I painted those images and words, and the good thing is, people started coming forward, talking about how the same thing had happened to them. Cops would pick them up when the bars closed and would dump them, ten, twenty miles out of town. They identified Turk and a half-dozen others by name.

So I'm sitting in county, and I don't know where Turk is, but he's been suspended without pay while the investigation goes on, and it looks like they've got to deal with this fair and square because everybody's on their case now, right across the city—whites, blacks, skins, everybody. They're all watching what the authorities do, writing editorials, writing letters to the editor, holding protest demonstrations.

This isn't going away.

So if I've got to do some jail time, I'm thinking the sacrifice is worth it.

My cousin Tommy drives my mom down from the rez on a regular basis to visit me. The first time she comes, she stands there looking at me and I don't know what she's thinking, but I wait for the blast I'm sure's coming my way. But all she says is, "Couldn't you have stuck with the boxcars?" Then she holds me a long while, tells me I'm stupid, but how she's so proud of me. Go figure.

Some of the Creek Aunts have connections in the city and they found me a good lawyer, so I'm not stuck with some public defender. I like him. His name's Marty Caine and I can tell he doesn't care what color my skin is. He tells me that what I did was "morally correct, if legally indefensible, but we'll do our damnedest to get you out of this anyway." But nobody's fooled. We all know that whatever happens to the cops, they're still going to make a lesson with me. When it comes to skins, they always do.

* * *

I see Walking Elk one more time before the trial. I'm lying on my bunk, staring up at the ceiling, thinking how, when I get out, I'm going on those last two vision quests. I need to be centered. I need to talk to the Creator and find out what my place is in the world, who I'm supposed to be so that my being here in this world makes a difference to what happens to the people in my life, to the ground I walk on and the spirits that share this world with us.

I hear a rustle of cloth and turn my head to see John Walking Elk sitting on the other bunk. He's still wearing the clothes he died in. I assume he's still dead. This time he's got the smokes and he offers me one.

I swing my feet to the floor and take the cigarette, let him light it for me.

"How come you're still here?" I ask.

He shrugs. "Maybe I'm not," he says. "Maybe Whiteduck sent my spirit on and you're just dreaming."

I smile. "You'd think if I was going to dream, I'd dream myself out of this place."

"You'd think."

We smoke our cigarettes for a while.

"I'm in all the papers," Walking Elk finally says. "And that's your doing. They wrote about how Whiteduck sent my body down to the city, how the cops drove me up there and dumped me in the snow. Family I didn't even know I had anymore came to the funeral. From the rez, from Pine Ridge, hell, from places I never even heard of before."

I wasn't there, but I heard about it. Skins came from all over the country to show their solidarity. Mom told me that the Warriors' Society up on the rez organized it.

"Yeah, I heard it was some turnout," I say. "Made the cover of *Time* and everything."

Walking Elk nods. "You came through for me," he says. "On both counts."

I know what he's talking about. I can hear his voice against the northern winds that were blowing that day without even trying.

Don't let me be forgotten.

Be a warrior for me.

But I don't know what to say.

"Even counted some coup for yourself," he adds.

"Wasn't about that," I tell him.

"I know. I just wanted to thank you. I had to come by to tell you that. I lived a lot of years, just looking for something in the bottom of a bottle. There was nothing else left for me. Didn't think anybody'd ever look at me like I was a man again. But you did. And those people that came to the funeral? They were remembering me as a man, too, not just some drunk who got himself killed by a cop."

He stands up. I'm curious. Is he going to walk away through the wall, or just fade away like he did before?

"Any plans for when you get out?" he asks.

I think about that for a moment.

"I was thinking of going back to painting boxcars," I say. "You see where painting buildings got me."

"There's worse places to be," he tells me. "You could be dead."

I don't know if I blinked, or woke up, but the next thing I know, he's gone and I'm alone in my cell. But I hear an echo of laughter and I've still got the last of that cigarette he gave me smoldering in my hand.

"Ya-ha-hey," I say softly and butt it out in the ashtray.

Then I stretch out on the bed again and contemplate the ceiling some more.

I think maybe I was dead, or half-dead, anyway, before I found John Walking Elk dying in the snow. I was going through the motions of life, instead of really living, and there's no excuse for that. It's not something I'll let happen to me again.

Science Fiction Anthologies

Don't Miss These Exciting DAW Anthologies

SWORD AND SORCERESS
Marion Zimmer Bradley, editor
☐ Book XVII   0-88677-891-3—$6.99

OTHER ORIGINAL ANTHOLOGIES
Mercedes Lackey, editor
☐ FLIGHTS OF FANTASY   0-88677-863-8—$6.99
☐ SWORD OF ICE: And Other Tales of Valdemar
                                               0-88677-720-8—$6.99

Martin H. Greenberg & Larry Segriff, editors
☐ SPELL FANTASTIC   0-88677-878-6—$6.99

Martin H. Greenberg, editor
☐ MY FAVORITE SCIENCE FICTION STORY 0-88677-830-1—$6.99
☐ MY FAVORITE FANTASY STORY   0-88677-905-7—$6.99

Denise Little, editor
☐ PERCHANCE TO DREAM   0-88677-888-3—$6.99
☐ A DANGEROUS MAGIC   0-88677-830-1—$6.99
☐ TWICE UPON A TIME   0-88677-835-2—$6.99

Margaret Weis, editor
☐ NEW AMAZONS   0-88677-887-5—$6.99

Prices slightly higher in Canada   **DAW:105**

Payable in U.S. funds only. No cash/COD accepted. Postage & handling: U.S./CAN. $2.75 for one book, $1.00 for each additional, not to exceed $6.75; Int'l $5.00 for one book, $1.00 each additional. We accept Visa, Amex, MC ($10.00 min.), checks ($15.00 fee for returned checks) and money orders. Call 800-788-6262 or 201-933-9292, fax 201-896-8569; refer to ad #105.

Penguin Putnam Inc. P.O. Box 12289, Dept. B Newark, NJ 07101-5289	**Bill my:** ☐Visa ☐MasterCard ☐Amex_____ (expires) Card#_____
Please allow 4-6 weeks for delivery. Foreign and Canadian delivery 6-8 weeks.	Signature_____

Bill to:

Name_____

Address_____ City_____

State/ZIP_____

Daytime Phone #_____

Ship to:

Name_____ Book Total $_____

Address_____ Applicable Sales Tax $_____

City_____ Postage & Handling $_____

State/Zip_____ Total Amount Due $_____

This offer subject to change without notice.